THE MARSHAL

43rd & 8th

CORY SANDERS

ACKNOWLEDGEMENTS

It's been a special privilege to work with the FDNY Bureau of Fire Investigation in writing this book. I'd like to thank former Chief Fire Marshal Louis Garcia, Chief Fire Marshal Robert Byrnes, former Assistant Chief Fire Marshal Richard McCahey, and Commander Bill Law for all their help. I owe special thanks to Commander Randy Wilson for his support and friendship. If there are inaccuracies in this book, or if The Marshal's actions are inconsistent with that of a true law enforcement professional, it is simply because I have taken creative license. I'm eternally grateful for the BFI's support. A portion of all proceeds from The Marshal will go to a fund in the name of the FDNY Chief Fire Marshal. Visit my website at corysanders.com for details.

To my good friend Mark Iussig for your encouragement and accommodations during my research trips to New York. To Jeff McTaggart for your technical expertise. To Charles Salzberg for your support and insight into the writing and publishing process. To Michael Neff for your excellent workshops. To all the fine people at Thriller Fest. To Dr. Bill Noah for your prayers and friendship. To Michael Diaz for introducing me to the BFI. To Allen Plunkett for being a great friend and fan. To Elin Barnes for your editorial work. To Mary Drenick for your editorial work. To my brother Nick. You told me I could do this and your words kept me going. To mom, my "Editor in Chief." To my children, my favorite fans. And to my wife Heather. It is not an overstatement to say I could not have done this without you.

And so, my dear reader, I present to you my first installment of The Marshal series. May you accompany John Kane on many journeys in and beyond New York City.

ONE

She ran nearly two hundred feet atop the water. Her stern bore two names. *Minnow* was painted in black cursive letters to port, and SHADDOW in block lettering to starboard. She was meant to service the mother ship with food, beverage, parts, and fuel – a supermarket on water for the ultra-rich.

As instructed by her escort, Coast Guard Cutter *Hudson Bay,* the captain pushed her at 2 knots through The Narrows, the tidal channel that separated Upper and Lower New York Bay.

The captain glanced nervously at his radio. The Coast Guard had boarded them in the Lower Bay. Documentation was inspected. The *Minnow* was searched from tip to stern. Purely routine for a ship of Panamanian registry entering an American port. But he was still nervous. He was quite certain his identity, Captain Enrique Gustalvo Uriarte, raised no flags in any of their databases. His true identity, Carlos Esperanza, was another story. The United States Drug Enforcement Agency surely had Carlos Esperanza on their radar.

"Coast Guard Cutter Hudson Bay to shadow boat Minnow, over," a voice came over his radio.

The captain picked up his mic and replied, "Shaddow boat Minnow, over."

"You are cleared to enter port, Minnow. Welcome to America."

"Captain and crew thank the U.S. Coast Guard. Minnow over and out." Esperanza put the mic back in its holder, made an entry in the logbook, and increased the speed to five knots. The ship's guidance system was about to turn them due north for a run to the top of the Upper Bay.

Two

They sat inside Panificio di Ferrari, an Italian bakery on the outskirts of Times Square. Marshal John Kane savored a small spoonful of lime custard. He pushed the last plump raspberry to her side of the tart.

Across from him sat Jackie Fairbanks. Last week an editorial team from a popular New York magazine named her the city's most beautiful investigative journalist. She was glamorous, there was no doubt about it. But it wasn't her looks that got him. She was top in her field for her intellect. He'd researched her and found that she'd earned many of her field's print and visual media awards over the years, ranging from the Alfred I. duPont–Columbia University Award of her alma mater, to the Yankee Quill Award from her childhood home of New England.

The magazine article had described her as a modern day mix of two women: take one part Margaret Fuller, the first American female foreign and war correspondent, who, in her time, was described as the most remarkable and greatest woman in America; and the other part Kelly Garrett, the Charlie's Angel played by Jaclyn Smith. Jackie Fairbanks was fearless and intelligent. If he had to make a list of attributes he found desirable in a woman, those two would be at the very top, and possibly in that order. Still, it didn't bother him that she resembled his favorite Angel.

They'd been to the Broadway play *Jersey Boys* earlier and Frankie Valli's song "Can't Take My Eyes Off You" played over and over in John's head. But every time he came to the words, "I love you, baby!" the song rewound to the start.

He put the song out of his mind, deciding that he didn't have to be in love with her right now. Tomorrow he retired from the New York City

Bureau of Fire Investigation. Tonight he was in the greatest city on earth with someone whom he enjoyed very much, and that was enough.

They'd met a month ago at a crime scene. She showed up out of nowhere to look into a case that was all but finished. She hung around. Kept asking him questions, nibbling around very soft edges. It finally dawned on him that she was flirting with him. He remembered being shocked. Not so much because *the* Jackie Fairbanks was flirting with him, but because he didn't quite regard himself a single man. He found himself saying, though, once the moment was upon him, "Ms. Fairbanks, would you like to go to a play with me?"

"Are we talking a matinee?" she'd said, playfully teasing him for taking so long to catch on to her intent.

"A play and dinner, Ms. Fairbanks," he'd said. "A date."

"I'd love to," she'd said with a big smile.

Calling him back to the present, his phone zinged, indicating he had a Twitter message. Since he followed only one person's Tweets, he knew who it was. She was the reason the song kept rewinding.

He broke off a piece of the tart and scooped some of the custard, playing it off as though the phone hadn't just gone off like a siren in his mind.

"What was that?" she said.

Fighting every urge not to, he pulled the skinny Droid from his front pocket and looked at the Tweet from his ex-wife, Peggy. This was her typical hour of inspiration. Lately she'd been Tweeting esoteric things. Yesterday she'd quoted some guy named Paul Hoover. Something about the ghosts we drag through our memories. This one looked to be an original. "A woman needs a little madness or else she doesn't dare cut the strings that bind," she had written.

He dumped the phone back in his pocket and hoped the people whom he'd hired to find her would soon have success. She needed medication. And strict supervision. But she was smart. And she had a lot of money. It was unlikely she would let anyone find her, let alone institutionalize her.

He looked at Jackie, letting her know that it was Peggy. Jackie reached over and put her hand on his. She looked him kindly in the eye, as if to say, you can tell me. He'd told her the entire story at dinner. He didn't know why he'd done it, told himself he wouldn't until at least knowing her for a few months. There was just something about Jackie Fairbanks. She put him at ease.

He smiled at her and shook it off. He didn't really want to talk about it. Before the phone had interrupted, they'd had a moment going, and he wanted to get back to it. He'd waited a month to find a night that worked in both their schedules to go out, and he'd be hanged if he was going to let anything ruin this.

Jackie took her hand away and put the raspberry in her mouth. She smiled at its sweetness and said, "Um. Thank you." After a sip of espresso she asked him, "What was your favorite song? I like "Sherry"." She took another sip of espresso and softly hummed the tune.

"Can't Take My Eyes Off You," he said, looking her right in the eyes.

She put her espresso cup down, leaned in, put her elbow on the table and her chin in her hand, and looked him straight in the eyes. "Why that one?" she said.

"Would you believe me if I said it was the trombones?"

"No," she said, maintaining her stare.

Reaching slowly across to her, he cupped the side of her cheek, and leaning in, he said, "Then the hell with it. You are too good to be true, Jackie Fairbanks." He moved to her lips and kissed her passionately for several seconds until he felt her completely relax.

Patrons began clapping and two young guys at the pastry case whistled loudly. John pulled away and looked at her. "Sorry," he said.

"For what?" she said softly with a smile.

"The trombone thing."

"You're funny, and a good kisser," she said. "What's not to like?"

John looked up and waved to the crowd to quiet them down. A few of them were still looking their way and clapping. "Let's get out of here," he said. Tonight was July 3rd. The day's overcast had broken while they were in the play and a downpour had cleaned things up nicely. A light breeze pushed cool air through streets that had been muggy all day. His daughter Katie was at home with her Aunt Mary, and he hadn't been out on a date with a woman for much too long. There was more to do than eat pastries in the City That Never Sleeps.

THREE

The offshore cruiser *Shootout* pushed slowly up the mouth of the East River. Amidst the usual cluster, *Shootout*'s antenna mast held an array of infra-red cameras and microwave antennas. Inside her cabin, two men and two women from the U.S. Drug Enforcement Agency sat quietly observing the *Minnow* from 400 yards.

Agent Paul Mackenzie had been tracking Carlos Esperanza since he left Panama. The *Minnow* carried no drugs, no weapons, no people of any interest, aside from Esperanza himself. Her bill of lading was for the delivery of the ship itself. The consignee, a Delaware corporation whose ownership checked out. So what was Esperanza doing sailing a 200-foot shadow boat from Panama to New York City? It had been nearly a decade since he'd moved any product that they knew of. What was he doing? Why move the king around the board? Completely unprotected.

One of the four flat panel monitors showed the *Minnow* tied to the east side of the South Street Seaport Museum maintenance dock. A couple of smaller barges were tied to the west side.

"Should we drop a buoy, sir?" the first female agent asked.

Mackenzie studied the screen. *Shootout* was fitted with a military-grade detector, which allowed it to capture facial details from 500 yards away. She could deploy camouflaged and motorized buoys that could do the same and transmit their data back to the boat, or other receivers many miles away.

"No," he said. "Not yet." It was pitch black on the river and the buoys would be hard to detect, if anyone on the *Minnow* were looking out her stern. But he'd already spent several weeks and ample resources tracking Esperanza, and he didn't want to blow it now.

"Here we are," the other female agent said. The main screen showed an image of a lone man emerging from the shadow of *Minnow's* open hangar. She quickly worked the controls and captured a set of facial points.

"That's Esperanza," Mackenzie said.

The woman uploaded the images into the BioID Database and it quickly returned a match. "That is affirmative," she said. "It's Esperanza or someone who's spent a lot of money to look like him."

"All by himself," the first female agent said. She was scanning the Minnow with infrared binoculars. "Very strange."

"He's got company," the male agent said. He worked the controls for a separate camera and zoomed in on the head of the dock. Four men stepped through the metal gate and walked south toward the *Minnow*. One very large man led the pack of four. He shielded the middle man, who was flanked by two men in the rear.

The second female agent fed the image of the leader into the database and seconds later a profile emerged. "Got a match," she said.

Mackenzie sat down at a separate work station and began clicking through pages. "Torval Tangval," he said. Aside from his enormous size, there was nothing of real interest in Tangval's file. He clicked on known associates. At the top of the list was the name Condor Walken. Mackenzie clicked on the link and said, "Condor Walken? What kind of a name is that?"

"Mysterious," the first female agent said absently. "Fitting for Esperanza."

Mackenzie scanned Walken's profile. "Yes," he answered. Then, after a half minute of reading, he said, "FBI's got a protocol running on him." He continued reading and said, "Somebody please get this Agent Santiváñez on the phone."

FOUR

John stepped behind her chair and assisted her to standing. A loud boom silenced the chatter in the small café. John saw the flash through the window. Across the street and up, on the corner of 43rd & 8th, the top of a five-story building blew. He knew what was coming next – falling and shooting debris. He shielded her to the back of the room and yelled, "Everybody get back!" Two young men ignored his order. They stared in awe at the flames shooting from the top of the building. John ran over and grabbed each by an arm and threw them from harm's way. Just then, pieces of brick and debris pounded the sidewalk in front of Ferrari's. Several large fragments crashed through the large plate glass windows. John was quick enough to jump back and miss being hit.

A few seconds later, the volley was over. John stepped over the broken glass and rubble to the front of the store and looked up. The entire fifth floor of the building on 43rd & 8th was an inferno. The next floor could go any time and the whole thing could pancake. These people were not safe inside the store. John pulled his badge and held it out for everyone huddled at the back of Ferrari's to see. "Everybody out of here!"

John stepped through the window and out onto the sidewalk, shifting his attention from the inferno, to helping the fleeing patrons, who filed out the door and open window frame, and then ran up to 42nd Street.

Jackie stood in the back of the shop listening to someone on the other end of her mobile. She appeared to be arguing with whoever was on the other end. He whistled loudly and she looked up. He motioned for her to get out. She shook her head, put her hand out and looked back down, intent on her call.

He didn't have time to argue with her. Pulling his own phone, he dialed 9-1-1. 8th Avenue was pandemonium. Cabbies and other drivers on the street, who had slammed on their brakes when the debris started to fall, now sped away.

Through the chaos, he heard the whine of sirens and wailing horns coming from The Pride of Midtown, the fire house just up 8th Avenue. The 9-1-1 message droned on, saying they would be on the line as soon as possible.

A man holding the back of his head staggered across the street and collapsed on the sidewalk. John ran to him and knelt down. He put his phone on speaker, set it on the sidewalk, and examined the back of the man's head. Part of the falling debris had carved a large swath of skin away. He bled profusely from the area and his skull was fractured. First aid procedure dictated not applying pressure to the area and not removing any debris. There was almost nothing he could do for this man.

He saw Jackie step out to the sidewalk. He yelled to her, "Get me a bucket of ice!" She disappeared and returned thirty seconds later carrying a large mixing bowl filled with shaved ice from the Icee machine.

"Nice job," he said to her. He held the man's head up and she dumped the ice in a pile over the pool of blood on the sidewalk. John positioned the wound on the ice so that gravity would draw blood away from the brain, and hopefully the cold would slow the flow of blood.

A 9-1-1 operator answered and told John to state his emergency. "Fire Marshal John Kane. I have one male adult. Head trauma, skull fracture. Corner of 43rd & 8th in Manhattan."

"We have units responding, Marshal Kane. Hold the line." He could hear her transmitting the emergency call to EMS. She came back on the line. "EMS has been notified and is en route. Are there any other injuries?"

John looked around. He spotted one man dressed in a security guard uniform who walked across the street holding his head, but appeared to be stable. "There appears to be one more." Aside from a bunch of scared people, that's all he saw.

A woman who had been watching him screamed over the sirens. "Should we give him CPR? We should give him CPR!"

"He's breathing," John said. "No CPR."

"I don't think he's breathing," she said hysterically. "We should give him CPR!"

John looked up at the woman. She was in shock. He stood and gently put his hands on her shoulders. "Let me have a look at you, ma'am."

FIVE

Just seconds before, some of "The Pride" firefighters were still watching passers-by five blocks north on 8ᵗʰ Avenue. Their first reaction was to step out to the street when they heard the explosion. Their eyes widened at the inferno they saw in plain sight less than a half-mile away. The Battalion Chief stepped into the bay and onto the sidewalk. "Mount up!" he yelled.

The firefighters ran to their protective gear. Things happened in reverse that night. Normally the teleprinter spat out orders and the "firefighter on watch" read the orders. Then he rang the appropriate number of bells. One bell signaled a Pumper Truck, two bells signaled both the Pumper Truck and the Ladder Truck to roll, and three bells signaled the Battalion Chief in his SUV to join them. Then the firefighters took the appropriate action. Now, every firefighter in the garage was dressed and in position on their truck. The Battalion Chief, sitting in the passenger seat of his SUV, ready to roll with his driver, looked at the small glass window in the door to the radio room. The "firefighter on watch" looked out the small window despairingly at him, letting him know the machine hadn't spit the orders out yet. The Battalion Chief signaled his driver to roll – one didn't need a piece of paper to find this fire. When the Battalion Chief's SUV started moving, the big trucks switched on their sirens and pulled out behind him.

The trucks from "The Pride" made their way south towards 43ʳᵈ. The Battalion Chief had no trouble calling the status. He was on the radio before they had driven fifty feet. He knew that dispatch, if it hadn't already, would be transmitting a 10-75. This was an active fire. "Battalion-9 to Manhattan," he said over the radio.

"Go ahead, Battalion-9," Manhattan dispatch came back.

"Responding to 10-60 at box 797." A 10-60 was a major explosion, and Box 797 was the code for the area at 43rd and 8th. It referred to the old boxes the city used before phones. If there was a fire in those days, somebody pulled a lever at a big red box and it sent a code over copper wire to dispatch, where a telegraph was sent out to the appropriate firehouse.

"Roger that, Battalion-9," Manhattan answered. Dispatch needed no further instructions. A 10-60 meant an immediate Second Alarm, which meant two more Pumper Trucks, two more Ladder Trucks, another Battalion Chief, a HazTac Ambulance, and three ambulances were called in. In addition, Con Edison, the utility company, was called to attend to any gas lines that might be involved.

The Battalion Chief still held the microphone in his hand. As they got closer, he could see a gas flame was shooting high up into the air from the top story of the building, which was completely aflame itself.

"Manhattan, this is Battalion-9. Ring in alarms three through five. Bring every Tower Truck available." Tower Trucks were the Cherry Pickers. They had the bucket that could hold three firefighters at the end of the ladder.

"Roger that, Battalion-9," Manhattan returned. "Truck twenty-two will be the fast truck." Truck Twenty-Two was a Tower Truck at Battalion-8, not far from the scene.

Truck-54 pulled to a stop in front of the burning building. The firefighters hurried to the hoses at the back of the truck and dragged them to the hydrants at the opposing corner. They connected the Pumper Truck to the Ladder Truck, which in turn shot the water. The Battalion Chief gave the signal to the firefighters to start shooting water up to the top. He pulled the microphone off his shoulder. "Battalion-9 to Manhattan."

"Go ahead, Battalion-9."

"Bring at least two Tower Trucks in from the west on 43rd."

"Roger that, Battalion-9."

Six

John waved his badge in the air. Three EMTs spotted him and sprinted over. John told one of them to get a blanket for the frail lady and check her for shock. The other two didn't need directions for the man on the ground. They hovered over him and checked his vitals.

"He's barely holding on," the first EMT said. He raised his head a little to look at the wound.

The second EMT placed a large gauze pad over the wound and they lowered him back to the ice. "Who are you?" she said to John.

"Fire marshal," John replied.

"Smartest thing you could have done, the ice. Good job. You probably saved his life."

"If he hangs on," the first EMT said. "Sir, come on. Stay with us. Open your eyes."

***

The wind was coming from the north. In addition to dousing the burning building, the men on the ground sprayed the buildings to the south to prevent any spread. The firefighters kept a wary eye on the front of the structure, a pancake collapse on everyone's mind.

A Con Edison natural gas service truck wove its way to the center of the action and stopped abruptly. The Con Ed engineer jumped out of his truck and flipped through pages in a large manual. He turned to another engineer, pointed down, and yelled, "The shutoff is under the pavement!"

The other man quickly ran to the back of the truck and pulled out a large saw used for cutting roadway and cement. He hurried to where the engineer stood and pulled the cord on the saw. Kneeling at the spot, he lowered the spinning blade into 8th Avenue and cut a large square in the pavement.

SEVEN

The fire had spread down into the fourth floor and it was growing. The Chief in Charge at the scene wasn't sending any firefighters into the building. It was all commercial, and the security guard said no one was inside. They'd let this one fall to the ground if that was what it wanted to do. All they could do was add more hoses to the problem, which they were doing as fast as they could stretch lines.

John now wore an FDNY windbreaker. He stood in the middle of 8th Avenue watching the firefighters do their work. This thing was getting worse, and Jackie was holed up again in the back of Ferrari's, probably talking with her producer or news manager.

He walked towards her with the intention of escorting her away from the scene, but the old building called out to him. It creaked and moaned, and he knew what was coming next. The bottom of the fourth floor collapsed into the third. The weight and the force behind it crashed the entire mess down through the second floor and to the ground level – a full pancake. Debris shot out from the mess. Like the blur of a fastball, John saw a large brick hurtling through the air. Rage grew quickly inside of him and he called out. It was no use. He watched helplessly as the brick struck a firefighter in the face.

The firefighter dropped to the ground. John ran to him and, as he got there, another firefighter wrestled the hose out of the fallen firefighter's grip. The guy's face was completely caved in and the brick was lodged deep. There was no saving him. Written in black Sharpie across his chest he saw the name J. Park. He was an old friend from the academy. He'd known Park for twenty years.

"Kane, get the hell out of here!" a firefighter yelled.

"Get a hat on, you idiot!" yelled a woman firefighter.

EIGHT

John walked towards Jackie. One group of paramedics carried Park away. Another moved the man on the sidewalk to a stretcher.

When he got close to her, Jackie took him by the arm. "Did you know that man?" she said.

He just shook his head and said, "He was a friend."

She saw one of her network's cameramen and a producer push to the front of the barricade, and she hated what she had to ask him.

After the explosion, she'd called into the news manager on duty. Barely through telling him to get a metro crew to the site, Kent Rogers barged in on the conversation. Kent was the chief news manager in charge of all the investigative journalists at the network, and a very bad, very brief mistake. Now he was cold and bitter at being rebuffed, and tried to rule her every chance he got.

"I'm sorry," she said to John. She pointed to the barricade where two men jockeyed for position at the perimeter line. "They want me to get in front of this. Can you let my camera crew in?"

Normally a request like this would be flatly denied. But he needed her more than she needed him right now. He whistled to the PD officers and motioned to let the two men through. The camera man, and another man he assumed to be the producer, sprinted towards them.

Before they even stopped running, the camera man brought his camera up to his shoulder and turned on the bright light. The other man handed Jackie a microphone.

"Slow down, guys," John said. Then, to Jackie, "These are crucial minutes. I need video of the crowd. I need you guys to take in everything you see."

Without delay, Jackie pointed her crew towards the barricade and they got to work.

John walked to the command post at 43rd & 8th. Across the street from the fire on the northeast curb stood a foldout-and-standup, magnetic whiteboard. The area and the buildings were drawn in black erasable marker. Magnets dotted the picture indicating truck and firefighter positions. The Manhattan Borough Fire Chief had assumed command. He stood in front of the board directing and monitoring movements.

Two cars led by two PD motorcycles approached from the south on 43rd. The motorcade stopped just yards away from the command post. Mayor Saltzman and Chief Fire Marshal Randy Fitzgerald stepped from the cars.

John caught Fitzgerald's attention and flagged him over. Fitzgerald was a tall and wiry black man. Dark black freckles spotted his face from the base of his nose back to his ears. "What are you doin' here?" Fitzgerald said. There was no mistaking his accent. He was Bronx born and bred.

"I was on a date. Sitting across the street when the thing blew."

"What did you see?" Fitzgerald said.

"It went off with a boom. No smoke that I could see."

"You know who owns this?"

John shook his head.

"Senator Michael Malley," Fitzgerald said. "Looks like someone on the Mayor's staff who knew Malley owned it was here when the thing went off. Called the Mayor's aide right away." Mayor Saltzman motioned for Fitzgerald to come over and talk to him.

"Stay right here." Fitzgerald left John and walked to Saltzman.

John watched him. Fitzgerald was doing a lot of nodding and Saltzman was doing all the talking. John knew he couldn't stop what was coming. Katie, he thought. My beloved Katie. I'm sorry for what I have to tell you.

After about a minute, Fitzgerald returned to John. He scratched his head, didn't want to look him in the eyes. "How do you feel about double time for the next few weeks?"

"Chief," John said half-heartedly. "I'm retired in less than 6 hours. I can't start a case."

"Who do you think I'm gonna drop on a deal like this? We got heavy written all over this thing and I don't have a senior guy I can call in here tonight. And you were here, and you're still on my clock for, like, 6 hours."

Fitzgerald said six hours. It was a few weeks when he walked up. This was no six-hour case. It was no three-week case, either. It might not turn into a heavy, as they called cases with heft. Or it might. You never knew. Saltzman and the Manhattan Borough Fire Chief were looking right at them. It was true that he had special knowledge, having been there when the thing went off. It was also true that there weren't a lot of guys Fitzgerald had to reach out to. Budget cuts for the 10th year in a row had done bad things to the department. They were half the size from a decade past.

"Listen," Fitzgerald said. "I'm not going to be breakin' your heels about checking in. This one's yours until I can rotate someone in."

Unlike a normal fire marshal who was tethered closely to the chiefs, he'd essentially been his own boss for the past decade on the JTTF, checking in with HQ weekly or even less frequently. A lot of times his cases were well outside of New York and the United States. He worked with the federal government mostly.

"You do what you have to do, Chief. I'll take care of this. Don't worry about a thing."

"Good. I think I can pull Jensen down off what he's doing and rotate some guys. I'll try to get you out as soon as possible."

"Let's just see what happens, Chief. Just don't worry about a thing. I've got this." John patted his shoulder and looked over to the mayor with a nod.

"ATF is on the way," Fitzgerald said. "FBI is sending someone from Federal Plaza. You get whatever you need on this. Mayor's been on the phone with Senator Malley. You're due at his place in Summit at nine AM. Treat him like the president. He may be one day."

Fitzgerald stood straight, shook John's hand, and walked back to the mayor.

John looked over at the street sign. Here he was, in the field again, at 43rd & 8th Ave in Manhattan, just like his early days. He wiped the sweaty dirt from his face. It was going to be a long night.

NINE

The current president's first term was up in seventeen months, and he was on the ropes with even the died-in-the wool from his own party. The economy was stagnant and job growth was negative. The only thing growing was the national debt, and everyone was calling for a change.

Malley was an Independent that caucused with the Democrats. He was being quiet about it, but he was staging a bid. John liked the simple way he presented himself and his ideas. He wanted to bring production back to our soil. Make the tax code more simple and fair. Provide for the needy, but make them work for it. He openly stated he wanted to take our country back twenty-five years, and John was all for it. The experiments of the last two decades had proved disastrous, and neither the Democrats nor the Republicans had a plan with any specifics that were going to stop the tsunami of debt and unemployment that was overtaking our country.

John walked up to the 42nd Street barricade. PD lifted the tape and let an unmarked Suburban through. There were two suits in the front. Chief said FBI would be there.

The suits got out. These weren't your average GS-13s. The average fibee was well-dressed and had an air of confidence about him that bespoke authority. Right away, he knew there was something different about these two. They looked at the burning building as if they knew something, as if there were some kind of back story.

"Stiles," said the man, flashing his badge.

"Agent Santiváñez," said the woman, not bothering to show her credential. "You the catching marshal?"

He nodded and gave each of them a card. "John Kane."

Stiles and Santiváñez looked at his card. Santiváñez read his information quickly, put it in her pocket, and then looked down to the fire. Stiles gave his card more respectful attention and then looked down the street in the direction of his partner's stare.

A few moments of silence passed and John became annoyed. Normal protocol would have been for them to produce their cards. State their business. Something besides just standing there.

"What unit are you with?" There were forty or fifty units in NYC's FBI and a few thousand agents – several terrorism units, racketeering units, corporate espionage units, public protection, public corruption, violent crime, arson, and a host of others. He'd worked with FBI agents every day at the JTTF but had never seen these two.

"We were in the area when the thing blew," Santiváñez said. "We know who the building belongs to so we thought we'd get a closer look."

She didn't answer his question. His annoyance was growing and he said, "Excuse me. But I saw your badge, Agent Stiles. I'd like to see some identification from you, ma'am."

Santiváñez produced her credential case and flipped it open for him to see.

John held out his hand, "I'll have a look at that if you don't mind." He knew agents like Santiváñez. If she was going to run a power play on him, he'd run one right back. After looking her badge over he passed it back and said, "Agent. Now, do you mind telling me what unit you're with?"

Fitzgerald had told him FBI was sending someone from Federal Plaza. Those guys would still show up. But these two were not just "in the area" as they'd said.

"I'm sorry, Marshal," Santiváñez said, now softening a bit. "It's been a long night. We're with Public Corruption. We were just in the area when it blew. Not an official mark here. We just wanted to get a closer look. See who was in charge. Public figure like the senator. We could end up getting involved." She gave him her card and said, "Please let us know if you need anything from us, Marshal Kane. Good evening."

John watched them get back into their Suburban and then turned away. He wasn't so much bothered by their manner, but because of certain uneasiness he felt. He knew he'd entered their world, instead of their entering his.

TEN

Santiváñez dialed Mackenzie's number and put the call through the Suburban's hands free system.

"Mackenzie," answered the other end.

"It's Maria Santiváñez, Agent Mackenzie."

"They ended up Midtown," Mackenzie came back. "'21' Club. I've got agents ready to go in now."

"Can we meet at the corner of 56th and 5th in twenty?"

"Roger that," Mackenzie said.

Santiváñez hung up the phone. She looked over at Stiles and then they each turned their attention to the fire.

Curiosity and boredom had brought them to this case. A few months ago, she and Stiles were sitting at their desks after handing off the Linea Cartel case to the U.S. Attorney. Waiting for a meeting to start, and nothing on their plate, Stiles was catching up on NBA stats. Never one to stay idle, Santiváñez started poking through the database in the open files section restricted to GS-15 supervisors and above.

The name Michael Malley sitting on a line entry all by itself stopped her cold. The file stated that five years ago, a Times writer had posted a controversial story about Michael Malley and a company named Immunex. He'd asked on a page-seven column why there was so much government money being spent on animal fetal tissue research, and why so much of it was going to a private company named Immunex owned by this man Condor Walken. And why the head of the Health and Human Services subcommittee, Michael Malley, had approved the appropriations. The writer promised an answer to his readers. He was later shown to have been backed by a republican. Shortly thereafter, he was killed in a boating accident.

Nothing but a Cease and Desist Order from Malley's lawyers and the writer's death ever happened in the case. Noting no suspicious activity on either the part of Malley or Walken, and no direction from above to investigate, the agent who created the file and took a couple marks left it open for inquiries.

She'd had to press her case with Tolliver, the ASAC, or Assistant Special Agent in Charge of her New York division, Public Corruption. He wasn't about to lay his reputation on the line and start looking into Michael Malley when another competent agent had already found nothing. In the end, she'd convinced Tolliver to let her take a peek into Walken only.

It didn't take her long to find out Walken enjoyed the night life – private clubs, women, wine, and what turned out to be her green light to take a deeper dive into him, his use and possession of cocaine. He had lots of it, and it was pure. So she commissioned one of her confidential informants, an irresistible high-dollar call girl, to get into his circle. A week ago, the CI reported that something was going on. Walken had changed. His mood had improved drastically. It was hard to get much when you just had sex and blew coke with the guy, but there was definitely something going on that was making him very happy.

Ninety minutes ago, she and Stiles were at Federal Plaza preparing to hang it up for the day when Mackenzie called. Minutes after that, the name Michael Malley and the address of the building on 43rd & 8th, followed by her case number, popped up on her phone. She, like every other Bureau agent, was linked to everything, always. All feeds went into the main database, a raw record of all key data. When someone said or wrote something that was recorded in print, on the airwaves, or the Internet, the database logic engine linked relational data and notified subscribers inspiringly fast.

"Are the two related?" Stiles said.

"I don't think so," Santiváñez said.

"So what's Esperanza doing here?"

"Vacation?" she replied. "Laying plans for a future enterprise? Mackenzie told us Esperanza hasn't moved anything out of the Medellin for years, but DEA's pretty sure he's continued to produce. He must have a mountain of product stocked up."

"Tell me more."

"I don't think Walken's change in mood had to do with Esperanza coming to town. Maybe Esperanza is the source of his cocaine. But tonight was not a delivery. Maybe they're old friends. But Walken wouldn't be happy about Esperanza showing up if he had something like this going. And I know he had something to do with this. No, Esperanza showed up out of the blue."

"Or the building was an accident. Buildings blow up. What if the building was an accident and you're reading into something a coked up, alcoholic CI is feeding you?"

"No. That's not it."

"I don't know. I'm trying to play devil's advocate here. But I think you're right."

"I'm always right, Stiles. You know that."

She was his superior in the agency, and not only did he respect her, he was in lust with her. She'd risen to a GS-15 faster than any agent in Bureau history. Period. She probably was right. And that meant his plans for the 4th of July with his kid were now shot. "This is true, Maria. This is true." He looked out the window at John. "Kane could be of help. He's smart." Stiles punched his name into the mobile computer.

"We'll bring him in when we're ready," she said.

Stiles scanned John's file. "He's no ordinary fire marshal. FD for ten years. Three years at BFI, he goes to work with us on the JTTF. Been there ten years. Computer Crimes section."

"Is he a fire marshal or a fed, Stiles?" she said.

"Both. He investigates arsons where computers are used and there is a potential for terrorist activity. Impressive case history. This guy knows computers, electronics, forensics, investigation – pretty impressive skill set. He's GS-15. Technically, ah, he outranks you." She shot him a look and he moved on.

He clicked on the personal section of his file. "Let's see what makes this guy tick." He read for a bit, then began paraphrasing to Santivánez. "Listen to this. His wife? Successful investment banker downtown. Diagnosed with schizophrenia ten years ago. Medication, counseling for both of them. She goes crazy two years ago. Attacks him with a knife. Actually cuts their daughter on the arm. Ruled an accident, but there was a restraining order. Temporary lock up. Gets out of the house last year, and… she runs off with all their cash. Five million in the bank. Still gone. Sends him divorce papers in the mail. Says here he signed them right away and sent them back to her lawyer. Also says he has a PI firm looking for her."

"Poor guy," Santiváñez said.

"This is odd. He's retiring… today."

"What's he doing here if he's JTTF Computer Crimes and retiring today?"

John stood on the east curb just up from them talking on his Droid. "Look at the skirt," Stiles said. "That's Jackie Fairbanks. She's not exactly dressed for camera. And he wasn't on duty. Look at the pants and the shoes Kane is wearing."

John wore tan linen pants, a fitted white button down, and woven boat shoes.

"They were here on a date when the thing blew," she said.

"He'll hand this off to another marshal if he's retiring," Stiles said. "Fairbanks could be trouble. She's aggressive."

Santiváñez looked Jackie up and down, sized her up. "Yes. She could get in the way."

"What do you think Tolliver's going to say now?" Stiles asked.

"I think he's going to say this is coincidence. That nothing has changed. To let DEA handle the drug connection with Walken and to let BFI handle the investigation of Malley's building. That we need to focus on a build-able case. And this isn't one."

"We better get something hard. And fast."

"Walken will make a mistake now. This is too big. It's just too much. Something will turn. Esperanza showing up won't help, either."

"What's the move?"

"Back this thing out of here. Let's see what Mackenzie has to say."

"Yes, ma'am," he said. She was the boss. A Supervisory Special Agent now, she had her sights set on the top desk, and he was pretty sure she'd get there. If he were lucky, he'd get her in the sack before that. In the sack or to the altar. He was in lust with her, sure. But he'd never felt this way about a woman. If it had been this way the first time around, he doubted he'd have gotten divorced.

Eleven

Now that Santiváñez and Stiles were gone, John walked over to Jackie. "Alright. I can get you a meeting with the brass. This thing's contained."

"Who were the suits?" she said.

This was where things were going to get tricky. He was supposed to be starting a romance with her, and now he was going to have to keep her at bay. Sharing case details with reporters was absolutely forbidden. He could say they were FBI, harmless enough. But then she'd ask more questions. He was trained to say nothing until the Chief or PR gave a statement. He scratched his head and looked back up 8th at the fire. "I can't say, Jackie. Sorry."

"Wait a minute. Are you catching this case? You're supposed to retire today."

He wasn't sure how to respond because he wasn't sure if he was catching the case or just filling in, and he couldn't really tell her either way.

Jackie's producer hung up his phone, stepped up, and whispered something into her ear. "John, does Senator Michael Malley own that building?"

"That must be a matter of public record."

"Wow. Well, what can you tell me?"

"Jackie, I don't know. Nothing. It's been less than an hour. It sounded like a gas explosion. Remember that boom? That's all I can tell you, and I can't even tell you that. All we're going to release is public information at this point, and that's not my job. You know how this works. You have to talk to those guys." He pointed to Fitzgerald and the mayor.

She did know how it worked. He could get her a shot with the mayor or Chief Fitzgerald, but they'd give her the same vanilla line she just got. Nothing of real use for an investigative reporter. But Michael Malley. This was no longer just a metro piece. She had a hundred things to do. She had to get to a computer. She turned to her producer and handed him the microphone. "Phil, take the spot John's going to get us. We'll take my lead-in we already shot, cut it with whatever you can get, and put a tail on later at the studio."

Phil fumbled with the microphone. "Jackie, I can't do this."

"Why not?"

"Because I'm not Jackie Fairbanks."

"You can do it, Phil."

Realizing this was his long-awaited shot to get in front of the camera, his smile grew and then his faced dropped deadpan. "Kent is going to lay an egg."

"I'll handle Kent," she said. "Now go."

Once they were gone, she kissed John's ear and whispered, "I'll take a rain check on whatever you had planned."

John watched her maneuver through the crowd of other press and onlookers. He was going to cash that rain check for her very soon. Now he had to keep his eye on the ball. Physicals would begin at sunup. Independent contractors for the cleanup would be ordered – all the rubble from the building would have to be hauled somewhere and inspected. That would take weeks. He was due in Jersey at nine. He'd have to pull insurance history, financial records – he'd subpoena those tomorrow. Even though Malley owned the building, they'd go through the normal procedures and look into his finances. There was a tremendous amount of work to be done.

Before disappearing around the corner at 42nd, Jackie turned and gave him a serious look. Her countenance turned to a smile, she bit her thumbnail, and he could have sworn that she growled at him. Then she slipped away.

He turned back to the fire and stood there for a few moments. He hated what he felt because he truly did not want to take this job. Duty was a hell of a thing.

TWELVE

The hostess led the party down the steps and into the '21 Club' subterranean kitchen. The aroma of balsamic vinegar, a tarragon-infused Béarnaise, and charred steak hit them at the bottom of the stairwell. Condor Walken breathed deep and let out a contented sigh.

He waved Torval Tangval and his two other men and seven female companions on. Torval stopped and looked back at Walken like a loyal guard dog, then took the next set of stairs to the sub-basement after Walken gestured him to continue with the group.

Walken invited his old friend Carlos Esperanza to the expediter's station. The chef put two plates under the warmer and said, "In the Wine Cellar tonight, Mr. Walken?" He was a trim black man from Louisiana with hazel eyes and a thin, gray pencil mustache.

"Yes, Chef," Walken answered.

The chef met eyes with Esperanza but did not inquire of his name. He was not the kind of man to become familiar with another until invited.

"I will see to your meal," the chef said, lowering his eyes to the garnish he was placing atop a shellfish appetizer.

"Thank you, Chef," Walken said. Then he moved down the line, looking over the counter to see what each cook was doing. Making their way towards the stairs to the sub-basement, he said, "What do you think?"

"One of the finest kitchens I have ever experienced," Esperanza said.

"It's why I bought her."

Esperanza stopped and turned in the middle of the stairwell. "She is yours?"

"I bought her years ago. Under one of my shells. Only Servaya Varvarushka and now you," Walken looked around, "and perhaps God, know of her true ownership." He and Esperanza had had many conversations about God. Walken was not a believer. Esperanza was a devout Catholic. He viewed his product as something God made. To be enjoyed responsibly. That some men could not do such was not his problem.

"You are mocking. I see you still have not found God," Esperanza said.

"Perhaps I am waiting for him to find me."

Esperanza raised his eyebrow and smiled. "Perhaps you will not like an unannounced visit from Dio, old friend."

"Well I am happy to receive yours," Walken said. Two hours ago he had been watching The History Channel when Esperanza called on the satellite phone and announced that he was entering port. "Continue on. Let me tell you more about '21 Club'."

"Con gusto," Esperanza said.

"She was built in the 20s as a speakeasy," Walken said when they reached the bottom of the short stairway. "Upstairs, they had shelves that would drop the bottles if the cops were to make a raid."

Esperanza said, "They would dump all their product down the drain if there was a raid?"

"Yes," Walken said.

"Well, we have some experience with that. Eh?" Esperanza slapped Condor on the shoulder.

Walken smiled big. "We dumped three hundred kilos into the ocean, Carlos. I could never forget."

"Ijo de la chingara," Esperanza said. "That was a lot of product at the time."

"At the time?" Walken laughed. "That was over a million dollars then."

"Simply bait for the DEA now." Esperanza looked around and then stepped closer. "You would not believe how many kilos I have."

"Is that why you are here?"

"In essence. But I am only here to pay a visit to you. I know you are a legitimate businessman now, and I would not involve you again in the trade."

"You know I would do anything for you, Carlos." Walken grabbed his forearm and squeezed gently. "You are my only true friend in this world."

Such a declaration demanded only their most familiar terms. "That is very comforting, Brian," Esperanza said. He was the only person in the world who knew Condor's real name. "Now show me more of this place. Where are we?"

"Step this way," Walken said.

A few paces down the hallway they came to an arched alcove. Covered with glossy gray paint, the walls were solid cement. Floor to ceiling, the apex of the arch rose five feet. It was just as wide, and three feet deep. Two ham legs hung from the ceiling.

"In the olden days, they stacked boxes at the back, too," Walken said.

"A very nice place to cure your ham. And store boxes," Esperanza said amusedly. He stepped to the back of the alcove and pounded the painted bricks. "There is something behind the wall? Si o No?"

"Take the skewer off the hook," Walken said.

Esperanza took a thin meat skewer off a screw in the wall, held it up, and looked around for a place to insert it.

Walken stepped into the alcove with him. "Let me show you," he said. He put his finger over a small hole in the back wall. "Here."

Esperanza inserted the skewer and pushed. There was a dull click.

Walken placed both hands on the wall and pushed hard. Part of the foundation of the building, the door weighed over four thousand pounds. "Welcome to the Wine Cellar, Carlos."

Inside, rustic and dimly-lit shelving held random bottles ranging from a 1933 bottle of bathtub gin with a type-written label bearing the name Lucky Luciano to a Sinatra Cabernet to a Merlot once held on reserve for Richard Nixon.

Walken led Esperanza around the corner to a rough opening in a two-foot-deep cement wall that was also part of the foundation. Beyond the vintage atmosphere of the first room lay the meticulously detailed Wine Cellar's dining room. From floor to ceiling, polished oak shelves held hundreds of bottles ranging in price from the tens to the tens-of-thousands of dollars. In the center of the room stood an oval table with twelve seats. At the far end, an intimate booth for two was carved into the wall. Adorned with pictures and artifacts mostly from the 1930s, it was a place which rich and powerful New Yorkers joined over the years to entertain, make deals, and lay secret plans.

The women held out their hands and assisted Esperanza down the two stairs into the sunken dining room. Four of them escorted him to the table, poured him wine, and lavished him with attention. The other three attended to Esperanza.

Walken motioned Torval over and nodded at the two other men. They were Terenty and Silanty. Two rough-looking Russians, brothers from different fathers, they were both six foot, two hundred pounds, and fit. Walken had met them in Moscow many years back. The brothers had tried to grab land when the Soviet government and economy failed. They drove around the country with crates of vodka and took peasants' acreage for a mere case of the mediocre stuff. But they hadn't bought enough land to really make an empire and they ran into cash flow problems when their appetite for Western indulgences exceeded their ability to produce liquid funds. Walken had met them one night at a club and they had partied and become instant friends. By luck, Walken had gone to use the bathroom as they were about to get their brains blown out by Russian shylocks. Walken bought their marker right there on the spot – twenty thousand dollars cash each.

He moved slowly with them, evaluating them as they got to know each other. The only flaw he could see in them was that their ambition exceeded their ability. He decided that they were good soldiers and had a place in his empire, as long as he kept them close. They were simply the kind that needed clear orders. They'd do anything and remain loyal and happy if supplied with what they wanted - a constant supply of nightclub life and all its trimmings – alcohol, cocaine, and women. They thrived in New York City.

"Have them stand guard outside," Walken said to Torval. "And have the Lithuanians take a look at the fire and report back." In addition to Terenty and Silanty, he employed people around Manhattan to do his bidding.

Torval simply nodded, motioned for the two Russians to follow, and then left.

Esperanza poured two glasses of a cabernet, handed one to Walken, and raised his. "To my old friend. I could not imagine a better reception."

"It must have been a long voyage, old friend," Walken said after sipping the wine.

"A long and very dry voyage," Carlos said.

Walken reached in his pocket, took out a long cigar tube, opened the top, and poured the cocaine in the center of the table in one long line. "Tu Puro," he said.

"To my best friend in the whole world." Carlos toasted Walken again, and then dipped his pinky in the white powder. After his sample, he invited his escorts to indulge at their pleasure, and the party was under way.

***

Three hours later, in a laughing storm, Walken and Carlos fell into the booth at the back of the room. The women, all wired on the powder, chattered away at the other end of the room. "What a night," Carlos laughed.

Walken smiled at his old friend, who was much more intoxicated than he. Carlos sat up straight and said, "Hey. Seriously. Let's catch up."

Walken opened his hands and said, "Okay."

"Tell me about the senator. How goes your plot to destroy Michael Malley?"

"Well, Carlos, it is funny you should come on such a night. I blew his building up four hours ago."

Carlos stood up and took the bottle and two glasses from the end of the table. He sat back down and poured the last of a chardonnay into the two glasses and said, "You blew up the senator's building? Here in Manhattan? *The* building?"

"The very one. Yes," Walken said as if it were a trivial matter.

Carlos drank his wine and shifted his head back and forth. He knew the history well and accepted it without further question.

It was a drama one hundred years in the making. In 1906, Michael Malley's grandfather – also Michael Malley – had effectively stolen the corner lot at 43rd and 8th right out from under Condor's grandfather – Harry Farrell. Harry Farrell, the "dirty Irish immigrant," was not fit to own land on Manhattan Island, old Senator Michael Malley had contended. He had used his influence to block the sale of the property to the "dirty Irishman," and bought the land himself, lest the working class think they could rise to prominence in New York City and be equal to the English.

It was a story often repeated in his family, usually not long after the whiskey started to flow, which generally began at the waking hour. Unable to rebound from the setback, his grandfather drank away the capital that he'd saved for the land and his grocery store. His mantra became, "no luck for the Irish." After his grandfather's premature death, his father got hard to work at becoming a bigger drunkard than his own father, proving his success by joining his father just a year later in the grave.

This was his nightmare. He'd seen it all and heard it all since he could remember. And while he had no respect for these men who wallowed in their self pity, he vowed at an early age to avenge their loss and embarrassment.

Tonight was but the second act in his play. He would take Malley's property, and if he chose, he would completely destroy him in everything that he was. It was fitting that the sins of one Michael Malley would come back to destroy another Michael Malley a century later.

"I think it was not such a good time for me to come," Carlos said. "I am a bad friend to show up unannounced."

"Nonsense," Walken said right away. "Now that you are here, I can't imagine it any other way. You took me in. You made my plot possible."

Carlos was all of a sudden very sober. "The senator wasn't in it when you blew it up, was he?"

Walken laughed. "No. You can't torture a dead man."

"Aye de me," Carlos said. "This could be a problem."

"How do you mean?"

"I mean, the Coast Guard boarded my boat and searched her. What if they know it is me and they are watching? It may bring attention to you."

"Old friend, I think the coca is getting to you. There is nothing. You know how I have planned. And I know how you cover yourself."

"We have to leave this place," Carlos said.

Walken chastised himself for not anticipating Carlos's reaction. The cocaine always made him paranoid. He took out his phone and texted Torval, who was in the adjacent room. Torval put his head through the opening and Walken motioned for him to take the women away.

Seconds later, alone in The Wine Cellar, Walken said, "Carlos, nobody is coming through that door. I would not have brought you to a place with no escape route. You taught me well." Esperanza had several hidden escape routes in his Medellin compound. He'd seen too many of his countrymen taken by the authorities and rival growers. Though he'd spent his adult life becoming a legitimate businessman, he'd molded his life in the city after his wily old friend.

"Let me show you a way out of here that only a dead man and I know about."

"And then I disappear," Carlos said. "I am going to Mexico to set up routes."

"As you wish, old friend."

THIRTEEN

It was 2:05 AM. The bar was empty, but for a couple in a corner booth. They were engaged in amorous conversation, oblivious to the waiter's impatient pacing. He stopped and put his hand on the bill wallet. "Pardon my interruption. The bar and restaurant are closed. Are you staying in the city? May I call you a car?"

The man looked at his watch. "Dear me, Charlie," he said with a British accent to the waiter. "We've overstayed ourselves."

"Oh, dash it," the woman said, also sounding like a Brit. "Charlie, be a darling," she said. "We got lost in all this." She circled her hand around the table. A half bottle of wine sat on the table, the fourth Charlie the waiter had brought that night. "I really wanted to see the Wine Cellar. Be a love and give us a peek."

"Madam," Charlie said. "We are closed. We have to lock the doors. City code."

The man opened the wallet. The bill was close to five hundred. He peeled off five one-hundred-dollar bills, and then five more, and put them inside.

Charlie looked over his shoulder to the bartender, who leaned against the back of the bar with his arms folded and head bowed. He was a man who wanted to go home and sleep.

The man pushed the wallet over the table to Charlie and said, "How about that?"

"Give me a minute," Charlie said, sliding the wallet off the table.

***

Mackenzie sat in the back of Santiváñez and Stiles' Suburban. They were parked at the corner of 56ᵗʰ & 5ᵗʰ. The female Brit's voice came over Mackenzie's radio. "This is unit five. We just got the tour. There's nobody in there but the waiter and the bartender. Over."

Another voice came over. "This is unit two. The waiter and bartender are locking the front door now. There is nobody left in there. Over."

Mackenzie pressed the send button on his Nextel and said, "This is unit one. Return to base. Over and out." He dropped his Nextel on the seat and said, "Where the hell did they go?"

Santiváñez's phone rang. She hit the talk button and simply said, "Go." She listened for a few seconds and then said, "Hold your post." Then she hung up and turned back to Mackenzie. "Condor Walken just got out of a cab and took the elevator up to his penthouse. No Esperanza."

"You think they smelled us?" Mackenzie said.

Santiváñez thought for a moment. "I don't think so. Walken has done this to us once before. There one minute and gone the next."

"What did you do?"

Stiles turned over his shoulder and said, "We walked away."

"I don't think you tipped your hand," Santiváñez said. "That place was packed, and the only flag you could have raised was at the end. Walken and his people were long gone."

"My people are going to be furious," Mackenzie said, staring out the window. "You'll bring us in if you see Esperanza resurface."

"Of course," Santiváñez said. "I'll call you directly."

Mackenzie pulled the handle on the door and stepped onto the sidewalk. He shook his head, and without words just closed the door.

Inside the Suburban, Stiles said, "You think Esperanza will resurface?"

"He's gone," she said.

"What if Walken knows we're on to him and he threw Esperanza in as a red herring?"

"Walken doesn't know we're on to him, and that's one hell of a ruse. Sail him all the way up from Colombia? No, Esperanza showing up is unrelated, and now he's moving on. We won't see him again."

"I think you're right."

She looked over at him and raised her eyebrows, calling back to what she told him at the fire scene. "I am in error for restating that which has already been established," Stiles said with a bit of gallantry.

She mouthed, "Thank you," dropped the Suburban in gear, and took the center lane. 5th Avenue was a straight shot to his apartment by Madison Square Park, a ten minute drive this time of night.

Stiles cracked his window for some fresh air. He had more than lust for Maria Santiváñez. There was no question about it. He was completely in love with her, and he didn't know what to do about it. He felt helpless as he had when he was a freshman and in love with the varsity cheerleading captain. That hadn't worked out well. She'd put him in his place without mercy. Turned out to be not a nice person at all. Maria, on the other hand. He was sure she was right for him. She was everything he desired in a woman, and she didn't take shit off anyone. And he was sure enough in himself that he could take shit off her. He would take her just the way she was, lock, stock and barrel.

He yawned for effect and stretched. "Late. You want my couch?" Why had he said that? His couch? Like she was one of the guys?

"Don't do couches, Stiles," she said immediately.

He'd said it because it was late and he was genuinely tired. She had to be too, and she had an hour drive to get home. And of course there was also the pent up lust. What the hell, he was already one foot in the water. "Maid came today. Fresh sheets. I'll grab the couch."

She took a full five seconds to answer. "I'm okay to drive."

What had flashed through her mind in those seconds that seemed an eternity to him? A sexual harassment reprimand? Did she see them together in his clean sheets?

The sex would be great. There was no doubt about it. But what he really wanted was the morning after. The muted morning light peeking through the curtains. A fresh pot of coffee. Breakfast in his garden. And the mutual feeling that this was a beginning. He longed to have that kind of intimacy with a woman again. The few romances he'd had since his divorce had satisfied his carnal needs, but it was his soul he needed to fill.

They still had a five-minute ride, and he couldn't sit there and pine away for her all the way down 5th Avenue. "What about Tolliver? What's the play now?"

"That's bound to be a long conversation. I'll call him on my way home. Unless you want to be in on it."

"You take it." He yawned again. For real this time. "You mind if I hit the radio?"

She pushed the button on the steering wheel that turned the radio on. A hits station played something new and unfamiliar. She pressed the up arrow on the wheel and an old Styx hit played. "You like?" she asked.

"Definitely."

She hit the volume up a few times and let out a sigh. They each needed to put this day behind them.

FOURTEEN

The ranking chief-at-the-scene called the fire "under control." It was out and there was no chance for another flare-up. The remaining two trucks sprayed the pile of rubble.

It was dawn. The coffee John had downed during the night made him wired and rummy. He rubbed his eyes and stepped up to the curb in front of the building.

By the morning light, he could see the gas riser that extended up the north wall. There was a "clean burn mark" around what looked like a pressure coupling. The "clean burn mark" was the telltale sign that gas had poured from a pipe there. It was no secret that the pipe had bled fire – he'd seen it himself and plenty of witnesses had told him and the other marshals the same thing. But what was a pressure coupling doing there? Pressure couplings were against code in that type of installation because it was more likely that they would leak than a soldered connection. John took out a fresh notepad Fitzgerald had given him. He used the pink-covered, stapled department issue 4x8 pad rather than the spiral notebook that was allowed. It made complying with Rosario much easier. If you tore a page out of the pink pad, as they called it, it was very evident. He never tore a page from his pad. It made things much simpler. No defense attorney could ever claim he'd withheld evidence or that he was trying to hide something. Something their kind tried to do at every turn.

They'd need to know when the pressure coupling had been installed. Who'd done the work? A handful of other things.

It was the first real clue. He'd ask Malley about recent repairs. The gas lines were as old as the building, but that coupling wouldn't have been put on at build.

John put the notepad in his back pocket and stretched his arms over his head. He clasped his hands together and lengthened every muscle in his body. He was a strong man, just over six feet and two hundred twenty pounds. He lowered his arms down and shook his arms and legs out. He needed a protein shake and a workout to wake his muscles up.

"Kane!" John heard a gruff voice over his shoulder. He turned and saw NYPD Detective Jerry Atkinson approaching. A short and stout man with a hard gut and a pack of smokes always nearby, he was a great cop. He'd worked some undercover cases that were infamous within the law enforcement community. If you were any kind of cop, you knew of Jerry Atkinson.

"Jerry," John said with a clear lack of enthusiasm. "Top of the morning."

"Yeah? It sucks." Atkinson wiped his forehead with a cotton handkerchief and shook John's hand. Then he fished out a smoke and mumbled through lighting it, "Goddamn mess." He blew smoke out of his nostrils and squinted up to the clean burn spot. "Any ideas?"

"You're looking at it. Possible C&O. See that fitting at the end of the pipe?"

"Yeah," Atkinson said.

"Pressure coupling. Shouldn't be there."

"Yeah," Atkinson said, still squinting. "I use those on my sprinkler system when I cut a pipe wrong. What kind of asshole puts one of those there?"

"Not sure. The other half of it is gone. It could have come off when the roof blew away. We'll send it through metallurgy, look for the usual signs of tampering."

Atkinson grunted. That would take weeks. Both men hated waiting on forensics, but short of a presidential order, there was usually little you could do to prod them along.

"I heard you lost one of yours. I'm sorry."

He looked John straight in the eyes with as much sincerity as a man possessed. He could be a real character, but Jerry Atkinson had heart where it counted.

"He was a good man," was all John could say.

"Well, you know where PD stands on this. One of yours down, BFI takes the lead. Chief called me personally to deliver the message. Why don't we sit down when we can review your findings?"

"Sure thing," John said.

"Mean time, you get anything, you need anything from PD, call me directly. Chief's still going to be up my ass on this. I may have to call you if I need to feed him something."

"I'll keep you on top, but I may be gone sooner than later. I'm retired, you know."

"No shit?"

John just smiled at him and shook his head.

Every cop dreamed of retirement, and none were more ready than Atkinson to get out of the rat race and leave the big city behind. "You're a prick, Kane."

A firefighter named Michael Terry approached carrying the burnt remains of something. "Hey, John," Terry said. "Take a look at this. Woody asked me to bring it down to you." Woody was a junior marshal John had tasked with handling evidence collection. "Couple guys found it two rooftops over."

John took the burnt thing from Terry. Nearly a mirror image physically, he was fifteen years his junior. Aside from Terry's black hair, which he wore a little longer than John, they could be stand-ins for each other. Terry was in shape and ripped. The nicest guy in the world, but you could always count on him for a grueling bout in the workout ring. For John, it was like fighting his doppelganger. They both always ended up on the canvass when they fought. Terry was also studying to take the marshal's exam. He was a good guy and John had personally recommended him for the open slot that was being created with his retirement.

"Looks like a floor heater," John said, looking the thing over. It was about a foot on each side. The front was open and the heating elements were still intact. The power cord was a burnt nub of rubber. "Yep, that's what it was. You guys photograph this?"

"Yes," Terry said. "Woody's still up there. He has the whole thing diagrammed. Thought you'd want to take care of the voucher on this personally."

"Ignition source?" Atkinson asked.

"Perhaps." It was too soon to start making assumptions. But it gave him something else to pursue in addition to the pressure coupling on the gas pipe.

"Give me a card, Kane." Atkinson handed John one of his.

John pulled his money and a card out of his pocket. Leaving home earlier that night, he thought for sure there was no way he'd need cards, so he'd taken only a few and put them in his pocket. He handed Atkinson his last. It was a simple card with his information and the BFI insignia, which was a round emblem with the scales of justice in the center. Topping the scales were the words Veritas Ex Cineribus, which meant "truth from ashes." Older than the NYPD Detectives Bureau and Scotland Yard, the New York City Bureau of Fire Investigation stood on its 158-year reputation of keeping the Greatest City on Earth safe from arsonists, pyromaniacs, and criminals of all kinds.

FIFTEEN

It was seven AM. He had to get back to his house in Jackson Heights, shower, put on proper attire before visiting Senator Malley. He took 3rd Avenue north to the Queensboro, rather than the tunnel. The Upper Roadway moved along at a fair pace and gave him time to enjoy the view.

The Channels were busy with boats this morning. Soon enough he'd be out there with them. His forty-footer needed a lot of work, but rehabilitating the old thing he'd bought at an auction was his new job while Katie was in school. His plan had always been to buy a new boat. But Peggy had taken most of the money, left him with a little cash in the checking account, the house they owned free and clear, and his pension. He just hoped she was safe. She belonged in a hospital, not running around the world philosophizing on social media sites. One day she'd hurt herself, or worse, someone else. It was probably time to let her go completely. Abandon the fake identities he'd created on Facebook and Twitter to keep track of her. He could do it now. The animosity was gone. The anger. She was thoroughly sick, and aside from locking her up there was nothing anyone could do. And locking her up wasn't his job. So long as she stayed away from Katie.

He was almost over the river. So many times he'd imagined being out there with Katie. A light wind pushed them along at four or five knots. She was driving the boat, standing on a milk crate, which she almost no longer needed. There was nothing in the world happening but the lapping water against the sides of their boat and the warm sun on their skin.

When Katie was in school, he'd be on the boat and tinker with electronics. He was looking forward to more time with microprocessors and printed circuit boards. He had majored in electrical engineering in college, and now fancied that he might invent the next big thing.

He certainly wasn't going to miss bureau dress code. In addition to a firmly pressed shirt and tie every day, a marshal had to wear a coat. During the humid months, the coat was torture. From now on, it would be cargo shorts and open-collar shirts. Most days he wouldn't even wear shoes. For the winter, they might even sail to the south.

He looked into the rearview mirror. The Twin Towers used to stand above their peers not even a mile away from where he now was. He was in nearly the same place, but driving into the city, when American Airlines Flight 11 crashed into the North Tower. He left his car and ran over the bridge into Manhattan that morning. It took him seven minutes. He was almost to Ground Zero when the second plane hit, and he was preparing to climb the stairs of the North Tower with a group of firemen when it started to collapse and he narrowly escaped the crush.

He could still hear the screams and the freakish roar of twisting steel and crumbling, cascading cement. He and Peggy had both lost a lot of friends that morning. She was supposed to be in her office on the 95th floor of the North Tower. The doctors said it's what triggered her schizophrenia. It was a sickness that ran in her family. She had always been the strongest one. Until it crept in. He'd struggled to keep her together for years. Then the market crashed in 2007 and she had another "episode," as the doctors called it. It had been more than an episode. Her brain had transformed, and after that, she really started to go.

He looked back down at the water. He was making the right decision retiring. If he didn't do it now, not only would the milk crate be gone, but so would Katie, off to college, and then on with her own life. Katie was thrilled. Now he'd be there every day when she got out of school. He'd be at all her events. There would be no more midnight calls. And they would go sailing all the time.

Sixteen

The trip from Queens to Summit, NJ took forty-five minutes. He rolled down the window and turned off the air conditioner. The car filled with the sweet fragrance from massive flowerbeds. The Garden State truly deserved its name.

A sort of bedroom community of new money, Summit held a pocket of estates for the ultra-rich. Unlike the sprawling estates of neighboring Mendham, these homes were grouped tighter on one and two-acre lots. Aside from a few newer custom homes, the structures themselves were all fashioned in some early American architecture, 17th Century Colonial, 18th Century Georgian, and a mix of styles from the 19th Century.

These homes were all at least seven to ten million. Taxes on each were fifty to eighty thousand a year. He couldn't see spending that on a house. A boat maybe. There were some beautiful sailing yachts out there that were in that range, and you didn't have to pay property taxes on a boat.

A few news vans were parked along the road by Malley's estate. John pulled the Explorer up to the security post and pushed the little white button on the box. He immediately heard a beep, and the heavy steel gate slid open.

***

Two FBI field agents sat inside one of the news vans parked along the road in front of Malley's property. The first agent picked up a phone and dialed a number.

***

Stiles read the Saturday Wall Street Journal and Santiváñez picked through the Times' Business Day section on her iPad. They sat under an umbrella in an Upper West Side outdoor café.

She set the device on the table, finished the cold black coffee in the bottom of her cup, and signaled the waiter for a refill. She was ticked off that Tolliver had only given her the one team that she now had posted outside of Malley's in the news van. He was calling it a watch and wait.

The Assistant Director in Charge of the New York field office had personally spoken to Michael Malley. Malley was sure the whole thing was an accident. Was refusing protection. Couldn't justify the expense to the Bureau for something that was clearly not aimed at harming him.

So Tolliver wouldn't go to the U.S. Attorney for expanded tap warrants. Especially not on the 4th of July. Neither he nor the ADIC shared her hunch that Michael Malley was corrupt.

Her phone rang. She hit the answer button, listened, and then cut the call. "He's there," she said to Stiles. It wasn't Kane that worried her. Jackie Fairbanks, though, was trouble. She was the kind of woman who didn't quit. She was… very much like her own self. This case was going to turn, and it was going to get very complex. She didn't need some alter ego getting in her way.

Stiles closed his paper and drank from his cappuccino. "We should level with Kane," he said. "The quicker we know what he does, the better."

"Convince Tolliver," she said. "Until we concretely connect Walken to Malley or the fire to Walken, it stays in-house."

Stiles opened his paper again. He hated the Bureau when it did this shit. It was so old school. Kane was a good man. He had more experience as a fed than either he or Santiváñez. They could do more with him on board, and he wasn't going to take kindly to the brush off that was coming his way. Tolliver had been clear. Kane was a hybrid, and it was his opinion that he was acting purely in his capacity as an FDNY fire marshal on this case.

He glanced down at her thigh. She wore a conservative skirt and very thin pantyhose this morning. And heels. He loved the way her legs looked in heels. She could stay close to him in the 100 meter dash with those legs. Beat him in the 1600 last week. It was hard to concentrate on work sitting next to her.

"Mind on the job, Stiles," she said sweetly and sipped her fresh coffee.

There was a small sparrow hopping around on the cement beside her. He thought about playing it off like he was looking at the bird. But what was the use in being coy anymore? He had invited her into his bed last night.

No, it was time to get real. They'd been working together for six months now, and that was the first time she'd acknowledged his furtive looks. Sometimes he knew they were all out longing stares. He simply couldn't help it. So he looked her in the eyes and smiled nice and easy. And then returned to his paper.

SEVENTEEN

John drove up a small incline. To his left, notched into the gentle slope, was a professional croquet course and bocce ball court. A dense stand of tall pines bordered the property to his right. At the top of the hill, a palace. Fifteen-thousand square feet sat atop a five-acre lot, the only lot of its size in the area. The quick property report he'd run in his home office showed the estate was valued at fifteen million dollars.

A smartly dressed man stood near the corner of the east wing. A mansion unto itself, it was connected to the body of the main structure. The main body was three stories tall and reminiscent of the Colonial style, but it missed the bland symmetry of classic structures.

A west wing jutted out at a forty-five degree angle from the main house. It was similar looking to the east wing, only it was longer and had another smaller house on the end of it. Every blade of grass, every tree, flower, and every bush was manicured to perfection.

The man at the east wing motioned for John to continue his course. He drove through a trellised tunnel and followed a slate stone drive that curved around to the back. Individual gardens, a walking path, lawns, and fountains filled the back acres.

"Good morning, Marshal Kane," a man at the top of the stairs said when John put both feet on the ground. He was dressed the same as the other man at the east wing. Malley liked order, that was evident.

John pulled a box from the back seat and walked up the stairs. As a matter of protocol, he showed the man his badge. "Good morning. Here to see the senator."

"Right this way, sir," the man said and offered to take John's coat.

The heat was coming on and John would have loved to shed it. But it was part of the uniform, and he was going to see a man who one day might be president, so he declined the offer.

The man led John through the formal sitting room, down a hall, and to a room near the west wing at the south of the mansion. He pushed open both doors to Malley's study and stepped to the side. Both doors rested neatly at their stops. John noted the perfection and thought the guy should go on Wheel of Fortune.

Michael Malley rose from his seat and met John in the middle of the room. "Good morning, Marshal Kane. Thank you for coming out."

Malley looked exactly as he did on television. Topping a large, round head, he had a thick shock of course, white hair parted over to the left side. His skin was unblemished and olive color, as if he sat in a tanning booth for five minutes every day. The years were catching up with his waist line. John judged it at forty-two inches, his inseam twenty-six. "It's a pleasure to meet you, Senator."

"Listen, you call me Michael, and I'll call you John."

John agreed. Malley offered him coffee and they moved to a sitting area. A sterling silver coffee tray rested on a small antique table between two toile-covered chairs. They were French, John knew. Peggy loved interior decorating. She was halfway through giving their kitchen a French-Country look when she left. John had finished the kitchen himself, pouring through the magazines and books she had all over the house. It was his breakthrough, something the counselor had suggested to overcome the anger and grief. It had worked. He realized standing there, that lately he could go into her kitchen and not be overcome by the memories. John felt the fabric on the chair. "Very nice."

"My great, great grandmother bought these chairs in Paris, oh gosh, I forget what year."

"In between wars with the English?"

Malley laughed. "Yes, I suppose."

John noted the rest of the surroundings in Malley's office. There was nothing but the finest of everything. "I should have gone into politics."

"Oh, believe me, you don't get rich in public service. I inherited most of this from my daddy."

"I inherited a fireman's jacket."

Malley laughed again at the joke. "As a marshal, you were a fireman first," he stated.

"That's right. We all go through the academy, learn the ropes, fight fires."

"Know thy enemy?"

John dropped a couple sugar cubes in his coffee. He'd been drinking it black all night. "You know, in my line of work it's a little different. People generally start fires. Whether they mean to or not. And they're not really the enemy."

"Ah," Malley said. "Like politics. You embrace those that oppose you to win."

John stirred the sugar. "Sure. Something like that."

John studied Malley. He seemed relaxed, composed, like a man heading for the White House would be. At this point, everyone was a suspect. You were innocent until proven guilty, but it was his job to look for signs of the latter. Malley was cool, calm, collected.

They talked about everything but the fire for several minutes, until John had finished his cup of coffee. Malley offered him another. Any more he would become jittery. "No, Michael. Thank you. I'm sure you're a very busy man. Do you mind if we get down to business?"

"Of course."

John took out his notepad and pen. "Just the routine questions I have to ask."

"Of course. Go right ahead. I'd be offended if you treated me differently than anyone else."

"Okay. So how did you first hear about the fire?"

"John, it was the strangest thing. His Honor the Mayor called me personally. Woke me out of a deep sleep on my personal line. When I heard his voice, I was scared to death. I thought there had been another terrorist attack."

John took the note. "How about the financial condition of the building? You rent that building out?"

"It's been fully leased for years. Those poor people are now out of places for their businesses. Well, I guess there's plenty of space in Manhattan."

"Not in your location," John said.

"No. That was a pretty good location," Malley said appraisingly.

"How about insurance?"

"Same policy I put in place nearly twenty years ago. I review all my coverage once yearly with my agent. We keep it up to date. Premiums took a healthy jump this year. The cost to rebuild that building nearly doubled in the past two years."

"Imagine if you didn't believe in insurance," John said.

"Some men are foolish and underinsure," Malley said flatly, not expounding any further.

"So business is good. You're one hundred percent leased. What about the mortgage?"

"I own that building and land outright, John. Land has been in my family for a century. Watched my daddy and grand daddy construct the building nearly fifty years ago. Drank a lot of soda pop that summer, I remember. Sad to think it's gone."

There was a silence.

"What is really sad, John," Malley continued, "is that a man lost his life. Firefighter I understand. I'm still waiting to hear about his family situation."

John knew Jimmy Park had a wife and child, but he didn't feel like offering that up at the moment.

"Do you have any idea how the fire started?" Malley asked.

"There was an explosion – a loud boom and then fire. No smoke. It's not official, yet, but I'm fairly certain it was gas."

"Gas," Malley said looking into space.

"Was there any plumbing work done to the building recently?"

Malley thought for a few seconds and then said, "Yes. There was." Then he looked off into space again.

John waited for him to return to the conversation, but he didn't. After a few seconds he said, "Michael?"

"Yes," Malley said, and shook off his visible disquietude. "Yes. We had a gas leak repaired a few months back."

John took quick notes. "Where was the leak?"

"In my office. I smelled it one day and had my assistant Henry call for a plumber."

"Your office, on the fifth floor?"

"Yes."

"Where exactly was the leak?"

"Well, that's the north wall. In my office. It was about midway up the wall. They used this ingenious little tool to find it and then broke through the plaster and repaired it."

John took notes. North wall, midway up. That was most likely the riser that was gushing last night. He'd have to wait weeks for the metallurgist's results, but this thing looked like an accident. He looked up from his notes and said, "Michael, do you have any reason to think someone would want to kill you?"

"John, the FBI asked me the same thing. I suppose there are people out there. But who would go to the trouble to blow up a building? Why not just use a rifle? You know what I mean?"

"I do. But I have to ask. I've been arresting criminals for a long time, and they all have different reasons for what they do."

"Well, I suppose you're right. Wouldn't be prudent to rule out anything at this point."

"Is it possible someone was trying to send you a message?"

"That's a good question. But no. If anyone contacts me, you and the FBI are the first people I would call, though."

"Good. You know, in any case, you might want to consider your security."

"This place is tight as a drum. If a fox jumps onto my property, we know about it. Surveillance here is top notch, John. Until your department tells me there is something to worry about, I just have to believe it was an accident."

"What was the security like at your building? I didn't get a chance to talk to your security guard before they took him to the hospital. I understand he's okay."

"Yes, he appears fine, thank God. He's all we really had. None of the tenants demanded any kind of video surveillance. You know, there are more cops on the street in Times Square than any other place in the world. If the alarm rang, that place would be swarming with officers. Everyone seemed very comforted by that. Nobody really had much to steal in there. Most of the tenants were artists, dancers – artists' studios, you know?"

"Any way in or out, other than the front door?"

"There was a door on the roof. It was alarmed at all times. You had to have a code and a key to get in."

Again, John took notes.

"What was the nature of your business in the building?"

"I rarely ever went there. Kept my father and grandfather's business records in the office. Truth is, I kept the office as sort of a remembrance, a tribute to them. Seemed like they belonged there. Most of what they did was on the Island. Plus, I didn't know where else to store all the files. There was a lot of paper in there, John. I had it all scanned and backed up, but I'm old-fashioned. I just couldn't see getting rid of all that nostalgia."

John took that down in his pad. "That might explain why the other floors went so fast."

Malley looked off in the distance again, disheveled.

Henry Douglas entered the room and cleared his throat. "Excuse me, Senator."

Malley looked over. "Henry, come in. John, this is my personal aide, Henry Douglas."

"Pleasure to meet you, Marshal."

Henry's Blackberry beeped. He checked it and said, "Excuse me, Senator, but it's almost time for our conference call with Mr. Kipp."

"Oh, by golly, I almost forgot. John, it's the end of the day in Germany, and we've got a narrow window of opportunity to get our negotiations finalized. I'm importing ink and feathers for pillows and pens. Not very exciting, but it looks like a profitable venture. Trying to build on my father's legacy, you know."

"Sure," John said. Everything they had talked about was as he expected it to be. "I just have one more thing to discuss before I go." John pulled the lid off the box and held up the charred floor heater. "Does this look familiar?"

Malley looked at it closely. "Why, yes. That's my foot warmer. Kept it under my desk. Used to turn it on those cold nights, keep the blood flowing in these old toes, you know?"

"Was it on last night?"

Malley thought for a second. "You know, it could have been. I've forgotten to turn it off a few times over the years. Goes on when the temperature drops below the setting. But it would have been set far below the temperature of last night."

"Thermostats can break," John said.

"Oh, my. Do you think it sparked the fire?"

"It could have been the ignition source. Something up there had to set the gas off. Were there any other electronics up there?"

"Henry, what was up there?" Malley asked.

"Well," Henry said, "there were a couple of old phones. We could pull the phone records and see if someone called. There was a shelf stereo, that I'm sure was off. Not anything else by way of electronics. It was kind of a relic, really. The Senator liked leaving it as it was."

John took notes. He sensed an open and shut case. But the FBI? What were they doing there last night? What were they hiding? Maybe it didn't have anything to do with the fire. It looked like Malley was going to run for president, after all. The complexities were limitless. Somehow it was a relief. It would make it much easier to hand the case off if nothing were dangling on his end.

"To think I might be responsible for this, for the death of those men," Malley said.

John drew a small flag in his notepad at hearing Malley say that. His tone was a bit melodramatic. And why would he say such a thing? No man with his knowledge of the law and its protections would suggest responsibility for someone's death. But he closed his notebook and looked up at Malley.

"It's much too early to make any kind of determination. The fire was almost definitely gas. How it got in the building and how it ignited is another story."

Malley was still visibly upset.

"Senator," Henry said. "I'm very sorry. But Mr. Kipp will be waiting on the phone."

"John, I am sorry. Can you wait?" Malley said.

"I'll come back if it's required, Michael."

"I'll have a package delivered to you, Marshal," Henry said. "Rents for the building, financials, etcetera. You'll need those things, I assume."

"That's very good. I will need those for the file."

"Well, I took a forensics course in college."

"I'll tell you, John. Henry ought to be the one running for office. Always a step ahead of me."

EIGHTEEN

Henry closed the door to the study and stepped close to Malley's desk. "Can we step outside?"

"Sure," Malley said.

A minute later they were standing in front of the pond at the back of his estate. "What's on your mind?" Malley said.

Henry wasted no time getting to the point. "You need to sell him that property, Michael."

Malley looked back into the pond. The lilies were in bloom and the koi were growing fat. He'd built this pond with his father many decades ago and it had always brought him great peace. This morning, though, he was anything but peaceful. "Nonsense," he said. "They found the floor heater. It was an accident."

"That's just what they made it look like, Michael. You know that was no accident."

Malley knew the truth, and he knew what he was going to have to do, but he wasn't sure he wanted to admit it to Henry. Henry knew every last thing about him personally and professionally, and for some reason Malley began to question their future together. He turned to Henry with a stone face and said, "How can you be so sure?"

"He's a ruthless man, Michael. He wants the property. He keeps telling you and you keep telling him no."

"Something like this would be one hell of an audacious shot across my bow."

"And you think he's not capable? Michael, sell him the property. He said that would be the end of the favors. Just do it and let's get on with running for the presidency."

Malley chewed on his lip and looked back to the pond.

"There is another way," Henry said.

Malley didn't answer, but Henry knew he was listening. "Remove him," Henry said. "You know the people to make it happen."

Malley stared into the pond like a man faced with sending his country to war. There was a man to whom he could turn, and he'd thought of calling him many times to deal with this man who had plagued him for so many years. "You mean have him killed, don't you?"

"Yes, Michael. That's exactly what I mean."

"Murder is a trick of the devil, my boy."

"And what is this we're in? God's blessing? We're now a party to arson and the death of a firefighter."

Malley snapped his head around. "Compose yourself. I am not a party to anything. There is no way they can trace anything back to me. I didn't do this."

"Us, Michael. We. And we are not coming forward with what we know. So we are party."

"We've done nothing and I know nothing. They've found the ignition device. He even said that thermostats can break. We don't have to explain anything. And you should not have offered to send him my records. You acted nervously."

"What if they really start digging? We need to be very careful."

"The building will be proven to be an accident, and nobody is going to investigate it any further. You just keep your mind on your job. Do I have to remind you what that is?"

"No, Michael. I know what my job is."

"Good. This conversation is over." Malley walked away.

Henry put his hands in his pockets and looked down through the thick Kentucky Bluegrass. Condor Walken had promised him nobody would die, let alone an FDNY firefighter. When one of their own died in a fire, the FDNY made it personal. So said the urban legend, anyway. Marshal

Kane was a serious cop. They couldn't make any mistakes with him on the case. Any more mistakes that is.

His biggest mistake had been listening to Condor in the first place. Condor had proposed the scheme a year ago when he picked up the last case of money for a contract Malley had helped him win. His proposition was simple – help them gain access to the building so they could burn it down. With the building gone, the sentimental attachment Malley had to the property would be too, and he would sell. Then Walken could move on with his life and never bother the senator again. Henry could either help him do this, or, Walken said, he would simply kill Senator Malley and wait for his estate to settle out and buy it then. Either way, he was going to get the property.

He took out a pack of Camel filters, lit one, and sucked the smoke deep into his lungs. He tapped his foot on the grass and looked at the smoldering tip of the white stick. It was a habit he'd kicked in college, and only picked back up recently. The senator despised cigarette smoking. But what was he going to say? They had bigger problems.

He took another hit off the cigarette and fished a small pill box from his pocket. He'd always wanted to kill Walken, from the first time Senator Malley had introduced him into this nightmare. He'd spent many hours meditating about it. He suspected the senator had, too. How could he not?

He pinched a Valium from the case and swallowed it dry. Walking across the grass to his private quarters, he second guessed himself. Michael Malley was not the kind of man to have another murdered. He was a good man. Perhaps too good a man to become the most powerful man on earth.

He'd planted the idea in the senator's head. It was up to him to do the right thing now. He needed to lie down and think. All of a sudden, playing both sides of the fence had become very nerve wracking.

Nineteen

Since he was this close, John decided to take a detour to a stretch of the Passaic River he'd never seen. He held the Passaic River Rowing Club's title for single-skull head-to-head, a title which he defended every year for the past decade. Every year, some young upstart came gunning for him. But his years of built up endurance held them off each time.

He left the windows down and took River Road for a mile to Passaic Drive. Pulling to the side, he saw a much narrower stretch than they enjoyed by Riverside Park in Lyndhurst.

Something nagged at him. If it was the floor heater that set off the gas, it was a big coincidence, and arson investigators didn't believe in coincidences. A flag. The pressure coupling that didn't belong. A flag. Malley was a little melodramatic. There was something about Henry Douglas that didn't sit right. Flags? A forensics class in college, Henry Douglas had said. Offering up phone records? He was a little eager. Too many flags.

Malley as a suspect? It was unlikely, but not crazy. If he were somehow complicit, he would be a very worthy adversary. Harvard Law School. United States Senator. Presidential candidate. If he wanted to, his abilities to hide the truth were strong. He'd watched his every move, and besides the bit of melodrama, it didn't seem that he was hiding anything.

A man becomes a criminal two basic ways. Either very quickly by accident or poor decision making, or very slowly, over the years. It was doubtful that a man like Malley would do anything impetuously or by accident. His kind were slow and cautious. It was in their DNA.

On the slow path to crime, a man tells his first lie, starts to distance himself from the truth and what is right, and then he repeats his actions, growing in magnitude each time. He creates Cognitive Distance. From the truth. With each indiscretion, he grows bolder and bolder. Malley was squeaky clean. He had been a presidential candidate. Was sending signals he was going to run again. Had to have been vetted by the FBI and his own party. He appeared straight as an arrow. Appeared that way, at least.

There was of course that great destroyer of men. Greed. This old devil was the real criminal in most every case he'd investigated.

John rolled up the windows and turned on the AC. The straight ones were often guilty. Never superstitious, he always remembered his first day as a marshal. The guys had walked down from the old Lafayette fire house to Chinatown for lunch, something they commonly did those days when they had more time and manpower. The little slip of paper in the fortune cookie said in Chinglish, "Straight tree have crooked root." In this case, Chinese philosophy coincided with one of the primary tenets of Law Enforcement Standards and Conduct – Never believe what you see on the surface.

He took out his phone, called Woody, and gave him instructions to follow up on the plumbing company that had installed the pressure coupling and then set the phone on the seat. Most people were in their homes getting ready to barbeque and celebrate the 4th. He had to get some rest. He'd promised Katie and Aunt Mary he'd take them to the fireworks show on The Hudson tonight.

There was just one more thing to do. He'd interview the security guard, log the call, and then hang it up for the day. He really needed to get some rest before the show.

TWENTY

It was 10AM. Jackie stood in front of the Port Authority Bus Terminal at the corner of 42nd & 8th. She had been glued to her computer researching anything she could find on Michael Malley for the past eight hours. She had a lead. It was a big lead. Senator Malley was tied to a company called Immunex. Immunex's credibility was suspect. That much she knew. The New York Times had run an article on them five years ago that questioned why they were receiving so much government appropriation monies. There was one story and then nothing. The fact that Malley owned a building that had just blown up, and the fact that he was loosely connected to a company whose credibility had been questioned by the Times raised every suspicious cell in her body. But that didn't explain why his building blew up. She needed more. Unfortunately, she would have to wait weeks for the data from the BFI.

Her phone rang. It was Kent. She rolled her eyes and wanted to let it go to voicemail, but he'd just call back. She'd made the mistake of letting him creep up behind her and spy her computer monitor, and now he shared her suspicions. He'd call every hour she was in the field now wanting an update. She pushed the button and spoke her normal greeting, "Jackie Fairbanks." Always polite, always a little lift at the end, sending a positive message to whoever was on the other end of the line, even though she knew it was the shit-heel Kent.

"What do you have?" he said without a greeting, trying to sound jovial, as if they were on the same team or something.

"Well, Kent, not much. I'm just getting started."

This was his game. He'd pursue her until she got annoyed, he'd back off, to make her think that she was in charge, and then move forward, hoping he could get back into her good graces, until she finally shut him down, and then he'd get pissy. They'd been through a few of these cycles. He must read women's magazines, or maybe they were counseling that sort of thing in the rags men read today. She wasn't sure. She read neither. But she knew his game.

She waited for him to say something, wanted to hang up, but that would be rude, and she was at all costs, never rude to another person. Firm, yes. Direct when the situation called, definitely. But rudeness was base. And her father had taught her better than that.

Morning traffic buzzed by. Tourists crowded the corners and snapped photos of the fire scene down 8th Ave.

"Where are you?" Kent finally said.

She'd tried to play nice with him. She really had. But enough was enough. "Kent. Let me be very clear with you. I'm dating a new guy now. He's six foot, big, and he knows how to handle himself. If you continue to harass me I'm going to send him up there to have a word with you." The line was dead silent. "Kent, I'm joking. What I'm really going to do is go upstairs and file a complaint. I hate to do it, but this is why we have laws."

"You sure grew a set of jugs all of a sudden."

She simply wouldn't respond to a comment like that.

"Who is he?"

"Kent, this conversation is over."

"Turn in what you have by five."

The readout showed disconnected. "Poor form, Kent," she said. Sliding the phone back into her purse, she laughed out loud. She didn't need to send John to take care of Kent. She'd taken various forms of martial arts since she was six. Her father knew she was going to be a knockout, and he'd taught her how to fell any guy who disrespected her. If Kent messed around with her, she could put him to the canvass before he could get a hand up to protect his pretty manicured eyebrows.

She could see Ferrari's from where she stood, and the little table through the broken glass where she had sat with John just ten hours ago.

She knew far more about him than what he'd told her last night. It was a year ago that she saw him outside of One Police Plaza in Lower Manhattan. His fluid but strong gait caught her eye. He stopped to talk to another man in the south courtyard, and she stopped to watch him.

Discovering his name was easy enough. From there... it was what she did. She hated it now that she'd spied on him before knowing him, but she'd had some bad relationships and, well, it was her prerogative as a woman to check out a man she was interested in.

The computers told her a lot. People at the gym where she often went after work told her the rest. It was said he was about as tough as they came. That several years ago people thought he could easily rise up and take the UFC middleweight title. He was a boxer and a wrestler. His Jiu-Jitsu came naturally, guys said. He had a combined skill that was deadly. Would trade blow for blow with any guy, then take you down and either pummel or choke you into submission.

The story went that his wife got sick, and she didn't want him to fight. No one had seen him around a gym since. People said he'd stopped training in Mixed Martial Arts, stopped working out altogether.

He was no longer 185 pounds. She guessed more like 210. But he was in shape. He definitely hadn't stopped working out. She'd held onto one of his arms when they were walking down 8th Avenue from the theatre. It was rock hard and toned. She jabbed him playfully in the side once, too. It was hard to believe he ever fought at 185.

She stood there in front of the Port Authority Bus Terminal, the busiest station in the world. Greater than fifty million people passed through it every year, came in one way, changed directions, went somewhere else.

She was at a crossroads. Or wanted to be, at least. She wanted John to be that other road. She wanted to turn away from her career and retire like him. For a long time now she'd been ready to leave all the hustle and hyper pace behind and settle down. She didn't need the money. What she needed, what she wanted, was a man like John Kane.

She had to turn her thoughts back to her story and forget about John for the time being. Then she laughed loud enough for everyone around to hear.

She couldn't take her mind off of him. Her fire marshal. Her Marshal. She liked the sound of it.

With that, she walked west on 42nd from 8th Avenue. Just down from the drug store stood a building much like Malley's, but four stories and a little older. It had been untouched by the fire. She entered the lobby. On the wall behind a glass case was a simple black and white board that listed the building's tenants. Maclevey, Maclevey and Horshowitz, Attorneys at Law appeared to occupy the entire 4th floor. It was a strange place for a law firm, but this was New York City. There probably wouldn't be anybody there. It was Saturday, July 4th. She had no idea why she pushed the up button on the elevator, but she was going up. She had a lead. She was following her nose. It's what investigative reporters did.

The bell dinged at four and the doors opened effortlessly. It was an old building with a new elevator. She stepped into the lobby. The carpet was new. Hunter green with a simple gold inlay running the perimeter of the area. It was a newer firm. No pictures of the founding partners hung about the papered walls. Minimalist décor, but very finely done, suggesting they were the kind of firm that got right down to business and deftly executed their part of the bargain.

A young girl carrying a file box across the lobby stopped and looked at Jackie as if she were an apparition. She set the box down on the receptionist desk and said, "Can I help you?"

"Hi. My name is Jackie—"

"Jackie Fairbanks," the young girl cut her off. "I know who you are," she said, crossing her arms, extending her left leg forward, leaning back a little.

She was very pretty and well built. About Jackie's height – 5', 10." Natural blond. Early 20s. Definitely an intern. Was she being combative? It was hard to tell. Her tone was neutral, but her posture suggested a certain defensiveness. She couldn't be thrilled to be there carrying files around on the 4th of July.

She was tough, but her pose merely registered as what it was – a young girl trying to prove herself in the big city. Not much of an affront to a woman who had made it several times over in New York. Jackie took a few steps forward.

"I'm surprised to find anyone here on a holiday." Sometimes small talk got you thrown back out on the street. What would this young doe say?

The young girl caved pretty fast. Dropped her arms. Put her hands on her hips. "These guys never stop working. It pays double time. What are you going to do?"

"Take the money, sweetheart." Jackie liked the young girl right away. She was most likely from the northwest. She had no discernible accent. She annunciated her words very clearly. Her voice was clear and rich. She was strong. Probably had a wide vocal range.

"Can I help you?" the young girl said.

"You have me at a disadvantage. You know my name, but I don't know yours."

"Erynn. Erynn Kelly."

"Hmm," Jackie said. "Sounds like a stage name."

Erynn raised her brows and smiled, as if to say, "yeah." Then, "You're here about the building down the Avenue."

She would be out of luck as soon as Maclevey, Maclevey, or Horshowitz came around the corner. She knew she had better work fast. "Strange," Jackie said. "A building just blowing up like that."

"It happens," Erynn said, as if she had her own doubts.

A man walked around the corner and stopped when he recognized Jackie. He was surprised and it took him a second to decide what to do.

"You're the reporter on television." said the man. "From the conservative channel."

It was true. She did work for the "conservative" channel. "It is I. Guilty." She felt no guilt, but this guy was obviously a liberal. He practically spit when he said conservative. If the word had started with an s or p, he probably would have.

Extending her hand, she said, "I'm Jackie Fairbanks."

"Our firm has no comment on the happenings last night."

He was definitely Maclevey, Maclevey, or Horshowitz. "That's what the young lady was just saying. I'll just be leaving, then."

He walked to the elevator and pressed the button. The door took far too long to open for his liking. This guy really hated conservatives, or maybe it was just reporters.

She smiled and held her ground while she waited for the car to arrive. When the bell chimed, she walked to the car, stopped, and pulled a card from her purse.

"No thank you, Ms. Fairbanks," the man said. "We know how to find you if we require your, ah, services."

Jackie stepped into the elevator. The man stepped off to the side, but watched her as if he wanted to make sure she didn't escape the car. Erynn Kelly stood straight on to the closing doors. At the last minute, Jackie held up her card, shot Erynn a wink and let the card drop to the floor of the elevator car.

Minutes later, walking back up 42nd, her phone rang. It was a blocked caller ID. Maybe it was her Marshal. She felt a little extra bounce in her step and pushed the talk button. "Jackie Fairbanks."

"It's Erynn Kelly, Jackie."

"Erynn." She had called in precisely the amount of time it took her to take that box wherever she was going, get back to the elevator, call the car back up, get her card off the floor, and go someplace in the firm where she could talk on her mobile. "So was that one of the Macleveys or Horshowitz?"

"Horshowitz. Sorry. He's a real you know what."

"Not your problem, Erynn. But you didn't call to make small talk. How can I help you?"

"I think we can help each other."

Erynn was strong and assertive. She saw her opportunity and she was unashamedly taking it. She was a young girl ready to take on the big city, and Jackie admired her for it. "Let me guess. You're not in New York trying to make it in the legal profession."

"Stage name give it away?"

"What have you done?"

"Requisite stuff. High school plays, college, regional. All leads. Good reviews. Everything you'd expect from Simon to Shakespeare."

"I like you, Erynn. What can you tell me?"

"Quid pro quo, Ms. Fairbanks?"

"I know a lot of people, honey. The right people. I can help you. I will help you."

There was a silence. "They're pretty worked up in here this morning."

"Why is that?" A great smile grew over Jackie's face and she stopped walking. Her nose never failed.

"You can't say you heard this from me. Right?"

"Off the record."

"And you'll protect my name like a lawyer would his client. Right?"

"Better."

"They've all been waiting for that building to sell. The man who owns it, the senator from New Jersey, he's been the only holdout on the block. It's been years. Four to be exact. The partners own this building. Figure they just hit pay dirt. They figure he has to sell now, or would want to, at the least."

"You're saying someone has been trying to buy up the block? Who?"

"Yes. That's right. They don't know who exactly. It's a private consortium represented by a powerful firm in town. But they won't buy unless they can get the whole block. The partners think that whoever it is, they want to put up a high-rise."

Conspiratorial thoughts raced in Jackie's mind now. Immunex, a not-so-aboveboard company. A senator in charge of appropriations that could benefit a company like Immunex. A building that spontaneously explodes. A mysterious consortium. A new high rise. Money. Money. Money.

"It's very strange if you ask me. If the senator takes the insurance money and sells, then that will be very strange. I don't like that old man. And I don't like career politicians. Men like that think they can do something like this and get away with it, you know?"

"Well, if he did it. But I do know what you mean."

"That's all I have," Erynn said, and then the line went quiet.

Jackie looked at the readout to see if the connection had dropped. The counter still ticked on. She waited several seconds. Erynn remained quiet, and she would until Jackie repaid her. She was strong and proud. A girl like her would make it in this city.

"What's your phone number, honey?"

Erynn gave her number. Sure enough, a Seattle area code. Jackie committed the number to memory and then said, "You'll be receiving a call, Erynn. I know you'll make the best of it."

"Call me if you need anything else," Erynn said hurriedly. And then the line disconnected.

Jackie scrolled through her address book. Came to Maxwell Davis and pressed Talk.

"Hello, my lovely," a crisp American voice answered.

"Maxwell, darling. I need a favor."

"Anything, dear."

"Friend needs a break. Girl named Erynn Kelly. I think she has what it takes."

"Send her over."

"I want you to call her and invite her down for an audition."

"Give me her number."

"I'll text you."

"Looking forward to it."

"Can we catch up later?"

"Chasing a good one?"

Maxwell would love to hear some pithy twenty-word pitch, but she couldn't give him one now. "Later."

"I'll call Erynn, love."

"Thank you."

"Bye for now," Maxwell said, and she hung up.

Maxwell was the safest of all Broadway producers to whom she could send Erynn. He was on his 5th marriage, and he was a hopeless womanizer. But he wasn't the kind that would try and bed her down and then decide if he wanted to give her a break. He'd give her a break and then try to romance her. There was no doubt about it. But that was Erynn's decision. Life as she knew it was about to change.

Twenty-one

John pulled to a stop at one of the infamous "Projects" in Spanish Harlem. He'd been here before covering a rubbish fire in a hallway. He walked into the courtyard, keeping a watchful eye to the sky. These Projects weren't as bad as some of the movies had portrayed them, but you still had to stay on your toes. NYPD often reported falling objects when they entered areas like this – toasters, knives, chairs, televisions, and in one case he had heard of a falling bowling ball nearly hitting a cop.

John knocked at a door on the twenty-third floor and Mack Washington answered. His head was still bandaged and he looked sedated.

John showed his badge. "Marshal Kane, BFI."

"You police?"

"Bureau of Fire Investigation, Mr. Washington. I'm with the fire department." It was his standard opening with anyone he wanted to question. If you were with the police, nobody wanted to talk to you, especially in New York City, especially in The Projects. The police had a reputation for beating and shooting people. Police put people in prison. If you were with the fire department, you were one of the good guys – you were in the life-saving business. People wanted to talk to you when you said you were with the firefighters.

Mack opened the door. He and John sat down at the kitchen table and Mack said, "Can I offer you something to drink?"

"Yes. Please," John said.

"Got water, water, and water."

"I'll have water," John said with a smile. Mack's manners were brusque, but John could tell it wasn't his normal way. Mack had a gentle nature. John could see blood seeping through the bandage in the back of his head and he noticed a bottle on the table. The label said Percocet. "You took quite a hit. Meds doing the job?"

Mack took the small bottle, calmly got up from the table, and dumped the pills down the sink drain. Then he filled a clean glass with water and said, "I don't like any kind of drugs. They made me take those home." He put the water in front of John and took his seat again.

John looked at the water in the glass. It looked clear enough for drinking. New York City water was some of the best in the world. Unfortunately, the last mile of pipes could do strange things to it.

"Hasn't killed us," Mack said.

John took a drink. "Nothing like our tap water. Secret to the pizza."

"Yeah? I hope they filter it before mixing up the dough."

Mack was a funny guy. John liked him, and he laughed again. And he was wrong about him looking sedated. He was just tired, and sore. "Are you alright?"

"Yeah, yeah, I'm fine. I think it was a piece of brick. Man, don't ever run out of a building that just blew up."

"We're normally running in."

"Yes, and you guys have helmets."

"True," John said and drank more of the water. He took his notepad out and said, "Tell me what happened last night."

"Well, I heard a loud, I don't know, it sounded just like the top of the building blew off. Felt like it. Like an idiot I ran outside and got hit. You know, I'll tell you right now, I didn't have anything to do with that building blowing up."

"Did someone say you did?"

"Not yet. But I got a record, you know."

"What motivation would you have to blow up a building?"

"None."

"See. Don't worry. I'm just here as a matter of course. I just talk to people."

"Alright. Talk."

"Did you notice anyone suspicious go in or out of the building yesterday, in the past few days?"

"Not really. There's always someone going in and out of that building, though. The senator rents out space to many different people. Henry Douglas, the senator's assistant, was in and out periodically."

"Any more than usual of late?"

Mack thought a bit. "Not really."

"You keep a record?"

"Yeah, but it's burnt up with everything else."

"It's quite a mess."

"Maybe I should get down there and help clean up. I have to get another job. We have to have two incomes in this family."

"Did you work directly for Senator Malley, or for a security service?"

"I worked for the senator for three years."

"Has he been in touch?" John knew the senator's people had been in touch. It was second nature to ask questions he knew the answers to, just to see if you found discrepancies. A small lie or inconsistency was the first sign of someone hiding something bigger.

"His aide called me this morning to make sure I was alright. Heard I'd been checked out of the hospital. Said not to worry about anything, that Senator Malley would take care of everything. I've heard that before."

John took notes. He wanted to tell Mack that things would be okay, but he couldn't in all certainty give that assurance, so he said nothing.

"Anybody stand out, especially yesterday? Anyone come into the building who looked odd, out of place?"

"I don't know. Like I said, all kinds of people go in and out of there. It's pretty informal, you know? You think someone messed with a gas pipe and set it up to explode?"

It would be normal procedure to ask a person how they knew it was gas, or how they knew any kind of fire started, just to see their reaction, to see if they got defensive. But it had been all over the news that they suspected gas, plus this guy was one of the first to hear it go. There was no sense in trying to rattle him for a reaction, he'd clam up and then be of no further use.

"It's a possibility, but there's nothing yet to suggest an arson," John said.

"You know, there was one thing. I didn't think about it until this morning, but it's kind of been playing in my mind. Probably real crazy, but I stepped out to the 43rd Street curb to take in some air at about ten PM. This Town Car pulled out of the parking lot behind the building and drove past me. I saw a couple of really big men in the front. You know, like they were Mafia or something. It's been messing with me all morning. I've probably seen too many movies."

"Not crazy," John said and took a note. "Did you get a license plate?"

"No. Like I said. I didn't think about it until this morning."

"What was back there, by the parking lot?"

"Well, there was a ladder up to the roof."

"What was on the roof?"

"A door into the building. You'd have to have a security code to get in up there, of course, and it would register on the system if someone opened it. I'd have seen it on the readout at my desk if someone entered there, even if they did disarm the alarm."

"So you monitored that system all night?"

"Yes. If the door were to be opened, I would have to clear the notification on the system before it stopped flagging the breach. And you can be sure I'd be up there taking a look if it opened."

John knew that if you had the key code to disarm the alarm, it was possible to open the door without setting off the notification. All one would have to do is trick the sensor on the door jamb. Depending on how sophisticated the system was, it could easily be accomplished in a number of ways. He took a note to find out the exact configuration of the sensors.

"Do you think you could recognize the men in the Town Car?"

"I suppose so. What I saw through the windshield was mostly from the nose down, but they had pretty distinct features, you know? Big white guys. I mean real big."

"Well, it could be nothing. There's plenty of those kinds of guys driving around the city in Lincoln Town Cars." John said this to keep Mack calm, but alarm bells were going off in his head. He wanted to check on that security system ASAP. That information would be easy enough to get from PD. He'd call Atkinson.

Mack shrugged it off and tried to work his jaw around, but stopped because of the pain.

"What's your record," he asked, hoping he didn't offend Mack.

"I got in a fight and nearly killed three men. There were three of them and one of me. Stupid. Over twenty dollars I'd loaned one of them. Didn't even really want it back. All three of them were on drugs and had knifes. It got out of hand." Mack remembered back. "So stupid."

"Judge didn't buy self defense?"

"I think she wanted to set an example. But it's okay. My family is fine. When I was away, friends helped out with the little ones. And truth be known, I could have used a little more restraint. I try to serve as an example to kids around here. Most of them know who I am."

John closed his notepad and gave him a warm smile. "Mr. Washington, I want you to keep the memories fresh in your mind. If we end up needing you, it could be weeks, or months."

"Okay."

"Well, listen, I hope you get better. I'll be in touch, and you call me if you think about anything."

"Sure enough, Marshal."

They shook hands and John left.

***

Two nondescript men sat inside of a parked Japanese sports sedan. Sitting on the seat between them was a hand-held radio. "We better let Mr. Walken know about this," said the first man.

The second man took a silencer from his coat pocket and locked it into the end of his Walther P99. "Call it in," he said with cool indifference, as if he knew what the order would be.

Twenty-two

Many minutes later, the two men knocked on Mack's door. Mack opened the door and looked suspiciously at the men. They didn't look like cops, and they didn't look like the marshal who had just visited him.

"Marshal Kane asked us to stay with you. He'd like to arrange for a deposition."

"Deposition? He didn't say anything about a deposition. Show me some ID."

"Of course," the first man said immediately, and he reached inside his coat. He pulled out his silenced pistol and shot Mack in the heart. Mack dropped to the ground, but he was still alive. The two men entered Mack's apartment and dragged him further in. They closed the door. The second man took out a bag of cocaine, opened Mack's fist, and squeezed so the bag broke open. Cocaine fell on the carpet and Mack's hand. Then he took a clean bag and put the broken bag inside, sealed it and returned it to his pocket. The first man retrieved their transmitter from under the couch.

"He dead?" asked the second man.

They looked at Mack. He held on to life. The first man took out his gun and shot Mack between the eyes. Then they calmly exited the apartment and walked away.

TWENTY-THREE

John drove south on 3rd Avenue out of the Upper East Side. He'd just hung up with Fitzgerald, briefed him on the roof door development and told him about the floor heater. He was heading home. He was beat and all he wanted to do was get in a quick workout and take a nap before the fireworks.

His Droid rang. It was Jackie Fairbanks. "Marshal Kane," he said.

"John, it's me. Are you alone?"

"I am."

"Where are you?"

"Heading towards Midtown. What's up? You sound serious."

"Can we meet?"

"Sure. What is it?"

"Meet me at Armstrong's on 15th and 4th."

"About what?" he said.

"Lunch?"

"Is this business or personal?" he said. Tired as he was, he all of a sudden loved the idea of meeting her for lunch. But she sounded very serious, and that meant business.

"Can I help it if I want to see you again so soon?" she said.

"No. Of course not," he said. "So we've established the personal part. What about the other thing?"

"I need to tell you something I've found out. It's very much business."

"Fine. I'll see you at Armstrong's."

She said, "Fine," and the line went dead.

Twenty-four

He parked in the red zone across the street. It was the prerogative of a fire marshal to park anywhere he wanted when he was doing official business, and she'd said this was business. Crossing the street, he saw her sitting on the outside patio of Armstrong's. Two men at a far away table stole furtive glances at her.

John took a seat across from her. There was no greeting. As soon as he had settled she said, "Every building on the Senator's block is scheduled for sale. All except for his. Land developer wants to revamp the entire block. Probably put up a skyscraper. Malley has been the only holdout."

"How did you find that out?"

Jackie raised her eyebrows and said plainly, "John, I'm very good at what I do."

"Of course you are," he said. "So he didn't want to sell. He told me the land has been in his family for generations." He was slightly annoyed. She had told him something he'd normally find out days, maybe weeks, into an investigation. It's just the way law enforcement investigations went. Slow and methodical. Unless you were Perry Mason. Or, apparently, Jackie Fairbanks.

He put his ego down, breathed deep and swallowed the back of his throat. The motive flag was flapping in the wind now. But proving a United States senator conspired to blow up his building would take more than circumstantial evidence.

"You don't find that strange, that he was the only holdout and now his building blows up?" she said.

"We can't really have a conversation like that, Jackie. It's speculative."

"You know what I think?"

"I don't think I should hear this."

"I think there is a lot more to this than meets the eye."

"There always is. Now let's have lunch. You said you had something you had to tell me. You told me. I'd like some lemonade." He looked around and said, "Do you see a waitress?"

"I know something else that I probably shouldn't say right now. It may be a wild theory."

He scanned the menu, and trying to change the subject, he said, "Do you like tomato soup?"

"I'd like some. Yes, please," she said.

Jackie's phone buzzed. She held it up and said, "Do you mind? It's my producer." She pressed the talk button. "Talk to me, Phil." She listened for several seconds and then said, "And Kent knows nothing about this, right? Okay. I'll be there in twenty."

His Droid rang. It was Jerry Atkinson, probably calling back about the specs on the security system he'd called in an hour ago. "Hold on," he said to Jackie. He hit the answer button, "Kane."

"John. Jerry." He coughed and hacked off to the side. "This goddamn humidity. Killing me. Listen, one of my guys recognized a gunshot victim in Spanish Harlem as the security guard from your building explosion last night. One Mack Washington."

"I was just there talking to the guy."

"Sorry to say, but he's not talking anymore. Looks like a drug deal gone bad."

"Alright. I'll be there," he said. He hung up the phone and looked up at Jackie, sure that her call was the same as his.

"Something happen in Spanish Harlem?" she said.

"Why are you hiding things from this Kent?" he said.

"Kent is my news manager."

She struggled a bit. He watched her face and her body.

"He's very modern. I'm old school. He wants something we can run with right away. All about the ratings. I like to get things right."

He watched her. She wouldn't look him in the eye, as if she were hiding a small detail. His standard practice was to keep nodding, maintain eye contact. Say nothing. She finally looked him straight in the eye and said, "Kent and I had a couple of dates."

There was an awkward silence. He wasn't sure what to say. It would be silly to be jealous, but he was.

She spoke first. "You're the nicest man I've ever met, John. Kent was nothing."

Standing, he took her hand and helped her from the tall patio table. "That's good to know. Thank you for saying it like that. But now I have to go," he said. "I'd like to see you tomorrow." He wanted to invite her to fireworks tonight, but he hadn't cleared it with Katie. Katie knew he'd gone out on a date, and she was very supportive and excited for him. She was mature beyond her years. It scared him how much like her mother she was. There wasn't an academic subject she didn't master. She was always looking for more, always looking to be more intellectual.

"I know where you're going, John," Jackie said. "I'll probably see you there."

"Jackie, how about we go sailing? Do you like to sail? I think we could go tomorrow."

"I'd love to go sailing tomorrow," she said eagerly. "I have a boat."

"Good, we'll take yours. Mine's a work in progress" he said.

"Is it a crime if we walk out of here together?"

"No, it's not. Let's go."

TWENTY-FIVE

A few PD stood outside of Mack's apartment. Two men and a woman. Their stares were fierce. Coats bulky. They had automatics under there. When PD came into the Projects, they brought the heavy stuff.

John flashed his badge and stepped inside. Mack's body still lay on the floor, the cocaine spread on and around his hand. His wife sobbed on the couch. She was a nice-looking woman, dressed like a waitress from a fancy restaurant. His heart sank. That was two dead people in less than twelve hours.

Atkinson stood in the kitchen. He waved John over.

Stiles and Santiváñez emerged from the back of the apartment. Both with their phones glued to their ears. John looked at them and they both looked away. They appeared to be on the same conversation.

"Feds," John said to Atkinson.

"Coupla real assholes," Atkinson said.

"I don't believe this. I was just here."

"Wife says this is horseshit, that her husband would never be within a mile of any drugs."

"Yeah," John said. "He was straight."

"You never know. There's a lot of this shit floating around this neighborhood. Someone has to deal it out."

John looked around at the apartment. It was exactly as he remembered it. Clean and respectable, but there was no sign of anything extra. The television was modest. The couch was a bit worn. The pictures on the walls were of his children and family. On the bookshelf, displayed prominently above the television, was a chemistry study book, a book on spelling, more books for learning. This guy studied with his kids when he wasn't work-ing. He was no drug dealer. "I don't think so. Not this guy," John said incredulously.

"John," Atkinson said, "trust me. He could be the parish deacon and be dirty. We took down an Episcopalian pastor a few months back. Had two kilos stashed in with the communion wafers."

"Not this guy," John said. He was angry now. "When did the feds get here?"

"Don't know. They walked in, flashed their badges and got on their phones. One of theirs came in and swept for electronics, didn't find any-thing. Haven't heard a thing out of them since."

The paramedics prepared to take Mack's body away. Mack's wife moaned even louder at the sight.

"You find anything out about the security system at the building?" John asked.

"Company out of Canada – Detect, Inc." Atkinson consulted his notes. "A DS-1025."

"I know their stuff. The DS-1025 is one of their premier units. Almost impossible to beat."

Stiles and Santivánez both hung up their phones. Santivánez pointed outside and marched out onto the walkway. She wore a banker's suit today – a pinstripe blouse under a charcoal gray conservative skirt. Mod-est diamond earrings. Black pumps. She was hell on wheels, this one.

John stepped out to the walkway with them, expecting a download. What he got was two blank stares. He waited for either of them to say something. Anything.

These two had shown up at the fire last night before any other FBI. Now they were among the first responders here. They were investigating Michael Malley. That was a fact. He was also certain they would never admit to it.

"So," John said, "I'm guessing you don't buy the drug deal gone bad?"

Santivánez brushed the railing with her hand, shook it. Satisfied it was clean and sturdy, she leaned against it. "What do you think, Marshal Kane?" she said.

"I think you are investigating Michael Malley. And I'd like to know why."

"We can neither confirm nor deny that, Marshal," Santivánez said with a straight face.

He was tired and angry. Two people were dead, and they wanted to play games? "Agent Santivánez, you are Public Corruption. I am a JTTF Marshal. My security clearance far exceeds yours. I think you can trust me." That had only pissed her off and he wished he hadn't of said it like that.

"It is our determination that you are acting in your capacity as an FDNY fire marshal in this matter," Santivanez said. "This is not a terrorist case, Marshal."

"If we think someone blew up a building and killed two people, I'm pretty terrorized, Agent Santivánez. " John knew that was a silly thing to say. But he also knew it wasn't she who had made the decision to stonewall him. So he wasn't getting anywhere with her no matter what he said.

"Do you think someone blew up the building?" Stiles asked.

He thought about a snappy comeback, something about being unable to confirm or deny that, but he was in no mood for intra-agency games. And Stiles wasn't a bad guy. So he just said, "I'm not sure, Agent Stiles."

This would go up the chain. There would be a task force assembled. The FBI would be forced to cooperate before too long. But it wasn't going to start on the walkway of this apartment building in Spanish Harlem.

"Marshal Kane," Stiles said. "We don't want any hard feelings. We know your record at JTTF. You know how this works."

He could tell he and Stiles would get along if they went rowing together. But Santivánez, she was overcompensating for something. It would be interesting to find out what it was. She definitely had her sights set high. She was the kind of woman that absolutely would not lose. He knew women like her. They were rare with her skill set and ambition, and he had to respect her.

"Please keep in touch," Santivánez said. "We will be around." Then she turned and walked away.

And then she said things like that. They would be around? He raised his shoulders and calmly rolled them back. His neck and deltoids crackled.

Standing straighter, every vertebrae from his Atlas to his tail bone popped. Breath deep, he told himself. Then his Nextel beeped. The readout showed Chief Fitzgerald. He would want a report.

"Yeah, Chief?"

"What's the situation there?" Fitzgerald's voice asked over the radio.

John pushed the button on his Nextel. "Chief, we're going to need to call a meeting," was all he could say. The Nextel wasn't a channel for airing your grievances against the FBI. He'd do that later.

"It's already been called, John. I need you back to HQ on the fly."

"Roger that."

"Detective Atkinson's presence is required."

"Roger that."

"Over and out," Fitzgerald said to finish the communication

***

John walked out of the Project, still completely perturbed at being condescended to by Santiváñez. It was so old school. "We'll be around." He had to laugh it was so absurd.

Rounding the corner, he saw a news van parked in front of his car. The side door was open. Phil and the cameraman from last night sat inside with the air blowing on them. The day's heat was coming on and the humidity was growing oppressive.

Jackie poked her head around the corner of the van's open side door. As he got closer, he saw her sitting at the controls, watching video. She handed him a disk when he stopped. "Here's everything from last night. You can have the originals any time you want."

He took the disk and said, "Thank you."

"I talked to a couple of kids that live here," she said. "They say the deceased is Mack Washington. That he worked as a security guard in Malley's building."

"It would be better if that didn't get reported right now."

"I know. It's not going anywhere. Can you tell me what the FBI said? Kids these days. They pick up on everything."

"I'll call you later, Jackie. To set up our sailing date. Deal?"

She didn't answer.

"I really hate being like this, but I have to go," he said.

"Heading back to HQ?" she said.

"I'll call you later, Jackie," he said. He got in his car and turned his Nextel back up, beeped Woody, and waited for a reply.

"Go ahead," Woody came back immediately.

"Report," John said flatly.

"That plumbing outfit is a real winner. They've got a record of the call, but the guy that did the work on Malley's building allegedly got lonely and went back to his little village in the middle of the Andalusia. No way to reach him unless we want to hop a plane to Spain."

"Roger that. Get back to Citywide and wait for me. We've got something going on at Metro."

"10-4, over and out," Woody signed off.

Of course the guy was in Spain. Where else would he be? He put the car in gear sped away.

Twenty-six

Stiles moved in and out of traffic, southbound on the FDR towards Federal Plaza. He flashed his brights and took a Ferrari doing seventy in the far lane.

Santiváñez hit the end button and severed the call with Tolliver. She'd pressed for blanket wire taps on Michael Malley and Condor Walken, and he'd shot her down. He didn't buy Mack Washington as a bad drug deal, but he still wanted something more concrete before he went up the chain asking for permission to bug a United States Senator and a private citizen who'd really broken no laws except for possession of small amounts of a controlled substance.

She scanned the file on her computer screen again. Condor Walken was a complete enigma. They had no prints. No DNA. According to the records, his real name was Joseph Farrell. He changed that to Condor Walken decades ago. A medical ailment kept him out of Vietnam. He'd never done anything wrong. Never been in any trouble. "Who are you?" she said for Stiles to hear.

Younger brother Brian died around the time he was called up for service in Vietnam. His mother had simply vanished. Immigrant grandparents. Father passed on when he was young. Joseph Farrell never held a job until he somehow came up with a pile of cash and bought Immunex in the '80s under the name Condor Walken. Claimed it as gambling winnings on his tax returns. His company gave heavily to many politicians on both sides of the aisle. Michael Malley included.

Immunex was a private corporation. IRS had audited it two years ago. Books were squeaky clean. Paid its fair share in taxes. But where Walken kept his money and what he did with it was a mystery.

Stiles pumped the brakes a few sharp times and took the lane in front of a delivery truck. Then punched the gas and moved up several more cars.

She trusted his driving implicitly. Finally taking her eyes off the computer screen, she looked over at him. He was a great agent. Smart. Handsome. Athletic. He wasn't shooting for the top like she was. Not everyone wanted to be number one. Like a normal person, he had interests outside of the Bureau. Primarily, an ex-wife who always seemed to need more money, and a teenage boy who was very likely going to be the next Manning or Montana, according to the proud father at least. She'd never seen him play. Perhaps this fall they'd check out a game together. It would be nice to have an interest outside the Bureau with someone whom she knew. Her life was work, and keeping fit, which was part work. Her only outside interest was astronomy, her major at USC. She was fascinated with deep space exploration. After college, she'd had the choice to join NASA or the FBI. NASA had promised her a seat on a shuttle and a marvelous career. The FBI had really promised nothing but sound training and a tough road ahead. And that's why she'd joined. A career at NASA seemed pre-written. At the FBI, she'd have to earn her way to the top.

It was clear Stiles was in love with her. She'd seen the little crushes. Looks when he didn't think she could see. He was under her spell. And she didn't hate it that it was starting to go both ways. Yesterday morning she woke completely relaxed and happy. She and Stiles had just made incredible love in her dream. She'd relived it ever so briefly last night when he invited her to take his bed, too.

The sexual tension was building, as was the intensity of this case. They'd be working 24/7 now. That's when it always happened. The stress, emotion, the long hours. And she wasn't going to fight it if it happened. She needed a man. Wanted one badly. Lots of men in the Bureau had hit on her and she'd rebuffed them all, lest she earn a reputation she didn't want. But Stiles was a good man, and she thought she could trust him.

"I'm hungry," she said.

"My place?" he said.

She gently closed the computer. His place? He lived in a building by Madison Square Park. Probably kept his apartment clean, made his bed every morning, healthy food in the fridge. Stiles was a very well-bred man. It was tempting, but if she went to his place they'd do more than just eat lunch.

"Deli," she said. A vegi sandwich and soy drink would get her through the rest of the day.

Stiles looked over his shoulder and made the 34th Street exit. He'd surprise her with some place new. Last time he took her to a neighborhood grocery in Brooklyn with a deli counter in the back. He knew the owner and the guy behind the counter. It was the best sandwich she ever had. Stiles grew up on Manhattan. It seemed as if he knew someone everywhere they went, in any of the five boroughs.

"I know a place," he said.

Of course he knew a place. It put her at ease and allowed her to think on the case.

Michael Malley. A presidential contender. Who would believe he was corrupt? He'd be counting on that. Of course Condor Walken was the core of the issue. But somewhere along the way Malley had miscalculated. And experience taught her that miscalculations grew in severity over time. It was only a matter of time, then, until his errors caught up with him. She just needed time. And lunch.

Twenty-seven

Henry entered the dining room and sat down across from Malley, who was eating a late lunch by himself.

"Michael. We need to talk."

Malley put down his fork and wiped his mouth. He took a small sip of the wine. "I told you the conversation was over."

Henry shook his head back and forth and looked Malley fiercely in the eyes, letting him know he was serious and that he would not be dismissed.

"Alright," Malley said. He rang a small bell and a butler appeared. "I'm all finished here. Please have the Bentley brought around."

"Of course, sir." The butler removed Malley's plate and silverware with efficiency and disappeared into the kitchen.

"We'll talk in the car. I have to run into town." Malley got up from the table and walked out to the front porch.

One of the smartly dressed men drove a beautifully polished Bentley Flying Spur convertible around from the back of the mansion. The other smartly dressed man stopped in front of the porch and waited for Malley to approach. "Will you require a driver, Senator?"

"No. That will be all." Malley got in the Bentley, and barely waiting for Henry to close his door, he hit the gas and took off around the curved driveway.

"What is on your mind?" Malley was visibly changed now. They drove down the incline towards the gate.

Henry motioned around the car with a questioning gesture. "Is this?"

"Yes. It's fine. Henry, I told you. Nobody is going to investigate me. Us, if you insist. This car is not bugged. My mansion is not bugged. The service has checked everything. The FBI is not going to try and plant a wire around me. They know I sweep. If I found it they'd be done. That's imagining, even by the wildest stretch of the imagination, that they were investigating me."

"Then why won't you talk inside?"

"What is on your mind, Henry?"

They passed through the gate and made their way out onto the main road.

"Mack Washington was killed earlier this morning in what looks like a botched cocaine deal."

Malley's face dropped. His eyes darted around. "How do you know this?"

"It's on the news, Michael. I just saw it."

TWENTY-EIGHT

High atop one of Manhattan's most exclusive hotels sat a three-story penthouse. Condor Walken sat in his smoking chair, drawing on a long Cuban. His study was dark and heavy. His library of modern and vintage books sat on shelves of polished walnut.

A rare copy of David Copperfield sat on the table beside him. Everything in the study bespoke success, affluence, refinement, and power, but most importantly, the upper class. Never again would he be the "Dirty Irishman." There were props all over the penthouse that reminded him of this.

He'd determined early on that if there were no luck for the Irish, he'd have to work hard to create his own. And since the people in charge who were supposed to follow the law did not, he would not respect the law either. As a boy, he saw the world was a violent and corrupt place. It had been so clear early on that if you were going to get to the top, you had to be willing to be more violent and corrupt than the guy in front of you. More importantly, you had to be smarter. If he were to get his revenge on the Malley clan, he would have to be smart. So he went to school and excelled in all things academic. He did everything with the thought that one day he would use every bit of knowledge he had to make the Malley clan cease to exist.

It was 1965 when his father died from liver cirrhosis, leaving Brian – Condor's real name – his older brother Joseph, and their mother with no income and a few thousand dollars of debt, a mountain at that time. Still precious dollars to him today.

Joseph had been the mirror image of his father and drank away any money he made from odd jobs. Mother couldn't work in those days. Gout and rheumatoid arthritis kept her indoors on a recliner most of the time.

Condor puffed on his cigar. He was fifteen again. He loved his mother dearly and he was determined to keep them in their Northeast Yonkers apartment. He was fifteen going on twenty-five, he mused.

He went to school now only on Monday and Friday and worked eighty hours a week at the Tuckahoe Road Diner washing dishes and bussing tables. He kept a notebook in his back pocket and did his lessons on breaks, and he managed to keep his grades at the A and B level. He was keeping under the radar at school and keeping his mother alive, and that was all he could think about at the time.

He was at that dish pit spraying scraps from the plates. There was a knock at the back door. The cook quickly brushed by, greeted the man at the door, and handed him a wad of cash. He took a small envelope in return and then hurried into the bathroom.

Brian stepped over and watched through the crack as the cook chopped the white powder up with a razor blade and sniffed it up his nose. Though he'd never seen it before, he knew well it was cocaine. The cook turned and saw him through the crack. Opened the door. Said, "Want a hit?"

He also knew what the cocaine did to people. It ruined their lives and turned them into "cluckers." He'd heard that term on the street. "Cluckers" were the users that kept the dealers in Cadillacs and nice apartments. The cook was a clucker.

"I'm okay. You go ahead." He could still remember the choice he'd made standing there. Of the two – cluckers, or dealers with money – he didn't want to be a clucker. He wanted money and the power that would come with it.

"Sure? Shit's Colombian. Dealer cuts it pretty heavy, but the shit still gets the job done."

"Colombian, huh?"

"Straight outta the Medellin, so he says."

"You go ahead. How much did that cost, anyway?"

The envelope sitting on the ledge had about two tablespoons of powder in it. "That right there is an eight ball, my man. I can get you that for eighty – 'bout a hundred bucks."

This guy had just spent about a week's pay on that little pile of powder.

He left the dishes where they were and ran home with one thought in his mind. Colombia was just a plane ride away. And he knew exactly where Medellin was. Geography was one of his favorite subjects. He just needed a passport to get there. Luckily he looked very much like his older brother Joseph.

Walken changed his posture in the chair and tapped the ash from the end of his cigar. He never liked to think about what came next. But it was his past, and there was no changing it.

Walking through the door that day, he found Joseph holding a pillow to his mother's face. Joseph's face turned white when he saw his little brother home early from work, but not so white as his dead mother's when the pillow Joseph held fell to the ground.

"What have you done?" Brian said incredulously. Walken could still feel the fire in young Brian's heart rage, and he was very present to that fire cooling to nothing. He could see Brian's outward appearance. His face fell flat. He was calm. At that point he cared about nothing and nobody, and he knew what he was going to do. It was at that moment that he became a cold-blooded killer.

Joseph was drunk. There was an open bottle of Jameson's Irish Whiskey on the table. He normally drank the cheap stuff. He must have bought this bottle in celebration. How he hated mother, argued with her at every turn. He picked up the glass on the kitchen table behind him and gulped, spilling the whiskey down his chin and throat. "You're free now, Brian. Now you don't have to buy her medicine, or feed her. You can go to school and make something of yourself."

He had grown strong carrying the bus bins heavy with dishes. He was much stronger than this indolent nebbish who had summoned from a bottle of whiskey the courage to kill their mother.

He ran at Joseph and kicked him in the knee, hyper extending it back a full foot. Joseph fell to the ground screaming and cursing him, sobbing like an over-exhausted little boy.

Stepping swiftly into the kitchen, he pulled the utensil drawer open. Returned to Joseph with a table knife. Drove the dull, rounded end through the skunk's ear until his closed fist touched his brother's rotten flesh. He twisted the tubular handle. Cranked the knife around, lobotomizing the worthless piece of trash. "On to see dad and pa-pa, Joseph. Tell them the luck of the Irish is about to change." Walken could still see the dead and surprised look on Joseph's face. He could still hear his own words, his accent so thick in those days.

The dirty old apartment was silent. His breath was even, metered. Killing was easy. He knew from that moment there would be many more.

He walked to the bathroom and returned with a towel, Joseph's bath towel. He folded it in fours. Put his foot on Joseph's dead cheek. Pulled the knife out of his ear. Placed the towel under his head. Returned to the kitchen, washed the knife in the sink, dried it with a tea towel. His mother had loved to embroider when her arthritis wasn't too bad. On this one she had stitched in red, green, and yellow thread two boys playing stick with their dog. It was a scene she always said she wished for her boys. "Sorry, mum."

It was still daylight. He'd have to wait for dark to dispose of Joseph. The cops were likely to ask a few questions about his mother's death. For what he had planned, he couldn't have any loose ends. He had to get back to the diner and finish his shift.

Nobody knew he had been gone for that hour when he returned to the diner. He finished his shift and returned home after 10PM that night, carrying with him a twenty-foot strand of rope from the diner's utility closet. At 2AM he returned to the street and spotted a 1954 Chevy that he knew he could boost. Joseph had taught him how to get into cars and hotwire them when they were much younger. An hour later, Joseph sank to the bottom of the Hudson River with the twenty feet of rope tied around his waist and a heavy cinder block he'd picked up from a nearby construction site.

He cremated his mother the next day, paying the mortician at the funeral home an extra fifteen dollars to keep it quiet. He worked at the diner and went to school his normal schedule until his passport arrived in the mail a month later. Inside was his picture, his thumb print, but the passport bore the name Joseph Farrell, age 18.

With four hundred dollars of his own, and a thousand dollars that he stole from the diner, he set out to start making his fortune. Three days later he landed in Bogotá, Colombia as Joseph Farrell. Later that night, he killed two American businessmen with the hotel's steak knife and increased his money to over three thousand dollars.

The next day, he bought a small motorbike and a map. Just fifty miles up the highway, he stopped for gas. Inside the cantina was where it all began.

There were several teens and a few older men sitting at the bar. "De me una *Coca-Cola*, por favor," he said to the bartender. He'd practiced Spanish with one of the Chicano cooks at the Tuckahoe Road Diner. He knew basic grammar, had a fair vocabulary. Still, he sounded like a kid from Yonkers.

On some days a lone teenage paddy ordering a coke fifty miles outside of Bogotá, Colombia might go by unnoticed. That day there were several Colombian teens at the bar, all hopped up on their own product. One of them mocked him for his accent.

Walken could clearly remember simply looking at him with a plain face, drinking his soda. Not backing down and not provoking the kid, which was provocation enough.

Five of them stepped up. He had a knife under his sleeve and he was ready to slice all of them across their throats if they came too close. They'd see how quick a skinny kid from Yonkers was. They'd see what he was willing to do to get what he wanted. He'd killed his own brother just a month ago. Not a half day past, he'd killed two men in cold blood and taken all their money. He looked impassively at the five as if they meant nothing to him.

The original teen pulled out a switch and smiled menacingly until a voice from down the bar laughed and said, "Oye, quien es?" Brian couldn't see who belonged to the voice because he was watching the sharp blade aimed for him.

"Es una puta muerta," the kid with the blade said.

"No," the other voice said.

The teens backed off quickly. He turned and saw a kid about his age sitting at the bar with a bottle of *Coca-Cola* in front of him. "Come on over," the kid said, trying to sound American. He was by far the youngest of the bunch, but clearly the leader.

Brian took his soda and sat next to the leader. The kid was relaxed. He wore loose linen clothes. His skin was clean and fresh. A good-looking kid, the kind women of any age find irresistible. After a bit he said, "How you say in English? Um, What brings you here?"

"Si, es correcto. Qué le trae aquí," Brian said.

"Ah, your Spanish is pretty good."

"I know a little. I know your friend said I was a dead bitch."

"He is puta."

Walken laughed out loud. From that moment these two would always be best friends.

"So, gringo, what the fuck are you doing here? Long way from home."

"I'm looking for something."

"Um hm. Let me guess. Anytime we see a white man in these parts, he is looking for one thing. But you are no older than me. Very odd. So, again, what the fuck are you doing here?"

The kid had yet to face him. They looked at each other through the mirror behind the bar.

"I aim to start a distribution network in New York City."

The kid raised his eyebrows, shifted his head back and forth, and said, "Well, my friend, you have come to the right place." He turned and held out his hand. "Como se llama?"

"Me llamo Joseph Farrell," Brian said. He put his passport on the bar. The kid took it and looked it over.

"Well, Joseph, I do not believe you are eighteen years old, but that is okay. My name is Carlos. Carlos Esperanza."

Brian thought it was best to be completely honest with him right up front. "Real name's Brian. Brian Farrell. Joseph is my older brother."

"Where is your brother, Brian?"

"I killed him," he said.

After a few moments Carlos accepted this, as if killing your brother were commonplace in his world. He extended his hand and said, "Mucho gusto, Brian. Welcome to Colombia."

Two weeks later he left Colombia without his three thousand dollars and no cocaine. Waiting for him in front of his Yonkers apartment when he returned home was a Colombian man. He accompanied him up to the apartment, and behind the closed door, the Colombian handed him a shopping bag with three kilos of cocaine. "I will be back in two weeks with more," he said in very clean English. "You give me the money and I give you the coca." And with that he left.

Two years later, still living in his Yonkers apartment, he had amassed well over a million dollars in profit. He kept his operation small and moved slowly, selling to a few dealers and directly to Wall Street up-and-comers who had the cash to buy a few ounces at a time. He could have lived anywhere he wanted, had any car, any woman. But he remained cautious, smart. The money was for one thing, and one thing only – his revenge against the Malley clan.

It was 1969. Vietnam was raging. One day the postman delivered two certified letters from the Department of War. Both he and Joseph had been drafted. He was living as Brian Farrell, but they had taken his fingerprints when he got the passport as Joseph. They were going to come calling if both didn't show up for service, according to what he was reading in the papers. He'd have a tough time explaining where his brother was and why his fingerprints and picture were on Joseph's passport.

He'd anticipated this. He always kept the apartment in his mother's name. Always paid everything in cash. And he'd kept Joseph's school records, which showed that he suffered from asthma and required injections of epinephrine. His problem was nothing that cash couldn't solve. For a nice fee, a local doctor whom he knew was only too happy to create a case history that showed Joseph unfit for service. He also paid the mortician who cremated his mother to certify the death of Brian Farrell.

He left most of his money in his safe deposit box and flew back to Colombia where he thought he'd wait the war out.

Carlos treated him like a brother and he wanted for nothing in his Medellin palace. But he grew restless. He wasn't moving any closer towards his goal. He still needed much more money and much more experience.

Watching the news one day, he learned about the Afghan heroin trade. "You know, they have all that heroin in that part of the world, but very little of our product," he remembered telling Carlos.

Carlos was high, as he often was now. He was sober, as always. Carlos waved his hand around in the air like it was nothing. Said, "Go. Take a few kilos with you as a sample." They had a warehouse packed full of product that he could not move.

Two months later the El Jai cargo container ship docked at Karachi, Pakistan and he walked down the dock with a suitcase containing one hundred thousand dollars of pocket cash and three kilos of Medellin Puro, or 24k, as he called it when he sold it to dealers in New York.

Those were the days. So young. So free. So ambitious and free from constraints.

Torval entered the room and interrupted his thoughts. He handed him a phone and said, "It's Senator Malley on the secure phone, Mr. Walken."

Condor put his cigar down in the ashtray on the table in front of him and took the phone with a sly smirk. It was fun to keep the little fat man on edge. All his time running around the world, making deals, creating his fortune. It was all meant for this very time. Michael Malley was completely his, to play with at his will.

"Michael. I thought you'd be calling," he said.

"What is the meaning of this?" Malley said.

"You know my intent, Michael."

"We need to meet."

"We shall." Condor picked his big Cuban from the tray and puffed it a few times. "I'll have my man call you." Condor hung up the phone and smoked.

He laughed. Malley thought he still had control over his life. He did not realize it, but he was in a chess game, and the grandmaster was not only seven moves ahead of him, he was moving his opponent's pieces. It was no sport, really. The old man didn't even know how badly he was being gamed. Well, it mattered not. Revenge was indeed a dish best served cold. And when Malley found out that he was paying for the sins of his forefather, when he felt the hilt of his sword against his fat belly, the look on his face was going to be the sport.

TWENTY-NINE

Malley drove the Bentley up a country road in east New Jersey. No longer did he stalk the road with confidence. Now he held onto the wheel at its bottom, instead of the commanding one-handed, 12 o'clock-high position. He looked like a man who thought he'd had the stock market beat, only to find out that fate's capricious hand had come in and scooped up the gains for herself.

"The police are never going to buy this, so close to the fire," Henry said, growing hysterical.

Malley did not answer. He drove up the secluded tree-lined highway.

"Michael!" Henry said imploringly.

"Henry!" Malley cut him off. Then he breathed deep and regained his composure. "My boy. I told you. We've nothing to fear."

"Michael, he has been blackmailing you for twenty years. He just blew up your building, and now it looks like he's off... whacking people. We have everything to fear."

"I will take care of this."

"How, Michael? They are going to investigate."

"I told you before, nobody is going to investigate me."

"This is going to lead right to your doorstep, Michael. You need to remove Condor from the picture."

"Henry, I am going to be president of this country one day. I do not have people murdered."

Henry sat sideways in his seat and raised his voice. "Michael! He is gaming you. Don't you see? It's only going to get worse. He's laughing at you, Michael. Playing you for the fool."

Malley snapped his head over. "Just shut up!" he yelled. "You let me worry about things." Then turned his attention back to the road. He didn't need Henry to school him. He'd been playing this game with Condor for decades. But eliminating him, as Henry had so euphemistically put it, was becoming more and more of an option. He was suddenly feeling those murderous thoughts he'd had at the beginning of their relationship.

It was that fundraising dinner well after he'd been elected a senator. There was a young man, in town to meet the men to whom he had donated such wonderful sums of money. He had been only too happy to invite this young man with the strange name Condor Walken to a private function at the Washington Hotel. He was impressive that night. Very well-spoken. He talked of ideals – the American Way, equality, justice. How he must have done his research. He said all the right things. Believed in all the right things.

And then there was his beautiful friend – just a friend he had said. A Guyanese woman with chocolate skin, wavy brown hair cascading down to the small of her back, wonderful breasts, tall, strong, intelligent, but modest. Antoinette Lassaut. She was an exquisite blend of African and French ancestry. Condor had had to leave the party early that night, but Antoinette had stayed, much to his delight. They conversed for hours together, and somehow, after many glasses of wine, they ended up in that room in the Washington Hotel.

Thinking back now, even knowing what had been done to him, she was so incredible, it would be hard not to do it all again.

He'd woken that next morning racked with guilt over the intercourse, the oral copulation. He was prepared to profess his sorrow, his guilt. He was a married man and he'd never done this sort of thing. Then she emerged from the bathroom wearing that terry cloth robe untied in the front. Clean and oiled all over.

They made love again and again that day. Drank Dom Perignon from the bottle and literally swang from the chandelier.

She ran off that night while he slept, but called him the next day in his office. He confessed to her that his wife was ill and in bed in their home in Summit, and that he just couldn't express how very sorry he was, but that he couldn't carry on an affair with her.

Oh, she was a pro. He could hear her now as clearly as that fateful day more than twenty years ago. "I had a wonderful time, Michael." The sound of her saying his name still melted his heart. "But I shall never call you again." She hung up the phone softly and probably counted off the minutes until he called back.

He could remember how the thought of her – her scent and taste and sound – how it tantalized him, shackled every other thought and rendered him useless for anything else. An hour later, he had called Condor Walken and inquired how he might contact his "friend."

They spent most of the next two weeks together at The Washington, eating room service and making love. He bought her perfume and jewelry, clothes and flowers, then he whisked her away for a month-long "fact-finding mission" to the Italian countryside.

When they returned to America, going through customs, it struck him that he was in love with Antoinette, and that he was content to go on like this forever. Only he couldn't go on like this forever. He had plans. His secret ambition had always been to make a run for the presidency. And it could never happen if he were caught carrying on an illicit affair, much less with a black woman. Interracial unions were becoming more accepted in America, but it would spell certain death with a voting public in those years. He had to return to real life. To caring for his wife, who was all of a sudden failing fast, the nurses were reporting.

He tried to wean Antoinette off slowly at first, seeing her only every few days, claiming pressing government business. After two weeks she became concerned. Then enraged, as the charade continued. She made threats. She harmed herself.

Finally, he asked Condor Walken to talk sense into her. The next morning, to his complete horror, all the local papers ran a story of a black woman named Antoinette Lassaut who had committed suicide in her room at The Washington.

They met later that afternoon at some obscure crab shack down on the South River. The nightmare only got worse as Condor assured him he'd taken care of everything, and that any of the staff who had seen them together had been appropriately compensated to keep their silence.

It was a nerve-wracking month as he waited for the police to come calling. But they never did, and the papers dropped it as if she were nothing. That made it sting all the more.

And then came the payback. He was the head of the Health and Human Services subcommittee, so it was easy for him to get the votes and grant that first "Backdoor Contract" he arranged for Immunex. Driving up the road in East New Jersey now, he could recall the dread he'd felt every day walking the halls of Congress, hoping that his relationship with Walken was over, but knowing that a man like him would keep coming back for favors. He was not surprised when Walken showed up at his office a month later. His next favor was simple. Take a case full of cash to show his gratitude for helping him win the contract. Despite a protest that grew heated, he had no other option but to accept the case. Walken's suggestion that his part in the Lassaut affair may one day be exposed if he became unhappy was enough to force his hand to reach out and take it. Over the years, he'd done several more favors and taken the case of cash each time, just so he didn't have to listen to the threat about Antoinette again. For all he really knew she was still alive. He'd never seen the body, and there were no pictures in the papers, and he never believed for a minute that she'd killed herself. Over the years he'd thought about trying to find her, but it would only create more problems. The thought that she was still alive somewhere was enough for him. So he just went on with his life in politics, did Walken favors every now and then, and took the payments.

All of that money sat untouched, in his underground vault. And now that his father and grandfather were gone, only he knew of its existence. He'd always intended to burn the money. It symbolized his weakness. It represented years of secrets and lies and deceit. Cheating of the American people. But now it had a use. A redemptive use. Totaling almost thirty million, that much money placed with the right people could ensure a lot of loyalty, and votes.

It was a relief, really, having made the decision to have Walken killed. For all the years of torture he had put him through, and this latest stunt, he would ensure the killing was slow. Walken would feel pain for a long time. "Feel it, you son of a bitch," he murmured.

Henry was still looking at him, waiting for a response. "What, Michael?"

An edgy tune by The Bowery Boys, long forgotten by most, was playing softly on the radio. Malley reached down and turned up the volume. He remembered singing this song with a high school girlfriend years ago while driving his father's Rolls Royce up a very similar highway. Those were easy times. This was a mess. The firefighter and now Mack Washington. He really liked that man. Such a good soul. Never had anyone died because of his relationship with Walken. Now two innocent people were gone.

He turned the music up and tried to focus on the bigger picture. The country. The country needed him. He was going to do so much good when he had the reins. He simply had to clean up the mess of Condor Walken once and for all.

THIRTY

Walken sat back in his chair, smoking and thinking. Torval stood at attention. "Our friend is nervous," Walken said, breaking the silence.

"It appears that way, Mr. Walken."

"You know I detest nervous people."

"Rightfully so, sir."

"It's time to make him think I am rearranging our relationship."

"You have been talking about that, sir."

"Set up a meeting. Right away, in fact. On the river. Carlos has given me the Minnow. We'll take her."

"Yes, sir." And then Torval took the secure phone off the table and walked away.

Condor took a long pull from his cigar and looked into space with steely resolve. His empire had grown exponentially, and legitimately, over the past decades. That was the first part of the plan – use the Malley family to increase his legitimate fortune, just as the Malley family and people like them had used the backs of his fellow countrymen to increase theirs. The second part, taking back the property stolen from his family, would happen soon. Then he'd buy the entire block and start on his plans for his sky scraper.

He had to laugh because he was the puppeteer walking Malley deeper and deeper into his trap. He'd march him right into the White House. To have a president as a pawn. It was genius. He was a genius.

Walken laughed out loud because it was such a cruel plan. But he hadn't started this to play nice. *He* hadn't started this.

THIRTY-ONE

BFI headquarters at 9 Metro Tech Center was quiet. John and Atkinson walked past the Confidential Investigations Unit and down the hallway to a door marked Conference A.

Fitzgerald stepped out of his office and stuck out his hand to Atkinson. "Jerry, good to see you. Let me get a moment alone with John." He nodded to the conference room door.

Atkinson entered the conference room and Fitzgerald pulled John into his office. "You don't look good," he said.

"I'm tired, and I'm pretty well ticked off. I told you agents Stiles and Santiváñez met me at the scene last night claiming a random drive-by. They were just at Mack Washington's. They've got something working and they're not talking."

"We'll get that worked out. Listen, I can pull Jensen off what he's on right now. He's on his way in. You still want off this one, you walk out of here a retired man after we do this thing next door."

"You know damn well I'm not going to walk on this," John said.

"Yeah, I know," Fitzgerald said. "But you should. Go do what you got planned with Katie. You don't need to do this anymore. I got it covered."

It was a valiant effort from his old friend. He was trying to give him an easy out. But he never took the easy way out and Fitzgerald knew it.

"Let's go next door, Chief," John said.

Fitzgerald looked at him for a few seconds, thought about a rebuttal, and then simply motioned to the door.

John opened the door to Conference Room A and was not surprised at what he saw. Sitting around the large table were Mayor Saltzman, the

Chief of Police, and an erudite looking man named Stanley Wilks, the district attorney. Jerry Atkinson sat next to his chief.

Fitzgerald took the head of the table and John sat at his right.

Each man in the room had his own agenda. Each wanted to rifle off questions to John – especially Stanley Wilks, who shifted in his seat.

As a matter of protocol, they let Fitzgerald speak first. "John, I've briefed everyone here on what you've told me. Tell us in your own words where you are, and what happened with Stiles and Santiváñez at Mack Washington's."

John told them everything that happened that morning up to Santiváñez blowing him off outside of Mack Washington's apartment.

"I've been on the phone with the FBI, John," said Mayor Saltzman. "I was on the phone with them last night shortly after the thing blew."

"What did they have to say then?" John said.

"Their ASAC was very insistent that anything BFI found was rolled up to FBI immediately." An ASAC, or Assistant Special Agent in Charge, and pronounced a-sack, was just below a SAC, or Special Agent in Charge, and pronounced sack.

"It doesn't look like they're interested in rolling anything up to us," John said.

"That won't stand," the mayor said quickly. "Stanley, we'll need your office to negotiate the debriefing."

"Of course, Mr. Mayor," Stanley said.

"What do you expect for a response time?" Fitzgerald asked.

"If they're stonewalling John in the field, the decision has already been made at a pretty high level. This could take days," Stanley said.

"Excuse me, Chief," Mayor Saltzman said. "I'll be on those calls with you, Stanley. They're going to have less than twenty-four hours to come clean with the city."

Each man in the room knew that the calls would begin with the ASAC that managed Stiles and Santiváñez. From there they would go to the SES Section Chief in Washington and then back to the SAC in New York. The SAC would have to consult with a low-level Assistant Director in Washington, who would kick it up to an Assistant Director in Charge, who might have to go to the Deputy Director in case it had to clear the Director's desk.

"If they give us the run around I'll go straight to Director Jennings," Mayor Saltzman said. "This is happening in my city, and my people will be in on it. It's not going to be a request." His finality was certain.

"Let's talk about a task force, gentlemen," Fitzgerald said. "Marshal Kane will lead from our department."

"I'd like Detective Atkinson to represent PD," the Chief of Police said. "Is that okay with you, Chief?"

Not just anybody got on a task force. There had to be absolute faith that you were incorruptible, that you knew how to keep your mouth shut, and that you could be counted on in a tight situation. Fitzgerald turned to John as if to ask his permission.

John said, "Of course."

"Then we wait for debriefing from the feds," Fitzgerald said.

"Come hell or high water," Saltzman said, "they will be in this room by eight AM tomorrow or we will be downtown knocking on their door."

"Okay, gentlemen," Fitzgerald said. "We have a press conference to give."

Stanley stopped in front of John before exiting. A man uptight to his very last breath, he said, "Anything you get, anything, you run it by me."

"I will, Stan," John said. "Chief, hold up."

Fitzgerald let the door close and then sat down next to John.

"You should know there is someone else involved in this," John said.

"Jackie Fairbanks," Fitzgerald said. "I saw her last night."

"She thinks Malley conspired to blow up the building for the insurance. Says she talked to another owner on the block, and that Malley's been the only holdout from selling to a developer who wants to put up a high-rise. She also says she's got some other lead she wants to share with me, but can't yet."

"She's quick."

John just shook his head.

"Keep an eye on her while we're waiting for the FBI to come clean," Fitzgerald said. "She could be of use. She could also cause trouble."

"The latter is what worries me."

"Then keep her close."

.

THIRTY-TWO

John and Atkinson stood at the base of 9 Metro Center. Shaded by the full-bloom Black Locust and Empress trees, they both looked to the center of the courtyard where Fitzgerald and the Chief of Police had taken up court. Press jockeyed for position as onlookers gathered.

Atkinson was well through a smoke he'd just lit. "You're not retiring any time soon," he said.

"I'll see this through," John said.

"You think Michael Malley is dirty somehow?"

"You know how it is when there's that little thing going off in your head?"

"Yeah. Of course. But what if Washington was just a botched drug deal? Maybe the fire was just an accident?"

John saw Jackie striding toward them. He answered a bit distractedly, "That's a few big what ifs that we need to investigate."

Atkinson saw Jackie approach. "That's Jackie Fairbanks. She comin' our way?"

"She is," John said.

"She have anything to do with that little thing going off in your head?"

"She does," John said.

Atkinson reached for another smoke out of habit, but thought better in front of a lady. "Listen, I've got things I have to take care of at City Hall. I'm going to have to unload some casework to take this on. Call me later."

"Okay." John's attention was still on Jackie. She gave him a big smile as she walked. "You don't want to meet New York City's most beautiful investigative reporter?"

"Sometime later," Atkinson said and walked away.

"Hi," Jackie said when she got close. "I know you can't comment on anything but I'll tell you something if you want to hear. Since the FBI is not telling you anything."

He looked right into her eyes with a straight face. How could she possibly know that?

"You were very upset when you drove away. Then my little spies came back. Told me you had words with two suits on the walkway. From the description, they were the two suits at the fire last night. I'm sorry. These things just kind of happen for me."

"Go ahead and tell me," John said. This woman. If anything, they were a pair. She'd do anything to get her story, and he'd never stop until he got his man.

"There was a story in the Times five years ago about a company called Immunex. They were doing a lot of animal fetal tissue research."

"Okay."

"Only problem was we already knew more than we ever needed to know on the subject. And they were getting millions from the government for the research. Useless. A bunch of repetitive tests I bet never actually occurred."

"Is that what the article said?"

"Yes. It also questioned why Immunex was getting so much money from the government."

"I'm going to guess that Health and Human Services was responsible for the grants to Immunex."

"It named Michael Malley. He signed the orders as head of HHS."

"What happened with the story?"

"It went nowhere. Immunex filed a crate full of motions against The Times the day the story ran. Senator Malley's lawyers filed a cease and desist. The reporter died a couple months later in a 'boating' accident."

"Was the reporter the only one who died in this boating accident?" John asked.

"No. There were a few others. The whole thing just kind of went away."

"What do you know about Immunex?" he said.

"They do a lot of legitimate cancer genome research now, so they look pretty clean from the outside. But get this. A man named Condor Walken owns it outright. Condor Walken? Isn't that creepy? It's an old English surname, but nobody has it as a first name. Sounds made up."

"At Armstrong's you told me this development company wants to buy up the whole block," he said. "That Malley has been the only holdout. How did you uncover that?"

"Confidential, John. Can't say right now. I'm sorry."

If she said she had a source, he believed her. Her reputation as a professional was unimpeachable. "So what do you make of all of it?"

"I don't know," she said. "Like you, I'm sure, I try not to speculate at times like this. Tends to send me in the wrong direction. I need more information."

He respected that she wasn't quick to jump to theories. She was right, it's how he was. Standard detective training. But he knew a few things she did not. Like how suspiciously Henry Douglas had acted. And what Mack Washington had told him about the suspicious car. And the almost certain fact that two agents from the FBI's Public Corruption unit were investigating Michael Malley. He'd find out what the FBI knew tomorrow and things would start to come together. But for now, his radar was blaring.

They had reached the bounds of what they could discuss about the case. "You know what I'm thinking?" he said.

"Go ahead and tell me."

"I didn't have lunch. I'm hungry and I'm a little wiped out."

"You want to have lunch? Right now?" She crinkled her nose and said, "I have somewhere to be."

"We'll do it another day. You said we're taking your boat sailing, right? I'll bring the picnic. And Katie."

"Tomorrow?" she said with a big smile.

"Probably not tomorrow. Something just came up that might keep me busy."

"Well then, how about that sandwich today?" she said. "I need a ride across the bridge to get to where I have to be. I'll buy you lunch for a ride. Do you have time?"

He wanted to ask her if the place she had to be had something to do with the case, but of course it did. Under normal circumstances, he'd have to be very careful about consorting with a reporter who was involved in one of his cases. It was the kind of thing that could land a law enforcement professional in jail. But his chief had told him to keep an eye on her, so that's what he was going to do.

"I'll buy lunch," he said.

***

Two FBI radio operators sat in an undercover news van across the court-yard. Young guys, hungry, looking to break out of surveillance. Kam took off his headphones and lowered the parabolic dish that he had pointed through the window at John and Jackie. "Let's call Santiváñez," he said.

"Yep," said Charlie, the second radio operator. "She's going to love this."

"Big time," Kam said.

Thirty-three

Malley drank Macallan Scotch from a tumbler and picked through a few newspapers while Henry piloted the *Mary Anne* up the Hudson. He'd had the seventy-foot yacht built from Cuban mahogany. She was christened the *Mary Anne*, after his wife, in 1982. That was the year she began her bout with cancer.

It was just Henry and he in the wheel house. Most of the trip from dock had been passed in silence. His personal line rang. It was his Chief of Staff, Carl Peterson, calling from his office in Washington. Again. He hit the end button and sent Carl to voicemail, for the third time this hour. Carl was nervous. Everyone in the world wanted a quote about the building. How did it happen? Was it arson? Was foul play suspected? Etcetera, etcetera. His instruction had been for his office to refer all questions to the New York City Bureau of Fire Investigation. Carl would have to deal with it. He was on his way to see Condor Walken in the middle of the Hudson River on the Fourth of July, probably to accept more terms of his blackmail. Malley sucked the last stream of whisky through the ice and placed the tumbler in the captain's chair cup holder. Normally one to wait for the sun to set over the proverbial yard arm, he was on his second liberal pour. What the hell, he told himself. He was going to meet a gangster. A gangster, whom he would soon have executed for two decades of nefarious blackmail. Somehow blackmail and murder and Scotch whiskey seemed to go together.

They were getting close to Walken's boat. Malley pulled himself out of the chair and said to Henry before leaving the deck, "Hold her steady, my boy."

Henry kept his eyes focused on the large vessel off his port. A voice came over the radio. It was from Walken's vessel. "Mary Anne, this is Minnow. Please hold her steady while we tack beside you."

Malley had exited the wheel house. Henry engaged the auto pilot to keep her straight and followed him to the stern. He'd be damned if he was staying behind.

THIRTY-FOUR

Walken looked down from the wheelhouse at the *Mary Anne*. She was a beautiful boat, small, but a classic. Maybe he'd take her and put her in inside his gigayacht when she was finished. He'd already paid the German shipbuilder the full three hundred million dollars for her commission. The largest of her kind, she was a four-hundred-twenty-foot gigayacht. Next year he'd sail around the world with the *Minnow* in tow. Carlos had indefinitely left her in his care. Coming from Carlos, that was an outright gift.

"Hold her steady," he said to the husband and wife team piloting the boat. Like Terenty and Silanty, he'd recruited the Lithuanians from an otherwise dire situation and given them a new life. In their case, he picked them out of ghettos of war-torn Lithuania. He paid them well, didn't demand their services full-time, but when he called, he demanded they spring instantly into action.

Walken stood on the stern of the *Minnow*, flanked by Terenty, Silanty and Torval.

Henry dropped down the stairs onto the stern behind Malley. Malley turned and said, "Back to the wheelhouse, my boy. I'll handle this."

Henry shook his head and said, "No way. I'm in this thing, Michael. I want to hear what he has to say."

Walken was watching. This was no time to have a squabble. So he walked toward the port side of the stern and stared across at Walken. The Statue of Liberty stood in the background.

"Did you see the press conference?" Walken asked, breaking the ice.

"I did. What's this all about?" Malley said, trying to assert himself in the face of a much superior presence.

"I've made a decision, Michael."

"What's that?" They were yelling over the gurgle produced by the thrusters and afternoon winds.

"You and I will part company now. Forever."

They would indeed be parting company forever. On his terms, and not soon enough, Malley told himself. He'd stood face to face with him many times like this. Walken had always dictated the terms. This would be his final set of instructions, so he hoped Walken enjoyed them.

"Don't you want to know how? Why?" Walken said with a big smile.

It was hard for him not to smile wryly back, for he knew that tomorrow Condor would be dead. But he kept up the façade of being under his thumb and said with a solemn frown, "Go ahead and tell me."

"Immunex is moving in a new direction. We don't need government grants anymore. I'm taking her public."

"Then I wish you well," Malley said. Even if Condor walked away from his life forever, he would still order a tortuous end for him. He'd leave those details to someone else, but Condor Walken was soon to meet a very uncomfortable end.

"Not to worry, Michael. I'm going to compensate you one final time for all your friendship over the years."

"That's not necessary. Let's just be done with it."

"Michael, that's not how friends treat each other. We are still friends?"

"Let's just call that part of our relationship finished. Then we can be friends."

"It wouldn't be right, Michael. I always pay my debts. Send Henry tonight."

Walken gave a signal and the *Minnow* pulled away. "Of course, you will still sell me your property at the appropriate time. I will give you time to settle your affairs with your insurance company, and then my high-rise project begins! Imagine! At the top of the tallest building in Times Square — Immunex!" Walken motioned with his hands like the name Immunex was up in lights on Broadway. Then the *Minnow* was out of shouting distance and there was no time for a rebuttal.

Malley stepped under the cover of the top deck and watched the Minnow power away.

"Well I'm not going anywhere tonight," Henry said. "To meet with anyone. That's absurd."

"Just relax, Henry. I'm in control here." He turned and looked at him. "We are in control."

"Michael! We are in control of nothing. You know they blew up your building. We are complicit in multiple murders, Michael! And now he is playing you!"

Malley looked at him with a stone face. "I told you I have it under control."

"Enlighten me, Michael. Please."

"You're going to get your wish."

Henry stood back and nearly stuttered. "You mean? You're going to take care of him?"

"No, Henry. I'm going to have him murdered. Now turn this boat around. And lay off those pills."

THIRTY-FIVE

It was a quick drive from 9 Metro in Brooklyn over the Manhattan Bridge to the Lower East Side. They'd stopped for a Jamba Juice instead of a sandwich. John preferred the instant pick-me-up of mixed fruit and protein powder, and as it turned out, so did she.

They entered an elevator lobby from a subterranean parking garage and walked into a waiting car. He didn't ask her where they were going because he didn't want to know, for many reasons.

She pushed the button for the top floor, and while the door was closing, she turned to face him. "How long do you have?"

John looked at his Droid. He read a text from Katie and Aunt Mary. They were leaving for Manhattan shortly. They wanted to meet at Pier 94 to tour the Home Show before fireworks. "Half hour," he said. He hadn't told either of them that he'd taken on another case.

The door opened. In front of them stood a skinny kid with mop hair and big blue eyes. John could tell right away that he was packed with intelligence, but there was something a little off with him. Jackie walked out of the elevator. "John, Rodney. Rodney, John."

They walked through a maze of halls. The ceiling was covered with acoustic tiles and the walls were poured cement covered with white, high-gloss paint. The floors were made from an exposed aggregate and covered with a shiny sealer. There were no signs on the walls, no indication where they were or where they were going. An indestructible fixture casting bright white light hung by a rod from the ceiling in each hallway. John looked around for embedded cameras. He couldn't see anything, but they were there.

At the last door, Rodney looked into the eye of a retinal scanner, and after a few seconds, it opened.

The room was a hexagon, forty feet in diameter, the same ceiling, walls, and light fixtures from the hallway. There was a large fax/copy machine on one wall, and an opening on the far side that led to what looked like a break room. He saw a coffee pot and a microwave on the counter. In the middle of the room was a round work station. Four fifty-inch plasma monitors lined half of the round work station. Besides a couple of keyboards, John could see no other hardware.

"What is this place?" John said.

"We're a geo-stationary satellite monitoring post," Rodney said. He looked at John to see if he'd stumped him.

John nodded and walked around to the other side of the work station. His knowledge of satellite technology was encyclopedic. There were approximately 120 private companies in the world that operated about a third of the thousands of commercial geo-stationary satellites. Interestingly enough, none of these companies were American.

"Where's your ground station?" John said.

Rodney looked up, annoyed. "Calgary."

That meant they were a Canadian company, probably monitoring global warming. The Canadians were doing a lot of that these days for Greenpeace.

John came to the opposite side of the round station. What he saw stopped him in his tracks. It wasn't every day you found another propeller head. Spread out in the semicircular area was a work station set up for making various gadgets. There were small printed circuit boards, soldering guns, scopes, drawers with integrated circuits and passive devices. Everything an engineer needed to make stuff. He could hang out here for awhile.

Sitting in a small dish was a small handful of what looked like large pieces of brown rice. John picked one up with his thumb and forefinger. It was sticky and rough, like a cat's tongue. He tried to put it back, but it stuck, like a sticky piece of gum that you just can't remove from your fingers. In the middle of that same desk there was a magnifying lens and a spec of something directly below. To the naked eye the spec was only about a millimeter-and-a-half square. Looking through the magnifying lens, John could see it clearly. It looked like a miniature battery source connected to some kind of chip, both sitting on a flexible substrate. "Hmp," John uttered. It was indeed interesting.

Rodney turned. "Hey, hey. Don't mess with that." He ran over to John.

"Sorry." John extended his finger.

Rodney took a pair of tweezers from his pocket pen protector and removed the little thing from the tip of John's finger. "Most people understand you can't touch this kind of stuff."

"John's an engineer, Rodney," Jackie said, focused intently on the monitor in front of her. "He knows what he's doing."

"You? An engineer?" Rodney said.

"I have a degree in computer science from NYU. Took a two year course at a technical college for the double E."

"Well, then, you should really know not to touch stuff in a lab."

"Rodney," Jackie called over. Her tone suggested he better stop.

"Would you like to know what those are?" Rodney said finally.

"Please tell me, Rodney. And I'm sorry for touching without asking. I won't do it again." As a kid his favorite movie was "War Games" with Matthew Broderick. There was a techie guy named Malvin in that movie, and it was incredible how much Rodney reminded him of Malvin.

"It's an integrated ball on chip mixed signal device that modulates a GSM signal."

That was simple enough. It was a secure transmitter that operated on the frequencies that most mobile phones use. A very, very small transmitter. "Pretty cool. What's your battery life?"

"It depends on how I program it."

"Of course. Say you ran a 30-second duty cycle at 20dB."

"About four days," Rodney said with an irritated tone.

John knew how to work with Rodney, and it was best not to push his buttons, so he let it go.

"Now, if you don't mind," Rodney said. "We were right in the middle of something."

Rodney walked back to Jackie. She looked over the monitor at John and rolled her eyes. He just smiled.

He walked around the work station, expecting to find them looking at weather patterns. Maybe Jackie was working on a story about Global Warming. Instead, on the monitor he saw a picture of two men talking to each other on the backs of their boats. Rodney hit a key and the image continued to play.

"That looks like Michael Malley," John said.

"I tracked him from his mansion in Summit," Rodney said.

"You're spying on Michael Malley?" John said.

"Perfectly legal, isn't it?" Jackie said.

"For you."

"You weren't supposed to see this, John. And Rodney, you weren't supposed to say anything."

"Oh," Rodney said.

"This doesn't compromise your investigation, does it?" Jackie said with a straight face.

"What I saw was in plain view. No."

"Plain View Statute, right?" Jackie said.

He was not amused. But he was hooked. And it was legal. "Where is he, and when is this?" John said.

"They're on the Hudson." Jackie said. "Ninety minutes ago. Pretty strange time for a cruise and a two minute conversation in the middle of the River, don't you think? Zoom in on them, Rodney."

Rodney hit a few keys, worked his mouse and the view pulled in.

John squinted. The picture was a little grainy. "Who's the other guy?"

"I could give you a rendering of his face and find him through DMV in about twenty seconds."

"I don't think you're supposed to be able to do that, Rodney," Jackie said with a stare.

"Oh. Right."

John had full access to the FBI database and he could find out who the other man was. But he couldn't sign in from here. That had to be done in a secure environment on secure JTTF servers.

"What did you mean a two minute conversation?" John said.

Jackie told Rodney to rewind the video. John watched intently as the Minnow pulled away from the other boat.

Jackie said, "Did you get that body language? Michael Malley was uptight. The other guy looked loose, in control. I'll bet he's got something to do with Immunex. It's got to be Condor Walken."

He took out his notepad and documented exactly how he'd come to this point. It could be suggested later that he'd had a part in spying on a private citizen, and he hadn't.

He put his notepad back in his pocket and continued to watch. He didn't have the authority to tell them to stop spying on Malley, and he was entitled by law to continue observing. Obligated actually. Any case evidence derived from this was solid.

"I know you have to leave soon," Jackie said. "Do you want me to call you if we come up with anything actionable?"

"Actionable?" John said.

Jackie just shrugged. "You never know."

"Jackie, I do have to go. Please call me if—"

"If I'm thinking of doing anything crazy?" Jackie finished his sentence.

"If you are thinking of doing anything at all," he said. He needed to get out of there and call Fitzgerald. Complicated wasn't quite the word for what this had become.

THIRTY-SIX

Jim Dine's Venus de Milo sculptures rose from the pool behind them.

Santivánez took small bites of her mixed plate from the famous halal cart at 53rd & 6th. "Stiles," she said. "It would make me feel better if you dug into that thing."

"Hmm?"

"You always do this," she said.

"What?"

"Eat only as much as I do."

Stiles pondered the notion and took another bite from the round aluminum container. Then he took a modest sip from his Welch's Grape.

His impeccable manners intrigued her. Someone had taught him well. How had it been for him growing up? Certainly much different than her hard scrabble immigrant experience. Why did he have such a thing for her? If he knew her past, he most certainly would think twice. He probably had a mother who would not approve of her. She would be one of New York's social elites. Would want him to marry a girl named Tinsley or Derek. She couldn't stifle a smile.

Stiles studied her. "What's so funny?"

"Nothing," she said. Then she turned and looked at him, serious. "What's your mom like, Stiles?"

"My mother? Incredible. You would really like her."

But he didn't say his mother would like her.

"And she would like you," he said. "I already told her about you."

"You told your mother about me? What would you possibly tell your mother about me?"

"Well, let's see. I told her that you were ambitious, and smart, and, well, lovely."

Santiváñez looked him in the eyes. "Lovely?"

"I told her you beat me in the 1600 the other day."

"I think you let me win, Stiles."

"I absolutely did not. You set the pace the whole way and took off so fast on the back half of the last 400, I couldn't catch you. That was one hell of a kick."

"You were right on my heels." Santiváñez took a bite of rice covered with red sauce. Most people feared the hot red stuff the cart put out, but to her it was like catsup.

"I'd have taken you in the next 400," he said.

"You think so?" she said.

Stiles took a bite of his meal and nodded. He liked the white sauce with just modest droppings of the red.

"Good. I like a strong man," she said. Then, covering, "I mean a strong partner."

He looked over at her and waited for her to look at him. "You can have it both ways, Maria."

Her phone rang. She smiled and gave him a look to let him know she was done playing coy with him, but she had to take the call. It was probably Tolliver with the decision they'd been waiting for. Mackenzie and the DEA had replaced electronics in the *Minnow's* radar and communications equipment while the ship sat unattended. Nearly anything audible in the wheelhouse and on the deck was picked up and transmitted to DEA equipment on their off-shore cruiser *Shootout*. Mackenzie called her shortly after the rendezvous on the Hudson and transmitted the audio and video taken from *Shootout* to her. Since the recording was garnered from a legal DEA tap warrant, it was all admissible into her case and into a court of law. Tolliver was finally convinced and took it to the U.S. Attorney. She knew the mistake would come, but she didn't expect it to be this incriminating, or for it to come so soon.

Stiles took the tin of food from her hand and she picked her phone out of her jacket pocket. It was Tolliver, but she never took liberties with her superiors. "Agent Santiváñez," she answered.

"Maria, get your team down to Federal Plaza. You've got your warrants."

"We'll be right there, sir," she said.

"Good. We'll task up when you get here."

She hung up the phone. "We're on."

Stiles was already filling the plastic bag. He dumped the garbage and got into the Suburban. Santivánez's phone rang again before she shut her door. It was Charlie and Kam. She pressed the answer button and said, "Go ahead."

"Kane just left the building," Charlie said.

She pressed her speakerphone button so Stiles could hear the conversation. "Fairbanks didn't leave with him?"

"No. He's solo. He's driving toward Houston now."

Fairbanks had figured out a lot in one day and she hated to drop the tail on her. She'd told them about the developer's plans to buy up the whole block. She'd pieced the Malley/Walken relationship together from the Times story just as she herself had done at the beginning. She was smart. And she was aggressive. But she didn't know what the FBI knew, and she didn't have warrants from the U.S. Attorney waiting for her. By tonight this would all be over, and maybe, just maybe she would bring Fairbanks in and give her an exclusive on the story.

"Okay," she said. "We're pulling the plug on that operation. Hightail it down to HQ. We've got warrants."

She looked over at Stiles. He weaved in and out of traffic going westbound on 53rd. "Tolliver said to get the team down to HQ," she said. "You think I'm making a mistake walking on Fairbanks and Kane?"

"We don't have a team to cover them right now. And your ASAC tells you to pull your team, you pull your team. Your mentor preaches respect for the chain of command."

Her mentor was Tina Rollins, Assistant Director over the Office of Congressional Affairs. "You've never seen the woman speak her mind to Congress."

"I know you don't like Tolliver's style, but watch what you say to him. You may be protected from on High, but your next promotion goes through him."

"You think I'm protected?" she said a little defensively.

"I don't think you use it. But let's just say when and if it comes time to play politics in the Bureau, it's not going to hurt to have the friends you have in The Office of the Director."

She thought on that one for a few seconds and then said, "Thanks for saying that, about watching what I say to Tolliver."

"I've got your back."

She looked ahead in traffic to make sure it was safe, then looked over at him and pointed her finger back and forth from her eyes to his. "This isn't going to change things for us."

Doing fifty down 7th, he was glancing back and forth between her eyes and the road. "I sure hope not. You're the boss. But, ah, we'll get back to this," he pointed from his eyes to hers, "later?"

She smiled. "Eyes on the road, Stiles."

He looked forward and nodded. "Yes, ma'am."

THIRTY-SEVEN

The last remnants of sunlight filtered through the sheers. Malley sat alone in his den, still drinking scotch. But for the tempest in his mind, the room was still and quiet.

He'd tried to be a religious and spiritual man. Tried not to become his father. How had he been strapped into this bondage of iniquity? How had his life become so perverted from the right ways of God? It was easy to blame Condor. But his troubles traced back much further.

He'd always been given everything a person could want. But advantage came with a price. As parents of his generation were so accustomed to doing, they regularly talked about him in the third person as if he were not present when he was indeed standing right there among them. His mother, after the gin started to flow, and when displeased with his father, would point out to his father with great southern pride that their boy had inherited his 'short' English genes. She would dig further by noting that, though he was short, he had been passed at least one of her family's traits – it was clear he would far exceed his father in his capacity to satisfy a woman. His father, when equally inebriated, would point out that he had inherited the fine English features of his clan, luckily, because her genes were too weak to pass on the advantage of height which was the only reason he had chosen to mate with her. When especially drunk, he would shout at the top of his lungs that she gave the saying 'long in the tooth' a more literal meaning. Then they would sober up in the morning and at the breakfast table it would be as if nothing had happened just hours ago. Things would be cordial again for sometimes months, sometimes weeks, but often only days or hours before young Michael's genetic disposition was drug through the mud, and heralded, all in the same cross barrage of drunken slurs.

After Academy, his mother had turned a cold shoulder to his father, his alcoholism and philandering, and she moved back to the South with her parents. The year he returned home from law school was when it all really began. Alone with his father then, he began to practice law and lay the seeds for his own political career. His father was determined to lay the path for him, and they spent much of their time on the social circuit in New Jersey, New York, and Washington.

It was common to find his father passed out alone, or with a prostitute, or worse yet, a couple of times with another man's wife. It became his job to shield him from the press, gold digger women, and cuckolded husbands. And so he learned to contain his father's indiscretions, to fix his troubles.

It was 1976. Two years after being appointed to finish out the term of his ailing father's seat, he'd cruised to his first election victory. The Vietnam War was over and military spending was sliding at a rapid pace. Charlie Whitfield, a manufacturer of odd textiles, and an old family friend, had called for lunch. It was a date he was only too eager to entertain, as this man was connected in business like no other. If he had learned anything from his father, it was that one had to have friends in high places to make it in politics.

He hadn't finished his first bite of salad when Mr. Whitfield told him the reason he had called the meeting. He was there on behalf of another family friend, a Mr. Black. Mr. Black had done great favors for the Malley family over the years, but he was aligned with foes from the other side of the aisle. His company manufactured bombs and heavy artillery, and he was one vote short on an upcoming appropriations bill that could approve a large government purchase of his products.

He recalled placing his fork gently down on the table. Politely folding his napkin and placing it over his food, and looking Mr. Whitfield straight in the eye. He reminded him how he had just fought to end the war. That he promised his constituency to do everything in his power to stop it and any further American military conflicts. How he had marched on Washington. How he despised war and all of Nixon's bombing. The name Michael Malley was known to every anti-war activist in the country.

To ask him to vote contrary to his promises, at any time, but especially now? It was preposterous.

Upon arriving back to his office in Summit, there was a message from his father's aide waiting for him. His immediate presence was required at home.

He'd driven nervously back to the mansion, thinking his father's last minute was at hand. Instead, his father greeted him in the foyer wearing his finest suit, hat, and overcoat. They walked slowly out the back lawn. In those days the huge red oak spread its branches over the pond. It was the place his father had taken him over the years to discuss everything from misbehavior to mathematics. If there were a day he could trace to the root of his troubles, it would be that cold and dark day in November of 1976.

His father explained that day that there were long-standing arrangements between the Malley family and certain men of business. Favors had been granted that had benefitted the Malley family greatly. It was time to repay one of them. Never mind what the past favor was, but it was imperative that he grant Mr. Black his request.

His father had always provided everything he could ever dream of having, and he had never challenged his advice or his orders. But he was a man now. He was an elected United States Senator. "Father," he'd said with all the respect he could muster for a dying man. "I cannot. Those are not my favors. It is a new time in politics, the old way is not my way."

"Michael," his father said through a coughing and hacking fit. He spit two mouthfuls of flem and bile on the ground and wiped his mouth with the back of his leather glove. "I have always respected your idealism. It should do you well in this world. But I want to be clear with you. You must know something before I go. I bought your appointment to the Senate. Paid for in cash and favors by Mr. Black. Now, I have neither the energy nor the time to go into the details. But do a dead man one last favor and vote for Black. It will be the wisest thing you ever do."

His father then walked back across the lawn. He stood there and watched him enter the house. When the door closed and he was alone with his thoughts, he looked over at the old red oak. It was impossible to escape the absolute enormity of its symbolism. Impossible to escape his father.

In the house, just a few minutes later, he found his father sitting in an old ladder back chair in his den. He had expired sitting fully erect, in his best suit and hat.

A week later, the vote came down, and Mr. Black was awarded his contract. Sometime later, in the spring of '77, he was sitting in The Mall, eating a sack lunch. A man sat down next to him and introduced himself as Mr. Black. Said how sorry he was about his father's passing. Wanted to personally reach out and express his friendship. That should he ever need a favor, it was his for the asking.

He stood that day and said, "Mr. Black. Any favors my family may have done for you are fully paid and in the past. Good day." And then he walked away.

He set his drink down on top of the desk. The glass was wet with condensation. Left too long, it would ring the wood. He cared not. He would burn the desk soon. He'd cut that old oak down shortly after his father's death, had the wood milled and treated, and made the desk himself. It was to be a reminder to never compromise his values again. Yet, not ten years later he'd failed miserably and gotten into bed with Antoinette Lasaut, and Condor Walken.

He picked the Scotch up again and sucked the last bit of the syrupy elixir through the cubes. Perhaps this was all just his fate. Perhaps casting his vote for Black was not his undoing, but the wisest thing he ever did. His father's last words. Indeed, a man did have to have friends in high places if he wanted to make it in politics. His agreement with Black wouldn't just be for the removal of Walken. It would be an alliance. Black would continue to prosper under a Malley White House. In turn, in advance, Black would pay him in a politician's most valuable currency. Votes. Yes, he'd often been on the other side of the argument than people of Black's ilk. But perceptions could be changed. New arguments could be made. And with the money and power that Black had, votes could be got in a number of ways.

There was a knock at the door. Henry stepped in, closed the door quietly, and approached. Stepping behind the desk, Henry pulled his handkerchief and wiped the water off the wood. He walked to the wet bar and poured Malley a fresh drink, returning with a coaster.

"I'm not going anywhere, Michael," he finally said.

Malley was amused by the young pup's determination. "We need to remain calm," he said. "This is the beginning of the end for Condor Walken."

"Why don't you go yourself?"

"I would, Henry, but it's not a good idea for me to go there right now."

"And it is for me? What if the FBI follows me? What if they are watching us?"

"My boy, we've done nothing. I told you, nobody is going to investigate us. They had a press conference. The whole thing was an accident. Now I need you to simply pick up a package tonight. This is not a request. We will carry on as normal. Your trips to Immunex are normal, Henry. They do business with the United States Congress. Nothing will appear out of the ordinary."

Henry shook his head. He'd been with Malley for years, and Malley had never given him any indication where he was going to end up. He'd never asked. What would he be if they made it to the White House? "And what do I get for all this, Michael? I've been doing your bidding for years, and you've never told me where you see me ending up with you."

Malley sat up and affected a look of bewilderment. "Henry, my boy, you are my most trusted advisor. We are inseparably tied. You'll help make decisions that affect the world when I'm in the White House. You will be my chief of staff. And then the world is yours. Just help me see this to its end."

Malley stood and said, "Now, please excuse me, I have a personal call to make." He'd made the mistake of introducing Henry into his relationship with Condor. He wouldn't do the same with Black.

When Henry was gone, he picked up the phone and dialed. He pressed each key with deliberation, still a shade of doubt in the back of his mind over the bargain he was about to make.

A woman's voice answered, "Mr. Black's office."

"Senator Michael Malley calling for Mr. Black," he said into the phone.

A few seconds later Black came on the line. "Michael?"

Black was a good twenty years older than he, yet his voice sounded like that of a man still in his prime. It irked him that he called him by his first name.

"Yes, Mr. Black. It is I."

"It's good to hear from you, Michael. How can I be of service?"

THIRTY-EIGHT

Among hundreds, they lay atop Pier 94. Small pillows they had brought from home propped their heads. Katie held onto his wrist. Aunt Mary held his hand on the other side. This was his family. His heart pounded from the emotion of being with those he loved, and from the rousing show in the sky. All throughout the night, a full brass band pounded out American tunes, from The National Anthem to Born in the USA.

The sky went dark. After several seconds of silence, a strong pulse from the tubas began beating through the air. It continued, like a heartbeat. Tracers shot up in the air, timed perfectly with the thumping tuba blast. The symbolism wasn't lost on the crowd. John could almost feel the swelling emotion. It was as if they were all one organism packed onto the pier, feeling the same sense of pride in America. After a minute, the tubas faded. Drums and woodwinds had not been heard all night, and when the rat-a-tat-tat of a snare and a strong flute broke into Yankee Doodle, the crowd gasped with a collective release of happiness. Whether you knew the story of Yankee Doodle or not, the quintessential American tune hit the spot. Macy's put on one heck of a 4th of July show.

The final volley lasted over ten minutes. "Beautiful, Daddy," Katie said as the last stars fell from the sky. She held tight to his hand.

He hadn't lost touch with her grip the whole show, but he shared her presence with thoughts about Malley and Condor Walken and Mack Washington, and a burnt building that had killed his friend Park. Every time the Hudson lit up, he thought about the two yachts that had met in the waters so close to them, just hours ago. What had they said across the sterns of those two boats? And what was Jackie Fairbanks doing?

This was the reason he had to retire. He had never been able to separate work from home. The case always ruled his thoughts. He was a great multi-tasker, and Katie didn't know the difference for years. But in the late years, she called him on it. Not that she minded. She was a little Nancy Drew, and she loved being in on the detective work. But he had to give it up. He could never do things half-hearted. If there were bad guys out there and he was responsible for getting them, he was going to get them.

His Droid rang. It was Jackie. "I have to take this, honey." He sat up and hit the talk button. "Hello."

"Henry Douglas left Malley's estate two hours ago. He drove to the city. Made a few random stops. He's checking for tails. Appears very nervous. It looks like he's making his way to the Upper East Side towards the Immunex building."

"I'll be right there," he said.

THIRTY-NINE

The elevator door opened. Jackie leaned against the back of the car while Rodney unnecessarily pushed the "door open" button every couple seconds.

John stepped into the car, looked over at Rodney, who refused to make eye contact, and then back to Jackie. "I'm guessing you didn't track Henry Douglas with the satellite," John said.

Rodney laughed. "It's a geo stationary weather satellite. Not an infra-red military spy bird. Of course we didn't use the satellite to track him at night."

Jackie shot him a look and said, "Rodney, please push the button."

The car rose and quickly came to a stop. Rodney strode ahead of them. John turned to her as they followed and said, "How do you know Rodney?"

"He's my brother, John."

John cleared his throat. "Oh."

"We're twins."

"Intelligence must run in your family."

"Thank you," she said.

"So how did you track Henry Douglas into the city?" John said when they were inside Rodney's lab.

"One of Malley's neighbors is an old family friend. I asked them to call me if anyone left or entered Malley's estate."

"Then what?"

"I had one of our traffic helicopters keep an eye on him until he hit Manhattan."

"Then what?"

"I had Phil and one of my new recruits do a tag team. Quite simple, really."

"A new recruit?"

"Incredible young girl. Had a scooter. Took to foot. Three cabs. She's doing a great job."

"Doing?"

"She's still on him. Okay. Full disclosure. She's my source I couldn't tell you about earlier. Works for a law firm named Maclevey, Maclevey and Horshowitz in Times Square. Told me about the developer wanting to buy up the block. She's an actress. I helped her out, and I needed someone in a pinch. She jumped in. She's perfectly safe. And she told me I could release her identity to you."

Jackie's phone rang. She picked it up, listened, and then put the phone to her side. "It's Phil. Guess where Henry Douglas just landed?"

"The Immunex building."

Jackie just raised her eyebrows.

"Who's your informant? What's her name?"

"Erynn Kelly."

"Tell Erynn Kelly and Phil to leave the area now."

Without hesitation, Jackie put the phone back to her ear and said, "The op is over, Phil. You guys return to base."

"Base?" John said after she hung up.

"Entry to the Lincoln Tunnel. Where we picked him up."

"Stay here, please," he said. He walked back to the break room and dialed into his Asterisk-based phone system in his lab at home. When the auto attendant answered he hit a series of keys to tell the system to dial out with his Droid's caller ID. He got a dial tone and then he fished Santiváñez's card out of his pocket and dialed the number labeled "direct."

He was relaying the call through his own server which allowed him to inspect all the IP packets of the conversation. By knowing the IP address of the tower Santiváñez was using, it would tell him approximately where Santiváñez was, and maybe give him some clue as to what she was doing.

"Good evening, Marshal Kane," Santiváñez said on the other end of the line.

"Agent Santiváñez, you need to level with me."

FORTY

Their Suburban stood next to the curb at Chelsea Park in Midtown South. The call ringing in on her mobile had activated the Bluetooth transceiver and stopped the DVD she and Stiles were watching.

"Level with you, Marshal?" she said over the Suburban's hands-free system.

"What is going on between Michael Malley and Condor Walken?"

"Marshal, there is a debriefing scheduled for first thing tomorrow."

"So you don't have anything you want to tell me?"

Santivánez hit the mute button on the steering wheel. She and Stiles shared a look. "You think he knows something?" Stiles said.

"No," she said. "He's fishing." She touched the mute button again. "Marshal Kane, all I can tell you is to wait until the morning. The BFI will get a full download."

She could feel his agitation through the silence. But the conversation could go nowhere. "Good night, Marshal. And happy Independence Day." Tomorrow the BFI would get a full download. They would get the whole case served up on a silver platter by mother FBI.

When the call had cleared the system, the DVD resumed play. It was Malley and Walken talking on the back of their boats in the Hudson. DEA and FBI techs had filtered out all of the wind and engine noise, and the voice was a little choppy and unclear in places, but plenty clear enough for her purposes, and for the U.S. Attorney.

"I'm going to compensate you one final time for all your friendship over the years."

"That's not necessary. Let's just be done with it."

"Michael, that's not how friends treat each other. We are still friends?"

"Let's just call that part of our relationship finished. Then we can be friends."

"It wouldn't be right, Michael. I always pay my debts. Send Henry tonight."

They'd played it over twenty times in the past five hours since Mackenzie had turned it over, but she and Stiles had little else to do while they waited for Henry to leave Immunex.

Now she had Malley on tape acknowledging taking payments from Walken, for years based on what Walken had said. It sounded as if Walken were blackmailing Malley to force him to sell him his property, and that Walken had probably orchestrated the fire. That would come out, and John Kane would get his due when it did. But her job was public corruption and she had what she needed. Almost. Tolliver and the U.S. Attorney were of the opinion that Malley's admission could be considered ambiguous. To place the cuffs on the likes of Michael Malley, they wanted an ironclad case. So she had what she wanted, which was a blanket wire tap and funds to step up the scope of her operation.

Her plan was to stop Henry just before he entered the Lincoln Tunnel, right as he rounded that bend on 39th. Two SWAT vans would cut off Walken's men if they were running a tail and detain them until the thing was over.

She and Henry would have a nice chat on the drive back to Summit and discuss his options.

She watched the video. The *Minnow* was pulling away from Malley's boat. The audio was gone now, but the video was perfectly clear. Henry's body language told her everything she needed to know about how to work him. And Bureau techs had supplied her with a transcript of what he was saying based on their interpretation of his lip movement. She didn't have to look down from the screen to read the script that they'd given her. She had it memorized. She watched Henry's lips and spoke the words aloud as he did in the video:

"Well, I'm not going anywhere tonight. To meet with anyone. That's absurd."

154

"Michael! We are in control of nothing. You know they blew up your building. People died. We are complicit in multiple murders, Michael! And now he is playing you!"

"Enlighten me, Michael. Please."

"You mean? You're going to take care of him?"

She couldn't see or hear what Malley's responses were. She could guess, but she wouldn't waste much time on speculation. Henry would fill in all the blanks later. He'd come over to her side. He simply didn't have a choice.

Forty-one

John took the phone from his ear and looked at the readout. Had she really hung up on him?

Jackie tapped her foot impatiently and stared at him as he walked back to the hexagon. She had her purse slung over her shoulder.

"Come on," she said

"What?" he said

"We're going down there."

"To Immunex?"

"John, in my world you go where the action is."

"Jackie, in my world I have to have proof to do anything. At a minimum articuable suspicion. What do you think is going on there? The only thing we can say is a couple boats met on the river and now a United States senator's aide is running errands."

"Isn't consorting with a suspected criminal enterprise something? After a building blows up? Less than 24 hours ago?"

"Jackie, as far as I know, Immunex is not officially suspected of anything. Even if it were, that would be very thin." The whole case stank to high heaven to him, but he wasn't going to so much as stake out a parking spot with her.

"I'm going."

"Jackie, the FBI will be there. You won't see them, but they will be there."

"If there is nothing to suspect, why is the FBI going to be there?"

"Jackie," he said with as much restraint as he possessed at the moment, "if there is something going on, the FBI will take care of it."

"And I'll be first on the scene when they make an arrest."

His patience was wearing thin. "They're not going to arrest anyone! This isn't the way it works."

"Don't yell at me."

"I'm sorry." And he genuinely was. He couldn't remember the last time he raised his voice to a woman. They were a pair, there was no doubt about it. But years of law enforcement training had taught him to control his impetuous nature. It would take a dozen lifetimes to subdue hers.

"Jackie," he said, "things don't happen this quick. We need weeks of monitoring, maybe months."

"I'm out of here." Jackie walked towards the exit and stopped. "Rodney, keys."

Rodney pulled a Mercedes key fob out of his pocket and obediently tossed it to her. She caught it mid-stride and continued on.

John shot Rodney a look. Rodney shrugged and tried to say something, but could only look away and scratch the back of his head.

"Jackie," John said. She stopped and looked back.

"John, this is what I do. I watch. I look. I listen. It takes me months, too. But when I put it all together, it makes a story. I can't miss any pieces. So I'm going down there to get a visual on... my suspect."

Her suspect? He opened his mouth to say something, but it was too late. She was gone.

Rodney looked at John and said, "I grew up with it."

FORTY-TWO

Terenty and Silanty escorted Henry through the hallways. As always, the doors at the end of the corridors opened as they approached. The last led to Condor's office.

He sat behind a large marble-topped desk. The office was spacious and open, decorated in a modern high-tech decor. "Hello, Henry," he said as if he were greeting an old friend.

"Mr. Walken," Henry said much more conservatively.

Condor walked from behind the desk and approached Henry. "Jesus, Henry, you look like a fried squid. What's the matter?"

"You assured me no one would be hurt."

"The death of the firefighter last night was unfortunate. When you play with fire, you can get burned."

"The security guard. Mack Washington? Why?"

"He was a loose string. In my business, there are no loose strings. You're not a loose string, are you, Henry?"

Henry felt the back of his throat itch. He coughed and said, "Of course not, Mr. Walken."

"Someone get this boy some water. You're all choked up, Henry. You okay?"

Silanty, the larger of the two brothers, handed Henry a glass of water. He took it and drank it down halfway. "I'm fine," he said. He cleared his throat again. "Just a little parched. Hot out there, you know."

"So tell me. What is Michael Malley saying. You did as we discussed? Told him he'd have to sell?"

"He'll be ready."

"He'll be ready, or he is ready? Does he see the light or not, Henry?"

"He is ready. Just let things calm down. Let the fire marshal make his report. They found the floor heater. Looks like a perfect accident. Like you said on the river, let him settle things with the insurance company and then send him a purchase offer. He'll sign."

"Good. So here we are. I've made a decision to part ways with Michael. But you know that." Condor took a briefcase from under the desk, placed it on top, and opened it. "In here is five million dollars in bearer bonds. I want you to give it to Michael with my blessing and tell him it is a tribute for all his friendship. We will never talk again. He will never ask me for anything, and I will never ask him for anything."

Henry's eyes narrowed with concern. His lips parted ever so slightly.

"What's the matter, Henry? You look like you just shit yourself."

"That's… a lot of money," Henry cleared his throat again and tried to appear relaxed.

"Bearer bonds, Henry. Should buy a few votes."

"Mr. Walken, this is not a good idea."

"Henry, there's only one way to transport five million dollars in bearer bonds."

Henry looked over to the Russians. Their dead stares had always made him uncomfortable, and at that moment he was simply terrified of them. They were cold blooded killers. Yet, even more scary, was taking the case on Condor's desk. "I'm not taking it."

Condor stepped close to Henry. "Henry, you're a good boy. Don't cross me. I will have my people escort you back to New Jersey as usual."

"This is not usual. I don't usually carry five million dollars in bearer bonds the day after the senator's building blows up. Bad idea. This is a very bad idea. There have been too many mistakes."

"No mistakes, Henry. Now don't make one. This conversation is over." Walken returned to his desk and fingered the bonds. There had been no mistakes. He was conducting the perfect symphony. He closed the briefcase and put the handle in Henry's hand. "Drive safely."

FORTY-THREE

He'd been on plenty of stakeouts, but never one like this. He was parked about a hundred yards west of York Avenue on 61st, just up the hill from the New York Presbyterian Hospital. He'd inched up behind a black Cadillac Deville with consulate plates. Behind him to his left, the Queensboro Bridge ran across the water towards home, which was where he wished he were right now. A tramcar buzzed along the overhead cables, taking tourists and locals to Roosevelt Island.

He was ringing Chief Fitzgerald on his mobile. "Fitzgerald," John heard over the Command Unit's hands-free speaker system.

"Chief."

"Yeah, John. Go ahead."

"Yeah," he rubbed his neck. He was tired, and a bit embarrassed for calling Fitzgerald on this. "Ah, Chief, I just have to call in a report to you. Get a reality check."

"What's up? Lemme guess. Jackie Fairbanks? Where are you?"

"Upper East Side. She's got Malley's aide tracked to the Immunex building."

"Fairbanks is hawkin' the Immunex building? What does she think she's going to find?"

"I don't know. I told her to stay away."

"What do you think Santivánez is up to?"

"I called Santivánez and she shined me on again. She's here on the Island. I tracked her cell to a tower by Chelsea Park."

"Maybe she's got an op running. You have my permission to tell Ms. Fairbanks we're getting the FBI's download tomorrow. Tell her you'll feed her something from it. Get her out of there. You don't want that getting messy."

John said nothing. He stared down 61st Street to the curb where Jackie was parked in Rodney's white Mercedes SL55AMG.

"But like I told you," Fitzgerald continued. "Do what you have to do. Your call. Your case. I told you to run it your way."

"Roger that, chief."

John pressed the button on the steering wheel and disconnected the call. He tapped the wheel and told himself nothing would come of this. Henry Douglas would exit the parking garage before too long, and he would drive back to New Jersey. But why was Santiváñez out there? There was a lot of information in the IP packets that he captured on his phone server at home. In addition to her location, the logs told him that she'd muted the call for a full eight seconds after he asked her, "So you don't have anything you want to tell me?" She'd obviously turned to Stiles and said something.

He didn't want to tell Jackie that he'd feed her anything. Fitzgerald didn't know her like he did – all of the roughly twenty-four hours that it had been. You couldn't give Jackie Fairbanks a scrap. You had to give her the keys or keep her out of the castle. Unfortunately, she had already breached the walls of this one, and ushering her out was going to be a very difficult task.

FORTY-FOUR

Kent twisted back and forth in his desk chair. Where the hell was she? He'd instructed her to turn in what she had by five PM. It was past eleven, she hadn't called in, faxed, emailed, and she didn't answer his calls. The insolent little tramp.

Brian Rust, Chief Investigative Correspondent for the network stepped into Kent's office. Pushing sixty, he still looked fifty. "I saw the coverage of the Malley fire last night."

"Yes," Kent said. He left his fingers steepled out in front of his chest.

"Nice work letting Phil in there. He's wanted to get in front of the camera since he came to us, but been too shy to make a request. I like to see you bringing new people up."

"It was just a metro piece. He did a good job."

"You've got something on your mind. Does Ms. Fairbanks have something working on that? That's why Phil had to take the spot," Rust said knowingly.

"Yes." He furrowed his brow. "And she's being very uncommunicative."

Brian smiled. "She'll deliver. She always does. Leave her be until the morning." The old sage walked off.

He couldn't leave her be. He was infatuated with her, and she had blown him off as if he were some adolescent plaything. He picked up his Blackberry. Chose Phone/Options/General Options/Restrict My Identity/ Always. Hit the track ball to save the change. Scrolled to her mobile number. Hit the trackball twice to dial.

***

Her phone rang with a restricted ID. It had to be John. She could see him parked down the hill behind the Cadillac. "Jackie Fairbanks," she said into her phone, expecting her hear her Marshal on the other end.

"Why haven't you called in?" Kent's nasal voice grinded in her ear.

She took the phone down with an annoyed look, clicked the ear volume to its lowest setting, and said, "Nice trick, Kent. What are you in junior high?"

"I told you to give me what you had by five. This has nothing to do with you and me. Strictly professional, which you are not being."

"I'm on it, Kent."

"I want to know what you have," he demanded.

"Strictly professional, then, Kent?"

"Trying to keep it that way, Jackie."

"Oh good. Hold on one second and I'll get you a download."

"Thank you."

She took the phone from her ear, dialed the personal mobile phone of Brian Rust, and then conferenced the two calls together.

"Hello. Jackie?" Brian's voice was part concern, part intrigue.

"Hi, Brian. It's me."

"How are you, darling?"

"Well, Brian, I was hoping you could help me out of a jamb."

"Of course. You know, anything."

"I've got Kent on the phone."

"Kent?"

Kent cleared his throat.

"Brian, I was hoping you could explain to Kent here that when an experienced reporter tells her news manager that she is on it, he should really give her some breathing room to do her job."

"Let it go, Kent," Rust said.

"I was just --"

"No," Rust cut him off sternly. "I mean let it go. She's out of your league, pal."

Kent was silent.

"I'm not sure I hear anything coming out the other end of my phone, Kent. Is there some kind of malfunction?"

"No, Brian. I get the message."

"Good," Rust said. "Anything else, Jackie?"

"That'll about do it."

"Oh, Kent," Brian said. "Are you still there?"

"I'm here."

"Come up and see me. Now."

She disconnected the call and flipped the phone around in her hand. It rang again. Restricted ID. Kent wouldn't have the balls to call her and apologize. She pushed the talk button and said, "I see you back there, you know."

"What are you going to do, Jackie? Say it is Malley's guy. You going to follow him all the way back to Jersey?"

"I am," she replied.

"And what if that's it? What if he just pulls into Malley's estate and goes to bed? Which, I'll tell you, is exactly what's going to happen."

"Then I'd say it's been an eventful day. I'll go home and go to sleep and start again tomorrow."

***

Henry waited at the exit to the parking garage for a couple of cars to clear the street. All of a sudden, he didn't want to go to the White House with Michael Malley. Escape was the only word that came to mind. He could take the five million and disappear. The bonds were untraceable. But there was the issue of Walken's people behind him somewhere. He never knew who they were, or where they were, but he knew they always followed him back to the mansion. Still, the thought was appealing. Get away. Take the five million. Live very frugally somewhere. He could go to the unlikeliest of places, like the Alaskan wilderness. People lived out there. Put up a perimeter. Cameras. See anyone coming from twenty miles away. With five million, he could live forever in the wild. Maybe get himself a little wife.

He fished the small pill box out of his pocket and swallowed a Vicodin. Then he reached into the door pocket and pulled out a small bottle of red wine. He unscrewed the cap and downed the contents, then slid the empty bottle back into the side pocket. He could never escape, and he sure as hell wasn't going to live in the wild. He looked in the mirror and laughed numbly. A disaster was brewing and he could do nothing to stop it. He didn't care. If Michael Malley were too weak to stand up to Condor, then to hell with it. They'd all burn.

***

"Jackie, tell me something," John said. He was beyond tired and he was reaching the end of his patience with her.

"Yes," she said after he didn't complete his question. "And no."

"What?" he said.

"Yes, John," she said. "This is always how I am. But it's not how I'm always going to be."

"I want you to get out of here," he said. "Right now."

"There he is," she said hurriedly.

He could see the nose of an Escalade pull out into traffic and then make a quick left on 2nd.

"You could pull him over and ask him what he's doing down here," she said. "I'm telling you, there's something going on."

He just shook his head and cleared his eyes. "Pull him over? Jackie, I need probable cause to do something like that. I haven't a clue what he's up to."

"John, I know all about probable cause. I just have to tell you. When I get this feeling, I'm rarely wrong. There's something going on."

"Jackie, stay right where you are. I'm coming to get you." He'd had about enough of this. This woman needed a man to take control, and damnit, that's what he was going to do. They were out of there. He didn't care what Santivánez may or may not be doing. They wouldn't be following Henry Douglas to Summit. No following him anywhere. He was going to escort Jackie to her townhome and drive himself back over the bridge. The feds would be playing ball tomorrow. He'd be damned if they were going to stonewall him. He had his own power base in the FBI, and he could get to the Director himself if he needed to.

Putting his Explorer in reverse to back away from the Cadillac, his heart leaped from his chest. The white SL shot from the curb and turned south onto 2nd Avenue. He hit the redial button on the console. The phone started to ring. He punched the pedal to the floor. Pushed first and second gear to the red. Red light at the intersection. Cars lined up behind the crosswalk, a few in the intersection, making their way slowly down 2nd. Flipping the lights would bring too much attention. There was a Level-Two in the intersection directing traffic. He flashed his brights, held his badge out the window. Pointed south. The cop quickly stepped toward oncoming traffic, stopped them. Waved John through.

He gunned it around the corner and hit red again on Ramp 62. There were people all over the intersection. He hit the steering wheel and quickly flashed his reds. No horn. The cop did her work and cleared the way, and he sped on. Red again at Ramp 59. He crept through the intersection, and when clear, he blew through first and second and rode third gear at eighty to close the gap. He could see her ahead. Dialed her phone again. The first call had gone straight to voicemail. "Damnit, Jackie. I told you to stay put." He scanned traffic and looked ahead for yellow lights. Right now it was all greens ahead. Six rings. "Pick up, Jackie."

***

She was doing forty down 2nd Avenue, keeping up with the thinning traffic as they headed south. How could she get Henry out of the car so John could have a talk with him? She briefly thought of rear-ending him to get him out of the car. That was vehicular assault. She could get in front to him and cause him to rear-end her. That was also illegal. But she was sure if John could stop him and ask him a few questions, something would come of it.

She came up on his driver's side and slowed down. She looked over at him to catch his attention and he looked over at her. The top was down on the SL, and she could see him perfectly. He looked absolutely stoned, or smashed. Whatever he was on, he was wasted. She had a new idea.

She hit the answer key on the phone just before it went to voicemail. "John, this guy is stoned to high heaven. He looks like a dead fish."

"Get out of there, Jackie."

"He's wasted, John. Pull him over."

"Jackie," he rose his voice and spoke with authority. "I'm right behind you. I am instructing you to pull ahead and leave this area. Turn off of 2nd Avenue immediately. That's me speaking as an agent of the federal government, Ms. Fairbanks. I am completely serious. You are now interfering with a federal investigation. Am I clear?"

FORTY-FIVE

Stiles drove the Suburban down 2nd Avenue. Santiváñez unconsciously tapped her thigh with her thumb. Her assets were posted all along the route to the Lincoln Tunnel. All she had to do was pick up Henry after her SWAT team had secured the scene and then present her case to him while they drove through the Tunnel. He'd be ready to flip before they hit the Jersey line.

Her first post on 2nd had already reported that he had a tail. It complicated her plan that they had to keep Walken's people on ice until they had the confession from Malley, but they were prepared for it. As soon as Henry got back with whatever he was carrying from Walken and engaged Malley in conversation about it, she would have what she needed to drive up to the mansion and present the senator with her evidence. Her SWAT teams would take care of apprehending Walken.

Her Nextel chirped and the radio operator said, "You're not going to believe this, but the fire marshal and Jackie Fairbanks are following Henry. I tapped into their phone conversation. Listen to this."

A recording played over her Nextel:

"John, this guy is stoned to high heaven. He looks like a dead fish."

"Get out of there, Jackie."

"He's wasted, John. Pull him over."

"Jackie, I'm right behind you. I am instructing you to pull ahead and leave this area. Turn off of 2nd Avenue immediately. That's me speaking as an agent of the federal government, Ms. Fairbanks. I am completely serious. You are now interfering with a federal investigation. Am I clear?"

"Oh, for God's sake no, lady!" Santiváñez cried. "If you screw this up, I'll send you to hell!" Then, into her Nextel, "All units, we are taking him before the Tunnel. He is southbound on 2nd approaching 34th. Converge on the target. I repeat, converge on the target."

Stiles put the pedal down, flashed his brights and honked his horn. The Level-2 at Ramp 62 saw him coming, stopped traffic, and waved him through.

***

John hugged the Mercedes' bumper. He locked eyes with her in her rearview and jerked his thumb to the right. She gave him a look, shrugged her shoulders. Then she switched lanes and sped ahead to 34th and turned west.

There was a dented yellow van parked on the side of the street with a phony decal on the side. He knew Santiváñez and Stiles were close. There was no doubt about it. What did they have planned?

In all reality, he should just let it go. He had absolutely no reason to pull Henry over, and if he did it would probably only hurt any case he was building. But as angry as he was at her, he shared Jackie's hunch. And Park and Mack Washington had been murdered. This was where instinct took over. It told him to act. He brought his Explorer even with Henry's Escalade, dropped the passenger window and waved to get his attention. After a few seconds, Henry saw him and turned.

Jackie was right. Henry looked like a stoned fish. He pulled the PA's mic out of its slot and hailed him, "Pull it over, Henry."

Henry looked back and forth nervously, rounded the corner at 34th, and pulled to a stop a hundred feet west of 2nd Avenue.

FORTY-SIX

Santiváñez's Nextel beeped. "This is unit five. Kane pulled the mark over on 34th before we could get there."

Tolliver's voice came over the Nextel. "All units pull back. I repeat, all units pull back. This is Tolliver. Maintain protocol with the subject's tail."

Santiváñez covered her face with her hands and willfully drove her rage away. Now was not the time to lose her cool. It was never time to lose one's cool in the FBI. But when the shit hit the fan, it was especially important not to show emotion.

Her mobile rang. The readout showed Tolliver. She hit the answer button and put him on speakerphone, "We're southbound on 2nd, sir."

"Maintain a visual but do not engage with him."

Stiles pulled the wheel hard and went the wrong way down 35th, then the wrong way up the tunnel entrance. He eased them out onto 34th and stopped at 2nd Avenue.

"What's happening," came Tolliver's voice over the speakers.

Santiváñez found she couldn't speak. She motioned to Stiles to field the question.

"We're parked east of 2nd on 34th, facing the subject, sir."

"Okay. He pulled him over on a di-wee, I'm guessing," Tolliver said. "Where are Walken's people?"

A blue sedan with heavily tinted windows pulled to a stop at the corner of 34th & 2nd. "Their car just pulled to a stop across the street from us, sir," Stiles said.

"I don't hear anything from Radio," Tolliver said. "Maria, what are those guys doing?"

"They have their orders, sir," she said. She picked up her Nextel, "Radio One, what is your status?"

Charlie's voice came back instantly with, "Radio One. We are monitoring all mobile channels and analog frequencies. Kane just called in the DWI to Midtown South."

"Sir," Santivánez said. "I'd like to intervene and take Henry Douglas now. Our people are in position to handle the blue sedan. Marshal Kane has simply accelerated our plan."

"Just slow down. Let's not forget that Kane is one of us. And he's probably just pissed off enough to battle you right there in the street in front of Henry Douglas."

"Sir, I thought we were treating him as a local marshal. There will be no battle. We outnumber him ten to one. I have two SWAT teams in the area."

"I'm perfectly aware of the operation's assets, Maria. I put them together. Kane is still a federal officer, and we have no idea what he knows or what he's doing right now. We can't just barge into the middle of his operation any more that he can ours. Like he just did."

"Sir, our case trumps his. We could take this over right now."

"He is JTTF, Agent Santivánez. We don't know what he's doing. And he could call in a few people who might trump us all the way to the Director's desk."

"Sir, he's fishing. He knows nothing."

"He knows something, Maria. What's he doing on the Upper East Side on the 4th of July pulling our suspect over? Where did he come from? And the reporter? Why didn't you know they were there?"

She had screwed up by pulling the surveillance from Fairbanks, and she should have done a better job of working the entire area. She should have known they were there. But the right thing to do was to take this down immediately. She was on record now multiple times for requesting that. Tolliver was screwing this up.

"Maria? Are you there?" Tolliver said.

"I'm here, sir. I don't know where Marshal Kane came from or how we missed his presence."

"My office is trying to reach the BFI chief and Kane's ASAC, who is in Cancun, of all places, on vacation."

"Sir, I don't think he's acting in his capacity as a federal marshal right now. I strongly urge we intervene and take Douglas."

"We don't know what he's doing, Santiváñez. And truth be told, I was never crazy about your plan to try and turn Henry Douglas in the Lincoln Tunnel. What if he told you to fly the coup? We'd be done. And our tape on the Hudson of Malley is a very weak confession. We always needed more. This might work out better. Let Kane feel it out and we stay back, don't blow our position."

She didn't know how to respond to that. Tolliver couldn't make a decision if his pants were on fire. Staying back and feeling things out when it was time to strike was his way.

"And Jackie Fairbanks is still parked up ahead on the street?" Tolliver said.

"Yes, sir. She is sitting in the Mercedes Benz."

"No cameras? No other press?"

"Not that I can see from this far away. No other press."

"Radio," Tolliver's voice came over the Nextel. "Has Fairbanks made any calls?"

"Negative," Charlie's voice came back. "But two blue and whites and a tow truck were just dispatched from PD."

"Okay," Tolliver said over Santiváñez's phone. "Just hold on. I think this is Kane's boss calling me back on my other line."

***

The Lithuanians sat inside the blue sedan. The woman pulled an uzi from underneath her seat. Rapped the slide back and forth. "That's the fire marshal from the scene last night," she said.

The man took out a phone and dialed a number. There was a fast busy signal. "What is this?" He dialed again and got the same thing.

The woman took a Motorola radio out of the glove compartment, pushed the button and said, "The goddamn fire marshal from the fire last night just pulled him over." She released the button and waited.

***

In the back of the surveillance van an alarm buzzed on the radio console. The spectrum analyzer showed encrypted traffic on the 146 megahertz frequency. Kam punched in 146-174 on his keyboard and hit enter. That would blast a signal of greater strength on the frequency, jamming any communications.

"That was about two seconds of transmission that got off," Charlie said.

"Best we can do with these tools," Kam said. "I can't jam everything in the area. Police, fire, taxi, they'd all be screaming. I have to do it selectively."

"What's two seconds?" Charlie said.

"'Base, this is,' or something like that," Kam said.

"Let's hope that's all it was," Charlie said.

"We do the best with the tools and the rules they give us, Charlie."

"We should tell Santivánez what just happened," Charlie said.

"Good idea. But should you direct it to Tolliver?" Kam said.

"No," Charlie said. "Santivánez is moving up soon. She'll appreciate us going through her."

"Right," Kam said.

"You call," Charlie said.

"Why me? You've been on the radio all night to her."

"Because you can say what you did better than me. She's going to ask to get it straight from you, anyway."

"You're such a chicken shit, Charlie."

"Yes, but one with good political sense. I made the call to run it through her. So call. Before too much more time passes by."

FORTY-SEVEN

John walked up to the Escalade's driver door. Henry smoked a menthol and tried to act casual.

"Henry? Everything okay?" It was his standard procedure. Anytime he pulled someone over, anytime he questioned someone, he inquired about their safety, their health, their well-being. You never accused them of something right off the bat. That was a sure way to get them to clam up.

"Fine, Marshal Kane. Things are fine. I'm heading back to Summit. Was I doing something wrong?"

"Ah, I was just on the Island working," he said, not really answering his question. "You know. Pulling an OT tour on the 4th."

"Why wouldn't everything be okay?"

"There's just not a lot of people down here this time of night, and I wanted to make sure you were safe."

"Yes, Marshal, I'm safe. Just heading home."

There was squawk and then a suburban pulled up behind a blue sedan parked at the corner on 2nd. There was a voice over the loud hailer, "Move it on. Pull forward." The grill lights flashed on. John couldn't see inside the suburban, but he knew it was the feds. Probably not Stiles and Santivánez. This suburban was blue. Theirs was black. The blue sedan pulled out into traffic and both cars disappeared.

John turned back to Henry. He looked as if he'd seen a ghost.

"You okay, Henry?"

"Yeah, yeah," he recovered. "That was weird."

"Happens all the time. Cops don't want people hanging out on holidays. Potential for trouble."

"Right, right," Henry said, trying to be smooth. "Well, the senator is expecting me, Marshal. I better get going."

"I don't think so, Henry."

"What?"

"Henry, what are you on?" John followed his eyes as Henry turned away.

"Is that what this is about?"

Henry seemed relieved. Why did he say that? Stoned people always said the wrong thing, things that revealed the truth. That's why priests gave wine at marriage counseling.

"What else would it be about?" John said. Henry was silent. "What else would this be about, Henry?"

"Nothing."

"Step out of the car, Henry. I'm placing you under arrest for Driving While Intoxicated."

"I will not."

John reached inside, flipped the lock, opened the door, and assisted Henry from the Escalade.

"You can't arrest me!" Henry said. "You're a fire marshal."

"Henry, I have a badge, and a gun." John pulled cuffs out. "Handcuffs, too. I can arrest anyone I want." John took his arm and turned him against the car. "They didn't teach you that in forensics class?"

FORTY-EIGHT

After PD arrived on the scene, John assisted Henry into the back of the patrol car and closed the door. His Nextel rang. It was Fitzgerald, probably with the feds on the other line.

"Chief," he said.

"John, I have Dwayne Tolliver on the other line. He's the ASAC over Santiváñez and Stiles. You got Henry Douglas in the back of a blue and white on 34th Street?"

"That's affirmative."

"Are you alone?"

"Yeah, chief. We're clear." Phone to phone, BFI traffic was encrypted. He knew the FBI was listening to cell channels, but they wouldn't be able to hear this conversation.

"You pulled him over on a DWI?"

"That's affirmative."

"What else do you have?"

"Based on what I've seen, and what he said to me, I think he has involvement in the building at 43rd & 8th. What are the feds telling you?"

"They want to know what you're doing, and what you know."

"And what did you tell Tolliver?"

"I told him the FBI better come clean with us or Henry Douglas was going in with you. They're obviously scared or they'd have stepped in by now. Hold on, I'm bringing them in."

"Special Agent Tolliver, I have Marshal John Kane on the line," Fitzgerald said.

"This is Assistant Special Agent in Charge Dwayne Tolliver, Marshal Kane."

"This is John Kane."

"John, may I call you John?"

"Please do."

"Okay. Please call me Dwayne. It seems we have a little standoff here."

"Shouldn't be that way, Dwayne."

"You're right. You're absolutely right. Just tell me what you have planned. We need to know what you're doing."

"Dwayne, all due respect, Chief Fitzgerald told me the FBI was going to download BFI, right here, right now. Now are you going to level with me or not?"

"You're right, John. We have Michael Malley acknowledging payments from Condor Walken and Walken quite apparently extorting him. We have Henry Douglas clearly admitting having knowledge of the fire, and suggesting Malley had a part in it, too. And we think Malley is going to arrange to have Condor Walken killed. We were prepared to place a wire on Henry Douglas. We think he'll flip. We're still prepared to do that. But I'd really like to know what you know, and we'd especially like to find out what he has in that Cadillac."

They had Henry admitting to the fire? And they didn't call him immediately? He was enraged, but anger wouldn't move things forward. "So you got audio from their meeting on the Hudson. Good."

There was a silence. "How do you know about the meeting on the Hudson?"

"I'll tell you what, Dwayne. I know some things. You know some things. I'm having a hard time getting over you not bringing me in on the arson. But we're not doing this on the street. Meet me in the garage at Midtown South."

"Right. We need to convene and brainstorm," Tolliver said.

John looked at his phone and frowned. Brainstorm? Santiváñez must really hate this guy. He hung the phone up and motioned for both the tow truck and the patrol car to take off.

He got in his Explorer and followed. Slowing down next to Jackie, who was still parked on 34th, he simply pointed his finger forward. She was inside the castle walls to stay now. She smiled big and pulled out into the lane behind him.

178

FORTY-NINE

Midtown South parking garage. John followed the tow truck down the ramp. He pointed out his window for Jackie to park next to him. "Stay in your car," he said to her through his open window as they came to a stop in two stalls. She nodded, but he was not convinced. "Jackie," he said, "You're going to stay in your car, right?"

"Yes, I will," she said. "I promise."

He expected what came next. Three black Suburbans descended the ramp. Light assemblies behind the grills. Fed antenna sets. Blacked-out windows.

He walked across the lane toward the tow truck and put out his hand. The first Suburban came to a stop a few feet behind Henry's Escalade. Santiváñez stared straight ahead, refusing to look over at him. Stiles exited the driver's side, walked around the back of their vehicle, and opened the door for his partner. She wasn't getting out, and she still wouldn't look over at him. She was one pissed off lady, as well she should be. She had a protocol going on the street tonight and he'd just turned it on its head. Well, he was pissed off, too. So they were even.

A black BMW 750i rattled over the metal grate at the top of the ramp and sped down to them. Tolliver stepped out of the car, brushed a piece of non-existent lint from his shirt, and approached. He extended his hand and said in an officious manner, "Dwayne Tolliver, Marshal Kane. We're working together from here on in." Then he motioned for Santiváñez to join them. She stepped from her Suburban and approached with a stone face.

John motioned for the tow truck driver to lower the Escalade.

"We need to know what you know and how you came by your knowledge, John," Tolliver said. "I don't want to get in front of the lawyers and have this thing blow up on us."

"Any more than it already has?" John said.

"John, please," Tolliver said. "Let's work together. I've given you the condensed version of our entire case. I need to know what you've done. We know Ms. Fairbanks is involved, and it complicates the hell out of things."

He had a point about Jackie, and he had indeed given him the canned version of what they knew. A little quid pro quo was in order.

"Okay, Dwayne. Here it is. A few years back there was a story in the New York Times suggesting a link between Michael Malley and Condor Walken. Early this morning, Ms. Fairbanks uncovered some information that suggested motive for starting the fire. But you knew that." He stopped. He wanted to see if Tolliver would acknowledge listening to his conversation with Jackie outside of his HQ earlier. Tolliver shrugged, and that was good enough as an acknowledgement in his book. But he wasn't going to split hairs right now. He'd use that against Tolliver later. "Neither Ms. Fairbanks nor I believed Mack Washington was a drug deal gone bad and the suspicion started to mount. At roughly three PM today, I observed her monitoring a satellite feed that showed Michael Malley's boat meeting up on the Hudson with another boat of substantially larger size. We assumed that person was Condor Walken."

"Wait a minute," Tolliver said. "You observed a satellite feed? That's ill-gotten evidence. The rest of what you did is poison. Oh, Jesus God."

"Dwane, I'd appreciate it if you didn't take God's name in vain, first off. Second, I obtained that knowledge under the plain view statute. Ms. Fairbanks, her brother who was running the satellite, and I will all testify to it in court." John turned over to Jackie, who looked through the rearview mirror at them. "Isn't that right, Ms. Fairbanks?" Jackie held her thumb up in the air. "So just slow down, Dwayne."

"Okay," Tolliver said. "What else?"

"Then I called the thing into Chief Fitzgerald and went to the fireworks show."

"You went to the fireworks show?"

"With my daughter and sister-in-law."

"And how did you come to find Henry Douglas in the city?"

"Ms. Fairbanks, as a private citizen, without my knowledge or consent, managed to follow him into the city. She called me and informed me that he was here. Ms. Fairbanks, acting in her capacity as an investigative reporter, followed Henry to the Immunex building. I followed her to make sure she was safe."

Tolliver's face was screwed up into a knot. He let out a sigh and rubbed his face with both hands and said, "And then you observed him driving away from Immunex and pulled him over on a DWI?"

"That's right."

"And that's all you have, and that's all you did?"

"Until we talked on the phone on 34th Street."

Tolliver looked over to Santiváñez. She said, "Sounds clean. Nothing poisonous there."

"And how did Ms. Fairbanks find out about the sale of the buildings on the block?" Tolliver said. "What is her source?"

"I didn't tell you she found out about the sale of the buildings. Only that she uncovered something that suggested motive. Did you have a warrant to listen in on our conversation outside of my HQ?"

Tolliver put his hands in his khakis and stood straight. "Well, ah," he looked at Santiváñez.

"Don't worry about it. It lead to nothing. Not germane. We'll note it and let it go."

"Well, fine, then," Tolliver said. "I'd still like to know what her source is. It will become germane to the case."

John looked over at her. "Ms. Fairbanks, would you please join us?"

Jackie stood from the convertible and walked confidently to the group.

"You all know of Jackie Fairbanks. Jackie, you know who stands before you?"

"I do."

"Ms. Fairbanks," Tolliver said. "Have you made any reports of this case to your editors?"

"No I have not, agent Tolliver," she said.

"That will be special agent, young lady," he said.

John didn't care for his tone, but let it pass. She was a big girl and could handle herself.

"Can you tell me your source?" Tolliver said.

"You know I can't, special agent Tolliver. I have revealed her identity to Marshal Kane, as she gave me authorization to do so. But only to him. She will cooperate with us, though."

"With us?" Tolliver said, circling his hands around his space. "With the FBI, Ms. Fairbanks. It appears to me that your investigative zeal knows no bounds. We're going to need to change that."

"Hey Dwayne," John said. "Back off. The 'young lady' was doing her job, within the bounds of the law."

"Okay," Tolliver said. "Point taken. I thank you in advance for your cooperation and keeping things confidential until the Bureau is ready to release information to the public."

"Of course, special agent Tolliver. That's the right thing to do. And the Bureau is also going to give my network the exclusive when you're ready to break this."

Tolliver smirked. "We'll see about that when the time comes." Then he turned to John. "This is much bigger than a local arson, John. We'll get you your conviction, but Public Corruption is going to need to take over now. We've got a lot of ground to make up for here. This is a federal case of the highest caliber."

"I wholeheartedly agree," John said.

"Thank you," Tolliver said.

"This is much bigger than a local arson. We're talking willful destruction of municipal and federal property. Two counts of murder directly relating to the fire, one of which was perpetrated on my friend and fellow firefighter, Jimmy Park. We'll leave Mack Washington out for now. We have Senator Michael Malley and his aide's involvement in arson, insurance fraud, and a whole host of other crimes that I have yet to discern. We're talking about the use of electronics to gain access to the building and the intention to extort, blackmail, and terrorize this allegedly complicit federal employee. This case just became a federal crime of the highest caliber, that, I will remind you, falls clearly under my jurisdiction as a federal fire marshal charged by the FBI's Joint Terrorist Task Force to investigate such matters."

"John," Tolliver said. "We're not going to have a pissing match here. Be reasonable." Tolliver opened his hand toward the two SWAT teams that stood at the ready beside their Suburbans.

"Those guys?" John said calmly, looking down the lane at the men, all dressed in SWAT gear, all standing at the ready with their hands behind their backs. "You want to draw down on me, be my guest. But you'll find yourself in the middle of a shit storm that will begin like that," John snapped his fingers. The crack rang through the garage like the report from a sidearm, and Tolliver visibly jumped. "It will end just as quick with your career going down the elevator and into the employment ads."

"John, be reasonable," Tolliver said with a coaxing laugh.

He had him scared and he was going to take it to the finish line. "Another thing," John said, again leaving the emotion buried even though it ran all over his skin and up and down his spine. He could almost kill this guy for keeping him in the dark when they had good solid evidence on the arson. Plus he's spoken rudely to Jackie. Oh, how he wanted to pummel Tolliver. Not bloody him. Just slap him around. "You may or may not know that as a New York State fire marshal, I have the power to take sworn confessions and subpoena evidence in the field. My commission as a federal marshal amplifies that power, and gives me the authority to take evidence in my arson cases away from even the likes of you. So I'll be needing a copy of that conversation you took on the Hudson."

Tolliver looked to Santivánez with a half-open mouth.

"Right away, please," John said.

Santivánez walked to her Suburban and returned with a DVD. "It's all on here, Marshal."

"Thank you, agent Santivánez," John said. "And your exclusive lies with me, Jackie."

Jackie raised her eyebrows at Tolliver, turned right to John, and gave him a quick smile.

"Well," Tolliver said. He cleared his throat three separate times. "That out of the way, I hope we can still work together. We do have Condor Walken's people, and a plan to insert Henry Douglas back with the senator. We probably have the arson, but it is important to get the whole thing if we can."

"I agree completely," John said. "Let's speed this up." He turned to Santiváñez. "Agent Santiváñez, would you care to SILA the car?" A SILA was a Search Incident to a Lawful Arrest, and pronounced seela.

"Go ahead and do your thing, Marshal," she said. "I wouldn't dream of interrupting this."

John stepped to the Escalade's driver's door and opened it. He looked around and quickly spotted the bottle caps peeking up from the door's side pocket. Pulling them out, he held them up and said, "Two individual serving bottles of American Merlot, one opened, the other unopened."

He walked around to the passenger's side and opened the door. There was a hard briefcase lying on the passenger floorboard.

Walking to the back of the Escalade, he held up the case and said, "We'll need something to open this."

The NYPD tow truck driver, who was standing off to the side, stepped up and said, "I got a grinder."

John looked over and nodded to him. From one of the service lockers on the truck, he produced a battery powered grinder strong enough to cut through heavy chain.

John set the briefcase on the ground and let the driver do his job. A half minute later, he had both locks cut and popped open. John turned the case around to face Santiváñez and Tolliver and lifted the lid. He thumbed the edge of the stack of bonds twice. $100,000 USD played as a still image in front of them. Then he looked up and said, "Let's go see Mr. Douglas."

FIFTY

His stomach ached. His sinuses were draining and he was nauseous. Henry could see how wrecked he looked in the mirror.

So this was an NYPD interrogation room? It was sterile. Hopeless. All the times he'd seen a guy here on the television hadn't prepared him for this. It was a helpless feeling being locked in a room with the knowledge of what you'd done, trying to figure out just what the guys on the other side of the glass knew, imagining they knew it all, but being prepared to deny it all to the end.

Who was back there behind the glass? It had been twenty minutes since the two cops had deposited him here. Soon enough someone was going to come through the door and play tough cop. Probably Marshal Kane. He'd mocked him on the street. "They didn't teach you that in forensics class?" It occurred to him that before, he'd been amused by Kane's sarcasm. He wasn't sure what he felt now, but amusement wasn't on the list.

They certainly didn't care about a bullshit DWI charge. There was no doubt they'd found the bearer bonds. Should he demand a lawyer? Could the senator get him out of this? Would he? If Michael Malley found out what he'd done, he'd surely send him up the proverbial river. Walken would surely kill him now. He'd seen what Walken did with loose ends.

What did the people behind the mirror really know? Surely about Malley's relationship with Condor. He always knew that Times article would come back to bite the senator. Now they had five million in extortion money as proof. But why take him in unless they had a bold move to make? Unless they had a recording of a conversation between him and Walken where they were discussing his part in giving them access to the building, they didn't know about his part in it. But they'd find out. They always did. There was no death penalty in New York state, but he'd be looking at several life sentences. It was time to switch sides, if only to buy some time.

He had to stall. He was sure the senator had already put the plan into motion to have Walken killed. With Walken dead, his part in the building would never be found out. But for transporting some of the payments from Walken to Malley, he really had no part in Malley's illegal activity with Walken. He was just a helpless pawn in a twisted case of extortion and blackmail that he never wanted to be a part of from the beginning. He just had to wait it out. Give the people behind the mirror a little something to chew on while Malley got rid of Walken.

FIFTY-ONE

John studied Henry through the two-way mirror. He sat there emotionless, staring into the corner, not directly into the glass like some guys he'd kept on ice. Some guys stared you down, let you know just how innocent they were, lawyered up right away. Had attitude in lockup.

Henry looked like a man ready to bear his soul. His face was a blank page. Probably because he was so stoned. But the room was working on him. He was cool on the outside but a raging inferno inside.

"Let's see what you've got, Marshal," Santiváñez said.

Jackie sat in the far corner, legs crossed, sitting confidently upright.

John picked up a briefcase and a couple protein drinks he'd bought from the vending machine. He looked over at Jackie and winked, and then exited the room.

***

Henry turned when John opened the door. His face showed nothing, just a stoned, dead look. He looked at the case, and then casually away, as if it meant nothing to him.

Was he going to shine him on, or did he want to play? John put the drinks down on the table and said, "This will make your stomach feel better." Henry didn't reach for it. John unscrewed both caps and took a long pull from his. He'd been up now for nearly forty-eight hours. "Go ahead. Drink. It's good." John pulled the pill box and wine bottles out of his pocket. "It'll help counteract the effects of this stuff."

Henry looked at the contraband with disdain. He closed his eyes and let out a huff through his nostrils.

"I think I need a lawyer," Henry said.

If Henry had demanded a lawyer, he was done. Procedure was clear. Anything he obtained past that would be inadmissible, and build grounds for dismissal.

"Henry, I want to be very clear with you. Are you demanding a lawyer, or do you think you need a lawyer? Because I know you know how this works. So let's not mince words. Take a drink of this and think about it." John pushed the plastic bottle closer to him.

"Why would I need a lawyer, Marshal Kane? The DWI charge you hauled me in here on, or something else?"

He was home free. Henry was a smart kid. He knew his rights and he wanted to deal.

"Henry, do me a favor and drink some of that. It will make your stomach feel better."

Henry took the plastic bottle and drank for several seconds, then again until it was empty.

John turned the case around and opened the top. "That's five million in bearer bonds, Henry."

"Not mine."

"We found your prints on the case."

"Who is we?"

"The FBI, Henry. I'll tell you what we know. We know about Senator Malley's kickbacks with Condor Walken. We know Walken is blackmailing Malley to sell him that property, and that he blew it up to send a message to the senator. We know you knew about the building. I've got a nice tape of the three of you on the Hudson today. Parts of it are a little unclear, but we've got what we need. I'll tell you the last thing I know. This five million dollars is your payoff from Walken for helping him blow the building."

"That's absurd," Henry said.

"Really? Someone had to help them into the building. Someone had to call the right plumbing outfit to fix that leak. That someone was you. You told me that yesterday. That alarm system is impenetrable, Henry.

But from the inside, you could rig it so the bad guys could get in and out without security knowing. And that's what you did. Mack Washington told me you were in and out of there alone on several occasions. That's in my notes, which to any DA in this city are as good as a sworn confession. I don't need a live body to testify to it."

"Absolutely not. That is not my money. I didn't do anything of the sort."

"Two people are dead. One of mine. Millions of dollars in City infrastructure. What was the senator's part in this, Henry? We can help you."

Henry just shook his head from side to side as if the whole thing were too much to believe.

"I can be your best friend. The other set you have, well, they've been a very bad influence. They made you do some very bad things. I can help you, Henry."

Henry said nothing.

"It's your call, Henry."

"I want immunity. And protection," he finally said.

John sat down across from him. "Okay, I'll get you immunity. But you have to level with me right here and now."

He hadn't anticipated them pinning the five million on him. And they could probably make it stick. That was, if the feds got Condor Walken. Henry gave him his most sure look. If he was going to pull this off he had to convince himself. "I'll do it," he said.

"If you lie to me and I find out, all bets are off. Your continued protection is based on complete trust, the complete truth. Do you understand me?"

"How do I know you can give me immunity, protection? I want something signed."

"This whole thing is being recorded, Henry. You give me what I want and I'll see that you get a new start. I said I'll help you."

"What authority do you have? You're a fire marshal."

"Henry, you continue to underestimate me. I'm a federal marshal. I have the FBI in the next room. They're all watching. If I were telling you anything false, they'd stop it."

"I still want something signed."

"It doesn't work like that. You have to trust me. You could always go back to demanding a lawyer. But we both know that's a bad move now."

He could always get a lawyer later. There was one thing John Kane was forgetting. He'd pulled him over on a DWI. He was high on prescription drugs and alcohol. He could always claim a hallucinatory state. Tonight he could do anything and say anything and tomorrow sing a different song. "No prison."

"You deliver for us and no prison. I promise. That is if you tell us the whole truth."

Henry looked down at the table. "I need some water."

"Okay, we'll get you an Evian. There's a nice machine right outside. Now do you want to deal or not? Time is running out."

"What are we talking about?"

"The opposite of a cement cell and three squares a day, Henry. You know the deal. It's not going to be the Peninsula, but you'll have a new life."

"Okay."

"Henry, you are under oath. You have been read your Miranda Rights and you are about to give a sworn confession by your own free will. Do you understand?"

"Yes."

"Did you, Henry Douglas, knowingly or unknowingly take part in the fire that destroyed the senator's building last night?"

"No," he said. Kane was looking him in the eyes for a sign, and he wasn't giving him one. Lying when you were this sedated was easy.

"What did you mean when you said to the senator on the back of his boat, 'You mean you're going to take care of him?' Is the senator planning on having Condor Walken killed?"

He'd said parts of the recording were unclear. They obviously didn't hear Malley's answer, which was that he was going to have Condor murdered. He probably had a couple of strikes before they threw him to the wolves. He'd use a bluff here to see just how much they knew.

"Michael Malley would never kill anyone, or have anyone killed. He's the kindest old man on the planet. That's why I stayed with him despite his dealings with Condor Walken. What I meant by that was, would he finally sell Condor the property. Condor kept saying, 'Michael, I took care of you all these years. When are you going to take care of me and sell me that property?'"

"Okay. What about their dealings all these years? What exactly are we talking about?"

"It would just be easier if I told you the story from the beginning. At least the way the senator has told it to me."

"Go ahead," John said.

Henry told him about Antoinette Lassaut and the payments Walken had forced on him over the years. "Condor wants the property to build a high rise," Henry said. "I kept telling the senator to sell and be done with it. Condor promised it would be the last favor he ever asked. The senator just would not sell, and so I believe Condor blew the building up. We should have come forward earlier."

"You lied to me yesterday morning. Senator Malley lied to me."

"He still didn't believe Walken had done it. Then, when you showed him the floor heater, he was convinced it was an accident. It wasn't until Mack Washington died that he really started to doubt."

"You mean when Walken had Mack Washington killed? Did you or Senator Malley know anything about that?"

"Of course not. Walken killed him. He told me when I picked up the money tonight. I asked him why and he said he was a loose string. That he helped him do the building and he had to get rid of him. So you see, the money was not for me. Walken was again forcing it on the senator. Like he always did. I don't think the senator has ever spent a dime of the money Walken gave him. Michael Malley is a good man. I so wanted to see him become president."

"That's not going to happen now."

John took a Mont Blanc pen out of his pocket and placed it on the table. "Looks like yours," he said.

"Of course. They took it from me."

"This one's a little different. You have immunity. You have witness protection. We need you to get Senator Malley to freely acknowledge all payments from Walken."

Henry picked it up. "I'm late. And what about my tail? How is this supposed to work? "

"FBI has the tail, Henry. I think it's time you met the FBI." John turned to the mirror. "Agent Santiváñez, would you come in and meet Henry, please?"

Santiváñez walked through the door. She took a chair from the corner, placed a bottle of Evian in front of Henry, and sat down at the side of the table.

"I'm Santiváñez, Henry. We'll be getting to know each other."

"You want me to elicit a confession out of Michael Malley? Into a pen?"

"And Condor Walken," Santiváñez said. "We want him clearly admitting to blowing up the building to threaten Michael Malley."

"You're insane. They check me for wires every time I go near Walken. Malley sweeps. This will never work."

Santiváñez took the pen from Henry and said, "You turn it just past full retraction and the transmitter is on." She turned it to show him. "Turn it back and it's off. Turn it again and it writes. One more turn and it's on while you are writing. You can feel each step. When it's off, it will pass any RF detector. It's got enough ink for a few pages." She handed it back to him.

Henry worked it around in his fingers. "Feels about the same," he said.

"It's some of the very best technology we have, Henry. You'll be fine."

"What happens if I can't get in front of Walken?"

"We think he'll come calling."

"And what if the senator won't say anything?"

"We own you until he does."

192

FIFTY-TWO

Henry sat on a bed behind a curtain. They had moved to St. Vincent's Hospital on Greenwich.

John pushed back the curtain and stepped inside the area. "Malley is here. Are you ready?"

"This is never going to work, John," Henry said.

"It's a little late to get a case of the nerves, Henry. Just do like Agent Santiváñez said. Don't push it."

"I'm not a good actor, John. I told you that. I tried to tell Santiváñez."

"And she told you to just be cool. Right? Don't rush the performance."

"Oh, save the metaphor. This isn't Hollywood."

"Henry, let me tell you something. You better put on an Oscar-winning act. Your freedom is tied to results."

"Right. You get dead for flubbing your lines in this one."

"Relax, Henry. You'll be fine."

Stiles poked his head through the curtain. "Thirty seconds, John."

"Listen up, Henry," John said. "Plain and simple. Do what we told you and you'll be fine."

FIFTY-THREE

Henry paced behind the curtain. He looked angrily out into the hall. Malley would be there in ten seconds. Who did these people think they were? A fire marshal and some chick FBI agent? The senator was never going to fall into their trap. They didn't know him the way he did.

He rubbed his wrist and breathed deep. Five. He'd give it an effort because they were listening. But he wouldn't push Malley too hard. When they got back to the mansion he'd ditch the transmitter and tell him everything. Malley would have Mr. Black send in his assassins to kill Walken, and this whole thing would be over. They could get back on track with the bid for the presidency. Why not? Malley's lawyers would shove this so far up Kane's and the FBI's ass they wouldn't ever look sideways at the senator again.

The curtain opened and Malley said, "Henry, thank God you're alright. Are you? My God, you look terrible."

"I'm alright," Henry said. "Just a little shook up."

"What's this world coming to? You didn't get a look at the men that ran you off the road?"

"No. Just drunk drivers, Michael. 4th of July. Too much to drink."

"Well, let's get you out of here."

***

Malley and Henry climbed into the back of Malley's Town Car minutes later. As soon as the door shut, Malley's countenance changed to an angry scowl. "What is this?"

"Condor gave me five million dollars in bonds and then his men stopped me and tried to killed me is what this is," Henry said calmly. "I barely got away with my life. I'm done with this, Michael. I don't want anything more to do with Condor Walken or his money." That was just general enough that it looked as if he were trying to bait him, but he really hadn't said anything. "Just sell him the building, Michael, and let's be done with it."

Malley stared him long and straight in the eyes. The limo pulled away from the hospital. When they were out on the road, he reached across the limo and felt Henry's torso area for a wire.

"What's this?" Henry demanded as if this were an insult to his loyalty. "You think I'm wearing a wire? Michael, I've just been through the most traumatic time of my life. They tried to kill me!"

Malley waved him off, indicating that he would have no discussion whatsoever.

***

Santivánez, Stiles, John and Jackie, and Fitzgerald stood in a cordoned-off hallway in the hospital.

"Radio, do you have them?" Stiles said into his radio.

Charlie's voice came back, "Affirmative. But the mark is not saying anything. Our boy tried, but the mark clammed up and checked him for a wire. Over."

"Ten-four. Keep us posted. Team One out," said Stiles.

Tolliver rounded the corner and handed Santivánez a folded piece of paper. Santivánez opened it, scanned it quickly, and then handed it to Jackie.

"Ms. Fairbanks," she said through an exhale that suggested her exasperation. It was late and everyone was tired and emotionally drained. "Here is the 6E we promised you."

A 6E was part of the Federal Rules of Criminal Procedure. It ordered the recipient to keep anything they knew about a federal case confidential. The penalties for non-compliance were very unpleasant.

Jackie took it, scanned to the bottom and put it in her purse. "Clear enough," she said.

"Very well," Tolliver said. He looked down at his watch. "I will be monitoring this around the clock. You're back in charge, Maria." He nodded to her, shook Fitzgerald's hand and said, "Chief," and then he walked away.

Santiváñez watched him walk away with an impassive stare. When he had rounded the corner, she turned to John and said, "So this night is over, Marshal Kane. If something happens, we will notify you immediately."

"Maria," John said. "May I call you by your first name?"

"Yes, John," Santiváñez said. "Go ahead."

"Let's not drag this on too long," John said. "I want arrests within 72 hours."

"I do too, John," she said. "Let our guys see what Henry can do. I'll keep you informed regularly."

"I'm sorry for barging into the middle of your protocol," John said. "Would have been cleaner your way."

"We have five million dollars in evidence and a confession from Henry Douglas. The Grand Jury will indict both Walken and Michael Malley. Malley's career as a politician is over. I'm not sure about Condor Walken."

"You should have read me into this earlier."

It took her several seconds to answer. She finally said, "Tolliver."

"He's a real schmuck," John said. Santiváñez laughed and he said, "Don't take any more crud off him."

"Good night, John," she said, and she and Stiles walked away.

In the parking garage, Santiváñez stopped at the tail of their Suburban. "So," she said. "Those sheets still clean?"

Stiles connected with her stare. It was like they were back in front of the Venus de Milo. He took her hand and assisted her into the passenger seat, extended the seat belt and handed her the buckle.

In the driver's seat, he started the engine and then turned to her. He wished he could reach over and kiss her right there. "Care for music?" he said.

"That would be nice," she said.

He tuned in a smooth jazz station and said, "Our first date."

"And you haven't even bought me dinner," she said.

She was flirting with him and it was fantastic. He backed out of the stall and said, "I'll make breakfast." He looked at his watch. "When the sun comes up."

FIFTY-FOUR

Back in the hospital hallway, John and Jackie walked hand in hand. You want to get some sleep?" John said to Jackie. "I booked a room at the Hilton Times Square."

"Sleep? In time," she said, and put her head on his shoulder. She fought a yawn away and said, "You were my knight in shining armor in that parking garage."

"With Tolliver?" he said. "The nerve of that guy to speak to you like that."

She kept his hand and swung out from him. "I feel very safe with you. My very own Marshal."

"Last night, before you disappeared around the corner at 42nd. Did you... growl at me?"

She scrunched her nose like she did when she growled and said, "I did."

He looked her deep in the eyes. They were both tremendously worn out, but the connection was still electric.

"So I'm sworn to secrecy," she said playfully. "When do I get deputized?"

"You don't get deputized."

"That's no fun."

"Do you want to be deputized?"

"Yes."

"Have to check regulations on that."

She smiled and opened the door to the parking garage ahead of him. "Good."

A few minutes later, John dropped the front windows on the Explorer, letting in the smell of the grilled meats and the sounds of the night life. It was 2:45AM. Vendors sold pretzels and kabob on the sidewalk. Every race, shape, and size of humanity coursed through Times Square.

He turned right on 7th, took a quick right on 41st, and parked the car in the red zone. Walking into the lobby of the Hilton Times Square, the bellman asked John if he were staying in the hotel. He pulled out a card, handed it to the bellman, and just nodded. John pushed the up button on the elevator. The cars sat midway between 41st and 42nd. If they continued on another fifty feet north, took a left onto the 42nd Street sidewalk, walked down to the corner and looked north up 8th Avenue, they'd see Malley's building, or what was left of it.

Several floors up in the guest lobby, they both began to feel a sense of calm. The hustle and flow of New York City was out on the street, and they were now safe inside this quiet building.

The guest services lady stepped out from behind the front counter and greeted them with a smile. "Good morning, Marshal. Your room is waiting." She handed John a key, returned to the counter with his credit card, swiped it, and gave it back. "Enjoy your stay."

They made their way to the main elevator bank and stepped into a waiting car. John pushed the button for the forty-fourth floor. He stood in one corner of the car, was surprised that she stood in the other. "Where did they put that big boat?"

"You don't actually want to talk shop, now, do you?"

He smiled. It was comfortable with her, as though he'd been with her for a very long time and they didn't have to play games. It was good. He was just himself. Didn't have to worry about a thing. "No. But where'd they put her in?"

"South end of the Island."

She was unabashedly confident. And damn did he love it.

The elevator door opened and they stepped out into the vestibule. She took his hand. Led him to their room. Took the key from his other hand and opened the door.

Inside, the bed had been turned down. A lone lamp by the bed shed soft light. Through the window, it looked as if he could reach out and grab the necks of The Empire State Building and Chrysler Building lighted red, white, and blue for the 4th of July.

He stepped to the window and closed the heavy curtain. The light by the bed went out and she stepped in behind him. She put her hands on his chest, slid them down his stomach, and then back up again.

He turned to her. She cupped the back of his neck and pulled herself tight to him. She was strong and ultra feminine all at once. He savored the sensation of being that close to a woman, a sensation he had missed for a very long time. Then he kissed her, and made love to her, as if she were the only woman whom he had ever loved.

FIFTY-FIVE

Walken opened his eyes, immediately alert. It was his nature to sleep with an alertness that woke him on the slightest sound or movement. He'd been like this since boyhood. There was a second knock at the door. He pushed a button on a remote. The lights came up and the door to his suite opened. Torval entered, stood across the room, smoothed down the front of his coat. "They haven't returned, Mr. Walken. They're not returning any calls."

Condor still lay on his bed. "Tell me again what was said on the radio."

"'The goddamned fire marsh', and then there was nothing. Neither answered their phone after that."

Walken sat up in bed and said with a calmness that belied his agitation, "Ready a limousine." He put his feet on the ground. "And bring the fire marshal to me. We'll see what he knows."

"I have our assets working on his location. We were unable to enter his home in Queens. It's too secure. He does have a daughter."

"He's a smart one, this John Kane." He rose from the bed and stretched. Though he was over sixty years old, he was still in very good shape and strong for his size and weight. "Find the marshal. And let's go see Michael Malley."

FIFTY-SIX

Malley stepped from his Town Car and walked to the mansion's main entrance.

Henry followed close behind him. "Michael?" he said in a hushed tone. "We need to talk." The car ride had passed in complete silence after Malley had checked him for the wire. He'd refused to so much as look at him the entire ride back to Summit.

Malley stopped, and with his back to Henry, he said, "Get some rest, Henry. You've been through a lot tonight. I'll call doctor Anderson. You look like you could use a checkup." He held up his hand indicating he would have no further conversation and continued on.

The Town Car was pulling away and he stood alone in the still night. "You're right," Henry said for the benefit of whoever was listening at the other end of the transmitter. They didn't know the senator couldn't hear him. "I don't feel well." He watched Malley enter the mansion and then walked to his private quarters. Worst case scenario was he'd take the immunity from the FBI. If it came to that. More probable was that the senator would have Walken killed, he'd claim coercion and a drug-induced state, and this whole thing would go away. Would the senator try to distance himself from him after it was all resolved? Before this, they had had a bond of trust like father and son. But the senator couldn't afford to push him away now. He simply knew too much. They just had to get through the next day. And Michael Malley had to make sure Condor Walken was gone from the picture.

FIFTY-SEVEN

A white Mercedes limo Walken had never used passed through Malley's gate and drove up the incline. Walken looked out to the lighted grounds, to the opulence that Malley possessed, and it humored him. Malley's life had been so easy. As a boy, Malley played croquet on these lawns and slurped down lemonade from crystal glasses served to him on silver platters.

He had suffered as the grandson of "The Dirty Irish Immigrant," and his fate had been drawn by the hand of the senior Malley. While young Michael Malley was running around these lawns in his knickers, he was stirring his brother's brains with a table knife. And while Malley roamed his university halls, he roamed the world impersonating his dead brother, building his fortune with one goal in mind – destroying the Malley clan forever.

He was back on that dock in Karachi. The El Jai container ship at his back. Walking down the dock with a suitcase filled with a hundred grand and three kilos of Puro.

It was a 600-mile jeep ride to the small village of Chartusharib in the Oruzgan province of central Afghanistan. He approached the village the same way he had approached the cantina outside of Bogota years before. It didn't take him long to convince the tribal leader sell the Colombian cocaine to the same people who were buying his heroin, and he returned a few months later with four hundred kilos of Puro. Carlos charged them two thousand a kilo. The Afghans turned around and sold it to American, French, and Italian businessmen for double that.

His best customer, regular as clockwork, was a Soviet General named Servaya Varvarushka, who, in turn, took over the business with the Afghans. Brian didn't care, as long as the money came in. Each time he left the Middle East, he returned with a crate containing between eight and ten million dollars. Carlos was giving him forty percent to run the operation.

He made millions and millions. Then Gorbechev came to power and the Wall fell. The new breed of capitalist mafia became uncontrollable, and his Russian operation came to an abrupt end. Without the fear of the tyrannical Soviet Army, these new upstarts were uncontrollable and soon outnumbered the men who had run things before them.

It was then that he decided it was time to put the second part of his plan into action. He had more money than he thought he would ever possess. Now it was time to start laying his trap.

He created the identity of Condor Walken and returned to New York City in 1989. After seeing one of his old customers in Chinatown one day, and learning about the emerging opportunity in genetic sequencing, he bought Immunex, then a struggling pharmaceutical research company, for five hundred thousand dollars cash. He poured millions more into the business, intent on creating something legitimate to hide behind so he could carry out his play.

As luck would have it, Michael Malley had been appointed to the Health and Human Services subcommittee in 1985.

He'd been playing puppet master on the little man ever since, and up until about three hours ago, the play had gone precisely as he directed. But someone had rushed onto the stage uttering lines not in his script and corrupted one of his players – Henry Douglas. It was the fire marshal, and he'd deal with John Kane. But first, the plan to kill off Henry Douglas had to be rewritten.

FIFTY-EIGHT

Henry opened his eyes. The butler stood over him, shaking his shoulders. "Mr. Douglas. Please wake up. The senator would like to see you outside."

Was he dreaming? He closed his eyes again, but the man still shook him. Still spoke words he did not comprehend. Outside?

He opened his eyes and realized he was sitting in the wingback chair in his quarters. He'd fallen asleep there. "Mr. Douglas, the senator would like you to join him outside. You have a visitor."

"What do you mean?" he said. "Who would come here at this time of night?" He stood up and tried to compose himself.

"I don't know, sir," the butler said. "The senator asked me to summon you."

"I'll be right there," Henry said. "Let me put some water on my face."

"Very well," the butler said. "I will inform the senator you will join him momentarily." And he left.

Henry rushed to the bathroom and looked in the mirror. Walken was there. Santivánez was right. He had come calling.

Henry saw the pen sticking out of his pocket in the mirror. It was still transmitting. The feds knew he had been summoned. If he ditched it, he'd be in hot water with them. If he took it with him and left it on, Walken's scanners would find it. His best option would be to turn it off just before being scanned.

***

Henry stepped onto the porch. Malley waited under the covering. He wore loose jeans, an untucked knit, and loafers with no socks. A white limo pulled around the corner and came to a stop in front of them. "Michael, if that's who I think it is, this is a bad idea. I don't want to meet with him."

"Don't worry," Malley said. "I told you I'd handle it. Now let's go."

The doors opened and two of Walken's men got out. Malley descended the steps and allowed himself to be scanned by the men. Henry reached in his pocket and turned the top of the pen one click to the right. That was off, wasn't it? One more click extended the ball point, and one more turned it on while you were writing. He wanted to throw the thing in the hedge, but they were watching. While he walked slowly down the steps, he felt the bottom of the pen. No ball point. It better pass or he was dead, and maybe the senator, too.

He raised his arms and let them scan him. He knew the drill. He'd done it less than twelve hours ago and many times over the years.

The two Russians finished scanning him and he and Malley climbed into the back of the limo.

Walken sat calmly with his legs crossed. He smoked a cigarette. When they were still, he said, "So, Michael, Henry. Is there something you want to tell me?"

Walken was calm, as if he were trying to elicit a confession out of a teenage son whom he knew had deceived him. He'd be a dead man soon, and that smug look on his face would turn to nothingness. "Your men tried to kill me," Henry said. "They stole the bonds, and I barely got away with my life."

"They tried to kill you? Stole the bonds?" He smoked calmly, as if he were amused.

"Mr. Walken, your men crashed into me on the road."

"Crashed into you?" Walken said, exhaling smoke at Henry and Malley.

Henry stared at him through the haze. "Yes. They pitted me out, turned my car sideways, and then rammed me. The next I know, there's an Uzi pointed at me." Doubt crept into the back of his head. Who would believe such unbelievable stuff? Kane was crazy for putting him in this position.

"Pitted you out, Henry? I'm not familiar with that one."

"With a capital P-I-T. It's what the police called it. Pursuit Intervention Technique. Your guys hit me in the rear and spun me out."

"The police were there?"

"Yes. The police came," Henry said. He was calm and his tone was slightly patronizing. "Take a look at my car in the police impound. It won't drive. Look, Mr. Walken, your men attacked me and stole the bonds. I barely escaped with my life."

Walken looked at him for a long while. "Escaped?" he said. "Where to?"

"Where is there to go at midnight in that part of town but a hotel? The Wellington. Where was a cop when I needed one until I went back to the car to see if the bonds were still there, and one shows up?"

Walken laughed, as if entertained by a friend's fish story. "This is a lot to take before the sun even comes up, gentlemen. I haven't even turned on the world news to get me warmed up to this... pile of goat manure. My guys would sooner cut off their own dicks than cross me for five million dollars. They know I'd spend ten times that hunting them down."

"It's the truth," Henry said as calmly as he could. Goat manure was funny. Like Kane's crack about forensics class. How he hated them both now. And he hated Michael Malley all of a sudden. He hated the whole world. Use the hatred, he told himself. Fucking Kane and his Hollywood analogies. Well here you go, Marshal. Hate was his motivation.

"I don't know what to say," he spat with as much venom as he could muster. "You think I'd make something like this up?"

Walken tossed the proposition around in his head and then said, "Are you working for the cops, Henry?"

"That's preposterous."

"Maybe not. What's the fire marshal got to do with this?"

"The fire marshal? You mean John Kane?" he said incredulously, though he was crushed inside. "John Kane is investigating the fire. What does he have to do with this? Is there something you're not telling us? Like your decision to off Mack Washington? Look, five million dollars is a lot of money. I don't know how much you pay your men, but I think you should find them. I'm pretty fucking pissed off. They almost killed me."

Walken studied him. "You're either telling the truth or you're a damn good liar, Henry. So tell me, what do you think my guys were going to do with you if they had killed you?"

"I'm not sure. Maybe take me and my car to some auto wrecking yard and dispose of me. I didn't give them that chance."

"An auto wrecking yard? That's funny, Henry. I don't own any auto wrecking yards, and I don't know anybody who does. That's what the Italian gumbas from your state do."

"Maybe they were just going to leave me there to die, like Mack Washington."

Henry noted how Malley had been watching the conversation go back and forth. His disbelief was softening, and now he seemed to turn, like a juror who had just heard the defenses' alibi.

"Henry, if we were going to kill you we would have done it a whole lot cleaner than what you are describing."

"I'm not saying you had anything to do with it, Mr. Walken. All I can tell you is I'm still pretty shook up. If you find those sons a bitches… I'll kill them myself."

Walken put out his cigarette. Then he turned to Malley. "Michael, we'll speak alone."

***

Killing Henry had indeed been the plan. He knew too much. It was supposed to be just one more act in the Malley saga. But the Lithuanians weren't supposed to do it in downtown Manhattan. They were to wait until they got into Jersey. Do it on a back road. He thought they might have turned on him for five million, but they weren't so stupid as to have tried to take Henry in the City. And then there was the call – 'The goddamned fire marsh-'

Walken lit another cigarette and said, "Henry is working with the police, Michael. The FBI is probably all over this."

Malley said nothing. His eyes darted around the limo.

"Henry is a good liar. First class. Those Yale boys know how to lay it out. But when he told me he wanted to kill my guys if I found them, I knew he was full of shit. That boy couldn't kill a church mouse if its head was strapped to a guillotine, and all he had to do was pull the little fucking string."

Malley still said nothing. He continued to look distractedly around the limo.

"Michael, what's the problem? You think I'm recording you?"

"You're always the one so particular about bugs. How do I know you're not?"

"How about this, Michael? I blew up your building at 43rd & 8th in Manhattan for a reason I may one day disclose to you. I killed your security guard because he saw my men driving away. Henry, little fuck that he is, helped me gain access to your building. He called the plumbing outfit I told him to so we could put the pressure coupling in. He rigged the alarm so my men could get in again last night and let the gas build up. My people were supposed to kill Henry tonight, because he knows everything, but they were given orders not to do it in the city. I've been blackmailing you for 30 years, and I'm here tonight because five million dollars I was having delivered to you has now been stolen from me, and it is probably evidence in a case against us. That means we have some fixing to do, Michael."

Malley took several seconds to digest what Walken had just told him. But he was past being surprised. "What do we do?"

"We take care of it, Michael."

"I think I know what you are suggesting, Condor. But I don't have the foggiest clue how to 'take care' of something like this."

"Michael, do you think I'd leave something like this to you? I'll take care of it. You just need to keep him close until we can make it look right."

Malley thought for a long while and then said, "I can do that."

***

Henry paced in his bathroom and spoke into the Mont Blanc like it was a microphone. "This is bullshit. It's never going to work. Condor Walken is here, and the senator is meeting with him alone, in a limo, outside the estate, right now. I was just in there. I told him what you told me to, and he's not buying it. He is going to kill me, just like he did Mack

Washington." He stopped and looked in the mirror. He wanted to go over to the other side right now, but he was hiding so much. If they found out his part in the building, he'd find himself in a very bad place.

They wanted a voluntary utterance out of the senator for what amounted to kickback money? This was mice nuts compared to nabbing Walken. He could get Walken, right here and right now. Walken always spoke openly when he was sure there were no bugs. He'd go back to the limo, get scanned, demand to be let back in again, turn the transmitter on when he was inside, and bait Walken to spill the beans. If Walken accused him of conspiring with him to do the building he'd deny it, say it was Mack Washington, and that Walken was just trying to confuse the matter now. It was he who had ordered him killed to remove him from the equation because he knew too much. This was the only way out. He had to do it, and he knew he had to do it now. He spoke into the pen again, "I'm going back in. I'm going to get Walken to lay it all out for you. I want a goddamn brigade of SWAT guys here when he admits to it."

He turned and opened the door to the bathroom. Malley was standing in the doorway to his room about twenty feet away. "Michael," he said.

Malley entered the room and stopped in the middle. Henry met him halfway. Malley put his hands on his shoulders and said, "I'm so sorry you had to go through this, my boy. All I can say is, I am going to handle this. Things will be back to normal soon." Then he turned and walked out.

Henry opened his mouth to say something, but no words came out. Malley closed the door behind him and Henry collapsed onto his bed and passed out before he could think another thought.

***

The surveillance van was parked behind a donut shop in the east part of Summit. Coffee cups and food wrappers filled the small trash can in the back corner to the rim.

"Awe, damn," Kam said. "I thought this was going to get good." He sighed and rubbed his eyes.

"I think our boy's passed out," Charlie said, removing his headphones. "You call Santivánez," he said to Kam. "She sounded kind of funny when I called before."

"I'm not calling her," Kam said. "She hates me. Probably going to give me a writeup for dereliction of duty or some shit."

"You think she and Stiles are fucking?" Charlie said.

Kam took a big bite of his maple bar and sipped his coffee. "Man, I hope so," he said through the soggy mix in his mouth.

"I'd like to be Stiles," Charlie said.

"Yeah," Kam said. "I ain't even got a girlfriend." He took a gulp of Coffee, washed the donut down, picked up his phone, and held down the number one key to speed dial Santivánez. "I'll make the call. You really are a pussy."

Charlie shrugged, pulled Diet Coke from his straw, and said unapologetically, "I know."

FIFTY-NINE

One of many rooms in the three-story penthouse, the octagonal conservatory sat at the top of the building in the center of the floor. Tall walnut-paneled walls rose to a cornice. A ledge, also of polished walnut, rose at a forty-five degree angle from the cornice and ran around the octagon. It joined at each angle with detailed molding. Carved into the solid wood were intricate reliefs of antiquity scenes Walken had admired in Rome and Florence and Córdoba. A marbled promontory that made up the outer wall of the structure rose up a few feet. A stained glass dome with sturdy walnut ribbing rose to an apex and was capped with an octagonal medallion that looked as if it had been rescued from the belly of some sunken Spanish Conquistador's galley and restored to its original brilliance.

A polished walnut and ivory Bosendorfer baby grand piano sat alone on one end. On each panel was a portrait of one of the masters – Bach, Beethoven, Mendelssohn, Tchaikovsky, Brahms, Wagner, Bernstein, Joel. In the center of the room, opposite the piano, a simple pair of leather settees.

Wagner's "The Valkyrie," played loudly over the sound system. Walken sat alone on one of the sofas. Thoughts of war and subterfuge filled his mind.

The words from his men had been clear. "The goddamned fire marsh-" Who was this man named John Kane? And how had he let a fire marshal cause him so much trouble?

One thing was certain, life as he knew it was over. He had one option, and that was escape. How to leave things before he left was the question. There were three scenarios. The first was to let Henry live and leave things the way they were. Michael Malley would no doubt burn up in flames. That would be the easiest thing to do, and while it would serve the end he had sought for so long, that option left his mind feeling very unsettled.

He could kill Henry and let things unfold as they would. If the feds had a taped confession from Henry, and the bonds, even with him dead there would be enough to indict Malley.

Both scenarios avenged his grandfather Harry Farrell and closed a chapter in his life. They both left a new void wide open though. John Kane. Somehow, a fire marshal had turned his life upside down.

Immunex was gone, and so was his plan to build a skyscraper in Times Square. Much of his money would become irretrievable. He would have to go underground and change his identity again. His days of living as Condor Walken were at an end. When he was young, a pretty girl had made fun of him, saying that he looked like a condor, one of the ugliest birds on Earth. So when he became rich, he had surgery to fix his deficit. He'd called himself Condor because it sounded mysterious, and so that he would never forget his past. What would he call himself next?

His phone buzzed. They'd found John Kane. He stood and smoothed out his tie. He wasn't sure exactly what he was going to do with Kane, but he wanted to look the man in the eye and find out what he knew before he killed him.

He walked to one of the panels. Racked the gilded frame holding Beethoven's portrait back and forth in the proper sequence. The wall retracted and slid open. Walken stepped into the space between the outer and inner walls, pushed the wall back in place, and took the stairs down three floors.

SIXTY

John's eyes sprang open. He knew he had slept. He looked at the clock radio and it said 6:00 AM. He'd been out for just over two hours. All he could remember was incredible, passionate lovemaking. Yet something else was flooding his consciousness. Something just didn't seem right.

He was sure the FBI had its hooks firmly planted in Henry Douglas. But what was Condor Walken doing?

He eased out of bed and left her resting on a pillow. If he stayed, he'd wake her. He gathered his clothes and put them on in the bathroom. Two of the top buttons on his shirt were missing. He remembered back to the initial embrace. His shoulders rolled back. He breathed in sweet inspiration and could smell her all about. A powerful rush of contentment ran all through him.

Closing the door silently behind him, he walked to the elevator bank and took the car to the lobby.

***

There was a Starbuck's across 42nd Street. There was a Starbucks across the street from wherever you were in New York City. He scanned the headlines on the Times while he waited for his turn in line.

His phone buzzed. It was the Hilton's main number. "John Kane," he answered.

"Where did you go?"

"Did I wake you?"

"Mmm. I had the best dreams."

"About what?"

"You. And me," she said. Her voice, always clear and clean, cracked a bit. She cleared her throat. "So, I have a question."

"Go ahead."

"Does this mean I'm deputized?"

He smiled big. "Do you want to be deputized?"

"I do."

"Okay, you're my deputy."

"Oh, fun. Where are you?"

"Across the street. Starbucks."

"No room service?"

"Room service it is."

"I'd like a chamomile tea."

"Me, too."

"I do adore you, John Kane."

Before he could answer her, he heard her stretch and growl. She was like a sweet lioness to him.

"John," she said. She sounded halfway serious.

"What is it?"

"Did you leave so you wouldn't wake me?"

"That was the plan."

"Are you the kind of guy who wakes up at the same time every day?"

"With the rooster."

"I sleep in when I can."

"That's good. I like to work out in the morning. Be by myself."

"Promise me you'll always be like this."

Always. He could think about the rest of time with her.

"Don't answer that," she said quickly. "I know this is probably moving very quickly for you."

"It's not," he said plainly.

"So, no workout this morning?"

"I'm, ah, saving my energy."

He could hear her stretch and roll in the sheets. She purred and said, "Hurry back."

The line went dead. He handed the teller a twenty and said, "Two venti chamomile teas and the paper." Stepping to the bar, he dialed the last incoming call. The hotel operator answered. "Room service, please."

***

A cargo van pulled into the Hilton's loading zone on 41st Street. Terenty and Silanty got out and walked up to the guest entrance. The doorman was busy flagging a cab for a couple of businessmen on their way out.

At the elevators, the bellman stopped them, "Good morning, sirs. Checking in?"

"Just breakfast." Silanty gave him a big smile and handed the bellman a five. They walked into an open elevator and pushed the button marked Guest Lobby.

SIXTY-ONE

John placed his key in the slot at room 4415, stepped inside, and closed the door quietly. He set the drink tray on the entry table. The room was completely still. Empty bed. No Jackie. Her handbag was there, but her clothes were gone. He walked to the bathroom and turned on the light. The shower was dry. It had been no more than five minutes since he hung up with her. The hotel didn't have a gift shop, only a small area to purchase sundries right by the front desk. She hadn't gone for ice. He'd passed by the machine on his way from the elevator. She would have to have gotten up and dressed. And left the room? At this hour? After the conversation they'd just had on the phone?

The phone on the table rang. "Hello," he said.

"John, it's me."

"Rodney? Is Jackie with you?"

"No."

"Where are you?" There was a knock at the door.

"Open the door, John," Rodney said.

John hung up the phone and opened the door. "Rodney, what is going on?"

"They took her, John. They took her. That's her." He held up his Droid and pointed to a flashing J on top of a city map.

John took the Droid from Rodney and watched the screen. The blip was at 42nd and Lex.

"Did you see who it was?"

"No. Only that it was a white cargo van."

"You put one of your tracking beacons on her last night," John said.

"Of course I did. How do you think I knew where you were?"

"Relax, Rodney. We're going to get her back."

There was a knock at the door. John moved Rodney around the corner so he couldn't be seen when the door opened. "That will be them. Call agent Santiváñez." He pulled Santiváñez's card out and gave it to him. "I'll stall them and you get her. Do you hear me?"

John looked through the peep hole. It was a man whom he did not recognize. He opened the door and waited for the man to speak.

"Good morning." The man wore a tailored suit and spoke with a Russian accent.

"Something I can do for you?"

"As a matter of fact, yes." He pulled back his coat and showed John his gun.

John did the same. "You want to have a pistol jerk? What?" John said.

A broad smile grew across the man's face. "Call me Terenty. A pistol jerk? That's pretty good." He chewed gum rudely. "Listen," he said flatly, "I'm just the messenger. You want the girl? Yes or no?"

John stepped out into the hallway and let the door close behind him. "Let's go."

Terenty smacked and popped his gum while they waited for the elevator door to open. He laughed. "A pistol jerk? That was in a movie. The one with Kurt Russell about Wyatt Earp. I love the movies. Big movie buff. You?"

John tuned Terenty out. He didn't need to make small talk with the messenger. There was a soft chime in the far corner. John walked to the opening door, not waiting for the messenger to follow.

***

The message played through the earbud in Rodney's ear, "Please hold while the subscriber you are calling is located." In his other ear, he heard the door latch click.

At the same time he saw the man with the pistol, Rodney heard, "Agent Santiváñez." That was the last thing he heard and saw before the small caliber bullet entered through his eye socket and bounced around the inside of his skull.

The shooter stepped over Rodney and picked his earbud out of his ear. He held it close to his and listened. "This is Agent Santiváñez. Who is calling?"

The shooter pressed the button on the earbud, and then returned it to Rodney's ear. He took Santiváñez's card from Rodney's hand, read it, put it in his pocket, and then left the room.

Sixty-two

Santiváñez opened her eyes and sat up. Her Droid was ringing. Confident she wasn't dreaming, she picked it up from the night stand and slid the answer bar down. It was a blocked caller ID. Surveillance had called at 4:20 informing her that Walken was at Malley's mansion, and then again just after five telling her that Henry had ditched the transmitter. Stiles' clock said 6:32AM.

"Agent Santiváñez," she said into the phone. She looked at the read-out. The call timer was going, but there was only silence on the other end. "This is Agent Santiváñez. Who is calling?" The line went dead.

She wanted to wrap Stiles' arm around her and go back to sleep. Instead, she shook him and said his name. He wasn't moving. "Stiles," she said and shook him harder. "Wake up."

"Hey," he said through half-opened eyes.

"Open those eyes, big guy," she said. "We have to go."

He put an arm around her and pulled close.

She wished they could make love and drift away together again. He'd been fantastic once she let go. It was like her dream the other night. She was definitely the boss out on the streets. But in his bed, she had let him rule. She hadn't had a lot of lovers and she wondered if it showed.

He licked her stomach. "Stiles," she said sweetly and stroked the back of his head. "It's time to get up."

He made his way up her torso. "We have to go," she said.

"Do you want me to stop?" he said.

She wanted to say no, but seemed only able to say yes.

In the shower, she quickly washed both of them. When they were rinsed, she shut off the water and told herself it was time to get serious. "We really have to go," she said, stepping out of the shower. She handed him a towel and took one for herself.

"What is it?" he said.

"I'm not sure. But I don't like it."

SIXTY-THREE

The 41st Street entrance to the Hilton Times Square was used for taxi and valet service, and for general deliveries. More of a back alley, it was narrow, and lacked the bright lights and constant hum of foot traffic on 42nd.

It was quiet this early in the morning. A van unloaded produce at the delivery gate. Two businessmen climbed into the back of a waiting Town Car. The bellman took his tip and returned to his post.

John and Terenty exited the building. Terenty waved the bellman off and a stretch limo pulled into the taxi zone. John had left his Explorer in the red zone last night. It still sat there.

Terenty stopped John at the limo. "Give me your piece," he said.

"I'm not giving you my gun."

"Nobody's going to shoot you in there. You want the girl, right?"

"Who's in the car?"

"Play nice and get in. Don't make me force you. Come on. Be cool."

This guy thought he could force him. He knew soon they would come to blows, but now was not the time. He also knew Jackie wasn't in the limo, if what Rodney said was right. Hopefully Rodney was on the phone with the FBI now and they were forming some kind of rescue plan for Jackie, and him. He felt at peace that Katie was secure. He'd done the right thing by shipping her off last night. He took his gun from his holster and handed it to Terenty.

In the car, John stared at a man whom he had never seen, but knew was Walken. Next to him sat an enormous man with white hair.

"Do you know who I am?" Walken said when John was situated.

"I haven't a clue."

"I'm the man you took five million dollars from last night."

"I'm sorry?" John feigned ignorance. The head man coming in the flesh? They'd shaken the lion's den and the alpha male was coming out to fight.

"I could play you a video of that fine young lady. Show her in peril. But I don't want to have to do that. You know why you're here." Walken lit a cigarette.

"What's this about?"

"John, last night my associate here," he referred to Torval, "received part of a transmission that said, 'The goddamned fire marsh-' Then nothing. This was just before my five million dollars in bearer bonds were stolen. Now, I'm just an immigrant's grandson with no formal education. I may be wrong, but this stinks of cop. And I think you're the cop that knows something about it."

"I'm a fire marshal."

"My apologies. I think you're the fucking fire marshal who knows something about it, and I know the FBI is in this, too."

"What did she tell you?"

"Nothing yet. I can make her talk. If you don't want to."

"What do you want?"

"First, I want to know what you know. Second, you took five million of my money. That means you owe me five million. Now, listen. I'm not even going to charge you interest. You are just going to go wherever you are holding those bonds and bring them back to me. And for this I won't search down every member of your bloodline and introduce them to some very unfortunate times."

"Say I could help you. The BFI doesn't hold evidence. Your bonds are probably in an NYPD locker."

"You better find out where."

"Give me back Jackie and I'll try."

"No."

There was no use trying to play coy. The jig was up. "You might as well try to rob Fort Knox. Those bonds are locked so far away the President couldn't walk in there and get them... if the police have them."

"No, John, you might as well try to rob Fort Knox. Have the god damned President help you if you want. I don't care. But you will get me those bonds."

"And then what?"

"Then we'll have an exchange. The girl for the bonds."

"I could arrest you right here." John knew how preposterous it sounded, but he was stalling. If he could stay there long enough the FBI could get Jackie back.

"Arrest me? John, I could shoot you dead and nobody would ever be the wiser. But then we'd get blood all over my limousine. Don't make me ruin a perfectly good car." Walken pushed a button on his control panel. "Driver, proceed." Then, to John, "John, your little friend from the hotel? Well, he's not going to be any help." Walken seemed amused. "What was he doing in your room?"

"What did you do with him?"

"My man shot him in the forehead. Turned his brain to mush. This is what I do to people who get in my way. So, what's it going to be?"

He wanted to reach across the car and snap Walken's neck. He could do it before the big guy got to him. He could handle the big guy. But then what? They had Jackie, and they'd just killed her brother. If Walken were dead, his men might just kill her and then disappear.

"I'll ask you again. Who was the guy in your hotel room?"

"Undercover cop. Stayed in the hotel last night. I called him over when I got back and she was gone."

"Who is Agent Santiváñez?"

"FBI."

"Well, your boy got a call off to her, but he didn't say anything. So I don't think the Cavalry is going to come rushing in to save you. Understand?"

The limo started to move. If Walken himself were here, he would have taken significant precautions to evade detection. A man like this didn't wander into the fray unprotected. That meant he was on his own.

"So, John, where to?" Walken said.

"Why did you take Jackie?" was all he could think to say.

"We came for you," Walken said. "Didn't even know she existed. I was just going to find out what you knew and kill you. Now I see a way to get my five million back, and maybe you'll live to see her again. She's a beautiful woman. You have my respect. Do everything you can to keep it. Now, where to, John? Midtown South Precinct? I think that's where you took Henry last night."

John looked out the window. They were turning west onto 42nd street. Midtown South was just eight blocks away. "Just keep going."

"Good. Now, tell me about my people, John. Two people very important to me were following Henry last night. Where are they?"

"The FBI has them."

"Where?"

"I don't know."

Walken looked at him for a long while. Then, "I believe you. What did they say, the man and woman?"

"Nothing, as far as I know." For all he knew, this was true. He had no idea what the FBI had done with them.

"You're going to tell me everything that happened, John. But first things first." Walken looked pleased. He sat back and appeared to be enjoying himself. "You realize if we are pulled over and things don't go the way I like, the girl is dead?" Walken lightly snapped his fingers.

John looked out the window. He didn't need to answer that.

SIXTY-FOUR

Santiváñez wrapped the white bath towel around her torso and tucked in an end. She took another and vigorously dried her short brown hair, then stepped to the sink and ran Stiles' brush through it a few times. She squeezed some gel into her palm, rubbed her hands together and ran her fingers through to the back. She was still thinking about the hang-up call. Who had that been?

Stiles stepped forward, pulled open a drawer, and took out a new toothbrush and paste for her. He leaned forward and said, "Do mine." She ran her fingers through the half inch of hair on the top of his head and then over his sides. He grabbed his toothbrush and some paste and walked to his closet.

She brushed her teeth quickly and then walked to the bed stand and picked up her Droid. The clock flipped over to AM 7:00. Manhattan temperature was 72 degrees. It would be sunny and 90 today. The icons for Messages, Mail, and Voicemail all showed nothing new.

Stiles stepped barefoot out of his closet wearing black slacks, and a blue knit shirt. He placed a box and two bags from a Park Avenue women's boutique on the bed. "I, ah, got you some things," he said.

She reached over and took the top off the box. Inside was a classic 3-button black pant suit and an ivory sleeveless top. She dumped the contents of the other two bags. There were black nylon socks, panties, and a bra in the first, and shoes in the other. "When did you get this?"

He just smiled.

She picked out the pants and arranged the top and blazer on top. "You have very nice taste."

When she was dressed, she picked up her phone off the night stand. "I need to find out who that call was from."

"Step out into the garden," he said. "What can I do?"

"Breakfast? I'm starved."

"Sun's up."

She stopped and surveyed his "living room." She'd seen it last night, but only in a quick flash. The minute he'd opened the door, they fell into a hot romantic kiss that lasted to his bed.

The living room was the size of two of her apartments. It was actually two living rooms. Closest to her was a sunken area for watching television with the largest wraparound couch she'd ever seen. Further on and raised three feet was an area with a pool table, more seating, video games. Through the tall windows, she was staring straight at the Empire State Building a half mile off.

Stiles was flat rich. That much was clear. She stepped into the kitchen and her jaw dropped. She spent a lot of time on the stationary bike reading home improvement magazines. She was sure this kitchen was featured in last month's Kitchen and Bath. It had the cool green subway tile backsplash, the center island topped with veined marble slab, varied cabinetry, pendant lighting, domed ceiling, Viking appliances. Dark green foliage filtered light through the two windows at the far end.

She stopped at a grouping of photos hanging by the door that she could see led to the garden. One of the photos was Stiles and his... mother? She was black and about five feet tall. There was one of him and his boy in football pads. He was a spitting image of Stiles. Stood about an inch higher than Stiles, and the doctors said he still had a few inches to grow. This was his father's pride. A real good-looking kid. Probably would be the next NFL star. Would have the height of a Manning, had better looks than Brady, and according to Stiles, he ran like Vince Young and Tim Tebow combined.

There was no man in any of the other pictures. Just Stiles and his boy, Stiles and the woman, and the three of them together. Maybe that was his mom. It was a funny thought, but Stiles was as white as they came. Was he adopted? She opened the door and stepped outside.

The "garden," as he'd called it, looked west over Madison Square Park. She could see the Hudson and beyond, and everything between. The roof of the Midtown South precinct where they'd flipped Henry just hours ago was a mile away to the northwest.

Island-style fans hanging from the covering spun lazily. Two rows of misters hissed cool water vapor. The ten-foot deep roof ran south about two hundred feet until it stopped at a red brick wall which she couldn't see beyond. Urns with flowers and plants decorated the span. Sconces with plants and water features hung from the wall. At the base of the red brick wall, it looked as if he were growing vegetables in a raised bed.

Uncovered veranda stretched about eight feet beyond the covering and ran parallel all the way to the brick wall. At the rail, he had several tomato plants, and various herbs growing in all sorts of different pots and planters. Flowers and small trees grew in pots running to the north. Flowering Jasmine vines grew out of a huge planter and up into a trellis that wrapped around the corner. They were part of the foliage she'd seen through the kitchen window. She could smell the Jasmine's exotic freshness.

She looked over the rail. Below was more veranda, but it was cut up into smaller sections. The low rent floor. "Not bad. Not bad at all," she said.

She sat at a square iron table and called the surveillance guys. The hang-up call was probably Henry Douglas. Maybe he'd been interrupted and had to abort. It would be good if he were reaching out. He needed to make it happen with Malley. If they had to go with only Henry's confession, it was going to be ugly. And she detested ugly cases.

"This is Charlie," the other end answered.

"What's happening with our guy?" she said.

"All quiet. Not a thing to report."

"I had a hang-up call this morning. Blocked caller ID."

"Well we can trace that. All blocked caller ID does is send a privacy flag. The number will be in our switch or with the carriers."

"Call me back."

"Sure thing," Charlie said.

She stepped to a huge basil plant that grew next to a tomato vine. She could see the little marker in the pot indicating the tomato was an Early

Girl variety. They were ready to eat and she nearly picked one and ate it like an apple, so starved was she.

The basil plant was garden variety Sweet. It was nearly four feet tall and just as wide. It was beginning to flower all over with buds that ranged in size from the tip of her pinky to half her forefinger. Its leaves were two inches across and thick. She took a bunch at the end of a stem and buried her nose and face into it. It was an inspiration of sweetness.

"You like that?" Stiles said, rounding the corner.

"What do you feed this stuff?"

"Steer manure and Miracle Grow. Water twice a day. Good drainage." He grabbed a tomato off the vine and took some of the purple basil from a smaller plant lower to the ground. "I'll put this on your bagel."

She bent down to an oregano plant, pinched a stem at the base, and ran her fingers up, stripping the pungent leaves away. She dumped them in Stiles' palm and smiled. "This too, please."

He turned for the door and said, "Breakfast is on the way. What did you find out?"

"Charlie says he can get the number from the call earlier. I'm calling Kane."

"Good," Stiles said before disappearing into the kitchen.

Kane's phone went to voicemail. He was probably still sleeping. Probably next to Jackie Fairbanks. It occurred to her how they were two very similar couples now. She and Stiles were a couple? Well, she wasn't going to fight it. It was very nice so far. They'd probably ask Kane and Fairbanks out to dinner when this thing was over. Say sorry for keeping him in the dark. Kane was right. Things would not have gotten to where they were if they'd have brought him in at the start.

Her phone rang. It was Charlie. She hit the green answer bar and said, "Go ahead, Charlie."

"Call came from a Rodney Fairbanks. Originated from a Verizon tower in Times Square. Call lasted twenty-five seconds and then was disconnected from the originating end."

"Rodney Fairbanks?" she said.

"It's him. Her brother. The one at the controls of the Greenpeace satellite. What do you want us to do?"

"Not sure yet. Hold your position."

"Yes, ma'am," Charlie said.

She disconnected the line and dialed Kane again. How did Rodney Fairbanks get her number? Did Jackie have his phone? Had Kane used it to call her? His line went right to voicemail again. She left a quick message and hung up. Stiles wheeled a cart up to the table. First he opened his laptop, already signed into NCIC, and placed it on the far side of the table. Then he put down a place mat and silverware, and a soft white cotton napkin on her lap. In the center of the plate he set before her was a toasted and buttered bagel top cut in half and stacked, and then cut again in center. He'd turned the pieces so that the round edges touched each other. Arranged around the top of the plate were sliced tomatoes, a scrambled egg, two pieces of smoked salmon, and fresh berries in a mint leaf bowl he'd constructed with white chocolate as the base. He'd whipped this breakfast up in a matter of three minutes, but the mint leaf bowl he'd had in the fridge. She looked over at the mint plant growing in a five gallon white ceramic pot and thought, the guy can cook. Green thumb. The list of his perfection ran through her mind and she flushed. Is this what love felt like? Or was it just lust? She'd felt this feeling before, sort of. It hadn't ended well the first time. But that was almost two decades ago when she was a teen.

He'd minced the oregano she gave him and mixed it with the cream cheese. She could see minced capers and onion in there, too. He placed a ramekin of the stuff over the fork and then inserted the purple basil in the side. She laughed because it looked like something straight out of the movie Avatar.

Stiles simply smiled. He finished off by placing juice, water, and a cup of black coffee over the knife and spoon.

"Thank you," she said.

"My pleasure."

"It's the nicest breakfast I've ever seen."

"Welcome."

"Am I eating alone?"

"I have to call my mother. She's on medication. I call her every morning to see how she's feeling."

"Is that her? In the picture? With you and Marty?"

"That's Mom," he said and smiled big. "Parents died when I was a baby. She was my nanny. Been mom ever since. Now eat. And figure out what we're doing." He turned to walk back into the kitchen and she dialed Kane again.

SIXTY-FIVE

Midtown South Police Station. John walked uneasily down the hallway on the second floor of the old building. Every twelve or fifteen feet there were stained wood doors with frosted glass in the upper panels – each etched with names of detectives and administrative personnel. He passed a few cops, and then a lone plainclothes detective who wore an old blue blazer. The guy looked up from his file as he passed and gave him a nod. Walken had told him before he got out of the limo that he had a man inside the station, so if he wanted to "try any funny business," he had better think twice. That could have been the guy.

He came to the door marked EVIDENCE. It was a door just like all the others. Inside there was a waiting room and a clerk behind protective glass. There were four cameras that he could see. Whatever he did would be recorded, but nobody was watching right now.

He was all alone. Rodney was dead. Santiváñez and Stiles were still sleeping. Fitzgerald was sleeping. Nobody was coming to save him, and he was the only one who could save Jackie. He surely couldn't just walk out of the precinct and give Walken the bonds. Both he and Jackie were dead if he did that.

He put his badge in the pass-through. "I'm Marshal John Kane."

The clerk's badge said Youhanahie. He took John's credential and said, "How can I help you?"

"I checked in an envelope last night."

"Yeah, what's up?"

"Bearer bonds. Chief Clerk at One PP wants to verify the amount." It was standard procedure to deposit all cash taken as evidence into a safe, interest-bearing account. There was no way to deposit five million dollars in bearer bonds without cashing them, but it seemed reasonable that they'd want to take a look at that much paper.

Youhanahie slipped a form through the window and John signed it. Youhanahie left and quickly returned with the sealed envelope. "Don't lose it," Youhanahie said after he'd slid it through the opening.

John gave him a serious look. "Not on my life."

SIXTY-SIX

He was approaching the second-floor security gate. The same guy in the blue blazer was walking toward him, head still buried in a file. John put the envelope under his belt behind his back. When the guy got closer, John stopped. The guy looked up, stopped, and said, "How are ya?" His speech was slightly nasal and he pronounced his r. Probably grew up in Flushing. This was good. He could do Flushing if he had to. He was going to have about one opportunity to pull this off, and this guy was it.

"You know Condor Walken?" John said.

"Ah," the guy said. "Should I?"

"Look, I need your help if this thing is going to happen," John said.

The guy looked down at his shoes, then around and over his shoulder. "Whaddya need me to do?"

"Come here," John said. He put his arm around the smaller man's shoulder and directed him through one of the stained wood doors. The glass was blank. It was a meeting room.

Inside the room, John said, "What's your name?"

"Saul Morris," he said "How can I help you?"

John wanted to keep him talking as long as he could to figure out his speech pattern and accent. "How long have you been with Walken?"

"What is this," Saul said. "You need me to do something or not?"

"I need you to get the bonds. Where are they?"

"They're in evidence. Where else?"

"Who's working in evidence right now?"

"How am I supposed to know. You breakin' my heels here or what?"

He'd heard enough. He was whiny and nasaly. He drew out his consonants, but spoke clearly otherwise. He could make this work.

John looked into Saul's eyes and said, "I hope this doesn't break your jaw." Then he threw an uppercut that lifted Saul four inches off the ground. His legs buckled and John slipped in behind him to keep him from crumpling to the floor. He put in a choke hold just in case, but Saul was out. John checked his pulse and his jaw. Pulse was stable and his jaw seemed intact. He just wouldn't be able to talk for a few days. That wouldn't be convenient for the interrogations he was going to face when this was all over.

John took Saul's phone, wallet, and gun, and he left the room. He walked swiftly to the east alley stairs and took them slowly. For his plan to work, he was going to have to move fast, and he was going to have to get lucky. If he could get back to his room at the Hilton, where Rodney undoubtedly still was, maybe Rodney's Droid would still be there. That would tell him where Jackie was, and then he could try to race to her and fight through whatever, or whoever Condor had guarding her. If not, he still had the bonds as a bargaining tool.

He pulled out Saul's phone and went through the call history. Last number dialed was always very telling. He scrolled onto it and hit the talk button. The other end picked up in one ring but didn't say anything. He'd told Henry to put on an Oscar-winning performance. It was his turn to do the acting. Running up the stairs and putting his hand over the mouthpiece to create confusion, he did his best Saul. "He got the bonds, but he ran into the chief. Chief walked him up to the third floor. I think it's good, but I, I, I don't know. Whaddya want me to do?"

"I'll call you back," the voice said.

John took the stairs two at a time and stepped swiftly out into the alley. He ran to the corner of the precinct and looked west down 35th. There were too many cars and a delivery truck in the way, but he knew Walken's limo was still parked down the street. An unmarked Crown Vic pulled up and parked. John walked up to the driver who was closing the door and he said, "Federal fire marshal. I need to commandeer this car."

The guy looked at him confusedly and said, "What?"

John didn't have time to argue. He moved the guy out of the way, took the keys from his hands and said, "Call it in. Marshal John Kane. BFI."

He backed the car out and sped away eastbound across 35th. The Hilton Times Square was just two blocks over and six blocks up.

Just then, a white cargo van slammed into the back of him. Out of his periphery he saw another van speeding towards him on Dyer Avenue. He pulled the wheel hard to the right to avoid the jackknife but the van heading south on Dyer still hit him on the front quarter panel. The van behind him kept pushing and his Crown Vic spun around and wrapped itself around the traffic light pole in the center median.

Before he knew it, two guys half again as big as he were dragging him out of the Crown Vic. They threw him into the side of one of the vans and it sped away.

In the back of the van was the Russian from the hotel, Terenty, and what might very well be his brother. "Grab the fucking bar, asshole!" the other one yelled. John grabbed the overhead bar and held on as the van swerved in and out of traffic. Terenty took the envelope containing the bonds. Looked it over. He smiled, and then his eyes grew a little larger, like a wide receiver's eyes when he's about to catch a flying pass. John knew the Russian in back was about to strike a blow to the back of his head. He moved at the last instant and the handle of the man's gun came down on his trapezoid muscle instead of the back of his head. It didn't feel good, but it was better than a blow to the head. Reaching across with his right hand, he grabbed the Russian's wrist. Twisted the gun free. Ducked under him, and slid behind, using him as a shield. The driver slammed on the brakes. John had anticipated this. He kept his center of gravity low, threw the Russian he held into the metal grating, and hurtling forward, he delivered a crushing elbow into Terenty's eye.

The driver, seeing what happened, hit the gas again. John felt the sudden surge, quickly fell to his knees, and grabbed the bonds from Terenty. Terenty was still in la la land from the elbow he'd taken. John took his cell phone from his belt. Shoved it deep in his pocket.

Holding the bonds like a football, John threw the side door open, picked up the other Russian's pistol, and jumped. Rolling on the road a few times, he regained his balance and sprang to his feet. A motorcyclist came to a screeching halt right in front of him. In one fluid motion, John shoved the bonds under his belt and pulled the motorcyclists' left hand off the bar. This popped the clutch and killed the bike. Then he reached down under the man's leg with his right hand, and still gripping the Russian's gun, he flung the rider from the machine.

The van driver was just opening his door and one of the Russians was firing wildly out of the open cargo door. The gun he'd picked up from the floor of the van was a Glock 21, .45 caliber with extended clip. Straddling the bike, John placed two shots above both their heads, punching inch-and-a-half-wide holes in the van's steel and driving them back.

Pulling the clutch, he hit the start button with his right thumb and jammed the shifter down into first gear. Four more shots into the van, then he trapped the gun under his chin, bore down on the bike, pumped the throttle, dropped the clutch, spun the bike around and rocketed away. Safely in control after a couple seconds, he took the Glock with his left hand, turned his body and extended to his target. With four steady pulls of the dual action trigger, he drove the Russian and the driver back once again.

He'd used 12 rounds. If the Russian had a full clip and one in the chamber, that would leave him with only two more rounds.

In less than a minute, he was at the 41st Street entrance to the Hilton. He jumped the bike up on the curb, skidded to a halt, hit the kill button, and handed the dead machine to the doorman. "Park it," John said. He ran to the elevators.

***

In the room, he found Rodney lying dead by the side of the bed. His Android was still in his hand. He took it from his clutched fingers, removed his ear bud and closed his eyelids. "I'm sorry, Rodney."

He unlocked the Android. The clock said 7:30 AM. He hit the button for apps and scanned the screen. Adobe Reader, Amazon MP3, Angry Birds. He flew through a couple of screens and came to an app titled Rodney's Little Tracker. He pressed his thumb on it and waited for it to load. And there it was. A little blinking light on a white screen with a map imprint. The blinking light moved, indicating a new position. They were in Parsippany. John traced the route. They'd left the Island and taken the 280 west. He had a lot of lost ground to make up. He put the Android in his coat pocket and left the room.

His Explorer was still parked on the 41st Street curb and his keys were in his pocket. He thought briefly about calling Santivánez. She would surely have to get Tolliver involved, and he trusted Tolliver to do the right thing about as much as he trusted a four-year-old to make pancakes. He'd get up to Parsippany and survey the situation. If he needed backup then, he'd call it in.

SIXTY-SEVEN

"Chief Fire Marshal Fitzgerald," she heard through her earpiece.

"Chief Fitzgerald," Santiváñez said. "Maria Santiváñez. Trying to reach Marshal Kane. Have you heard from him this morning?"

"No I have not, Agent Santiváñez. What's up?"

"I'm not sure, Chief, but I received a hang-up call from Rodney Fairbanks this morning. Jackie Fairbanks' brother. Call was blocked caller ID and originated from a tower in Times Square."

"Hold on," Fitzgerald said. He came back a few seconds later and said, "Calls go right to John's voicemail. He stayed at the Hilton in the Square last night with Jackie Fairbanks. They could be at the top with bad reception. Try reaching her."

"Do you have a number?"

"One of us will have to call the network," he said.

"I'll call you right back," she said and hung up the phone. She hit her Internet icon, typed in the network in the Google bar and touched the phone number when it appeared on the screen with the other information.

"This is agent Maria Santiváñez, Federal Bureau of Investigation," she said when the receptionist answered the phone. "It is imperative that I speak to one of your reporters right away. Jackie Fairbanks."

After a half minute she heard, "This is Kent Rogers. I am the news manager over Ms. Fairbanks. How can I help you?"

"I'm looking for Ms. Fairbanks, Mr. Rogers. Can you please connect me to her?"

"What's this in regards to?" Kent said.

"I'm sorry, Mr. Rogers," she said. "This is agent Maria Santivánez from the Federal Bureau of Investigation. I need you to connect me to Ms. Fairbanks directly. Thank you."

"And I asked you what this is in regards to, Agent Santivánez."

"Mr. Rogers, can you connect me with Ms. Fairbanks or not?"

There was a long pause. "I can't reach her. Calls began going directly to her voicemail at about 2AM this morning. I think she took her battery out. I assume you know she's working with the Bureau of Fire Investigation investigating something to do with Michael Malley and a company named Immunex. Now I have half a story I'm sitting on here. We're going to run something by five PM, and it would behoove you to let me in on some details. Because she sure as hell is not."

"Mr. Rogers, it would do you well not to speak to me in that fashion. You will also serve yourself and your network well if you do not report anything for the time being."

"Report on what?"

"Mr. Rogers, Kent, I've given you my advice. I suggest you take it. I'm hanging up now." She hung up the line. It was 7:20.

Fitzgerald was calling again. "Hi, Chief," she said.

"You get Fairbanks?"

"No. Her news manager said her calls started going to voicemail at 2AM."

"Well, that makes sense. The guy kept calling her all night and she was keeping quiet like you told her. Her phone probably went dead. I know she was running low because she showed me the screen the last time he called. Real asshole, this guy. Excuse my French."

"I spoke with Mr. Rogers," Santivánez said. "What about John's phone?"

"I don't know," Fitzgerald said. "He's not answering his Nextel or broadband. His personal goes right to voicemail. Can you send a unit over there?"

"Yes, hold the line." She hit the mute button on her screen and called out, "Stiles?"

He poked his head out the door.

"Can you bring me another phone?"

He disappeared for a second and returned with a wireless land line phone. His mobile was up to his ear. "Hold on, Mom," he said. He took his phone away and guarded the earpiece. "Do you need me?"

"Pretty quick," she said.

He put his mobile back to his ear and said, "Mom, glad you're feeling well. Gotta go. Love you." He hung up the phone and said, "What do you need?"

"Send a team over to the Hilton Times Square. Kane is staying there. Get them up to his room. Better yet, send three units, one goes up, and I want one at each entrance on 41st and 42nd."

Stiles held down his speed dial for FBI dispatch.

Santiváñez hit the mute button and said, "We're dispatching three units to the Hilton now, Chief Fitzgerald."

SIXTY-EIGHT

The ride from Summit to the Newark airport had been all business. Malley carried on with him as if nothing had happened, and Henry didn't push him. They were due in Washington for tomorrow's debate on the President's budget request for the FDA.

He'd left the Mont Blanc back at the estate inside one of his loafers. He'd tell the FBI something. By then Walken would be dead, and he'd confide in the senator, who would have no choice but to protect him. Now and forever.

It was 7:35 AM. The Bentley pulled to a stop behind the CJ 525. The smallest of the Cessna business-class jet family, it served Malley's needs for short hops to and from Washington. It was the least ostentatious plane he could fly and still provide the speed and comfort he required. He liked to keep a low profile. Appear the frugal old man. It was key to his image, part of what he thought would make him so attractive a candidate.

Comfortably seated aboard the jet now, Malley opened his brief case and said, "Let's have a mimosa."

Henry poured a split of champagne in two flutes and topped them with juice.

Malley scanned through pages of text and sipped his drink. The feds had said they owned him until they got Malley. But they didn't own him. He wasn't on their side. They weren't going to get Michael Malley. And they weren't going to get Condor Walken, because Black's men were going to kill him. They probably already had. So the scourge would be gone. Things would change with Walken gone.

The pilot closed the flight stairs and asked the men to buckle up. It would be a short taxi to the runway and they were cleared for immediate takeoff.

Sixty-nine

It was 7:50. John raced westbound out Highway 124. Rodney's Android showed the beacon was stopped in a commercial area of Parsippany. He could be there in ten minutes if he kept up the triple-digit speeds he was driving.

The Russian's phone he had in his pocket rang. Walken should be calling right about now. If he answered it, they might be able to track where he was and then his element of surprise would be shot. John noted the number, pushed battery release button on the back of the phone, and let the battery drop to the seat. Then he reached over to the glove compartment and took out his Nextel. It was on and still had one bar of battery life. Fitzgerald had called him four times. He wasn't sure if he should call him or not. If he told him what he was doing, he'd demand he pull back and wait for backup. That was just how he was, and that wasn't going to work. Well, he'd be the first person he called when he saw what he was up against in Parsippany.

Getting off the ramp at Parsipanny, he plugged a hands-free set into Rodney's Droid and dialed the last incoming number from the Russian's phone.

"Hello, John," Walken said.

John looked at the map on the Android's screen. The blinking dot indicating Jackie's position hadn't moved in twenty minutes. "How do you want to do this?"

"Do what, John?"

"You have something I want, I have something you want."

"John, do you take me for a fool?"

He'd thought about this on the drive out. His plan made sense in his mind, but not for Walken. So he said quickly, "Look, I had to get away. You think I was going to let you take me? I'd be a dead man, and so would Jackie. I couldn't do that anymore than I could go back to my own people."

"Where are you, John?" Walken said.

"I'm in the city. In a cab."

"Very smart." There was a long pause. "Okay," Walken said. "We're both in safe places then. What do you have in mind?"

"One of your guys and Jackie. Me and the bonds. Open field. One gun each. Even exchange."

"You'll go to prison."

"There's more."

"Go ahead."

"I need ten million dollars in cash. I'll be on the run the rest of my life." He'd bumped the amount from five to ten million at the last second. Somehow it just sounded better. He looked at the Android. Almost there. She was just around the next block.

SEVENTY

Her Android rang. "Agent Santiváñez."

"We got a dead guy in Kane's room. This is Brian Barlow, Maria."

She knew Barlow well. "ID?" she said.

"Fairbanks, Rodney," Barlow said.

"Cause of death?"

"Bullet through the left orbital."

Her call waiting rang. She looked at the screen. It was Fitzgerald. "Hold on, Brian. Chief, Rodney Fairbanks is deceased in Marshal Kane's hotel room. Shot in the eye."

"I just got a call from Midtown South. John commandeered an unmarked there about thirty minutes ago. Now it's wrapped around a light pole on Dyer and 35th. Witnesses say two men drug another man out of the unmarked and it sped away."

She stood from the table and closed the lid on Stiles' laptop. He took it from her hands and walked in front of her. "We're on our way to Midtown South now, Chief."

"There's more," he said.

"Go ahead."

"John checked the five mil of bearer bonds out of evidence. Told the clerk he was taking them to One PP for verification."

"Can you meet us at the station, Chief?"

"Already on my way."

SEVENTY-ONE

John looked from the Android's screen to a white cargo van parked at the curb in front of a Parsippany barber shop. The blinking dot indicated she was inside the van. Walken was still on the line.

"It will take me a while to get that much cash together," Walken said.

John pulled to a stop behind the van and got out of his Explorer. "There's bound to be five thousand cops looking for me now. Make it quick." He hurried around the front of the van while still talking to Walken. He put the Glock 21's barrel in the passenger's ear. She looked unsurprised. He looked over at the driver. She took her phone away from her ear and nodded to the back.

"John, are you there?" Walken said.

"Yeah, I'm here," John said. He kept the Glock pointed into the passenger's ear. With his free hand, he motioned for the two women to be quiet.

"John," Walken said, "open the door. It's okay. There's nobody back there."

A cold chill ran down the back of his neck. He reached out and opened the door. The van was empty. It started, pulled away from the curb, and drove off at a normal speed. John was left standing there on the curb.

"You lied to me, John. We found the transmitter. Great stuff. I'm very impressed. Not bad on the Jewish Queens accent either. You had us going until we saw you come out of the alley. I have people all over the place, John."

"Bring her out here. This is a good place for an exchange. You get the bonds. I get Jackie."

"John, how do I know you're not working with the FBI?"

"You see any FBI around here?"

"I can't see you anymore, John."

"You saw me leave the precinct. I left alone. I just want Jackie. I'll give you the bonds."

"Oh, this is interesting," Walken said.

There was a ten second silence.

"Okay. I'll bite. What's interesting?" John finally said.

"The FBI just showed up here."

"You see, I'm not working with them."

"Yes, I can see that. My, my. That must be agent Santiváñez. Very pretty lady. Not quite in the same league as your Jackie Fairbanks. But very lovely. Okay, you'll get the girl back. Be in front of Port Authority. It'll take you the better part of an hour if you don't drive like a maniac. You must have hit speeds in the hundreds driving out there. You gotta slow down. You're going to kill someone, John. Or get pulled over. Don't get pulled over."

"What's the deal? How are we going to do this?"

"Some of my people will be there."

"The two women I just saw in the van?"

"No. They're off for the day. I'll send men to do this job. They'll tell you where to go."

"I'm not getting any blindfolds put on me. And I'm not getting into any cars."

"Relax, John. You'll receive directions."

The line went dead. If ever there were a time he were stuck, it was now. One thing was sure, Walken wouldn't be giving the orders. Let him think he was, yes, but let him lead? That was a death sentence.

There was a saying in his line of work about the point in a case when you went from desperation to inspiration. It was a horrible feeling, desperation, and he refused to feel it. He flashed back over the past thirty-six hours and quickly saw his plot unfold. "Get ready, you son of a bitch," he said out loud. Then he got back in the car, flipped a hard u-turn and dialed Michael Terry.

"Hello," Terry answered. He sounded winded, was probably pumping iron.

"Michael, it's me, John."

"What's the word, Marshal Kane? How can I help you?" That's how Terry was. Always ready to jump in.

"You on duty?"

"Just got off."

"Are you ready to be a marshal?"

"You know it, John. What do you need?"

"Take the Red Line to the South Ferry stop. Meet me up on the street."

"I'm leaving now."

"Keep this under your hat, Michael."

"Sure thing, John. That will take me about twenty minutes. Do you need me to bring anything?"

John thought for a second. He wasn't sure why, but he said, "Your keys."

"See you in twenty," Terry said.

John hung up the phone and took the onramp to head back to the city.

SEVENTY-TWO

It took him twenty-five minutes to get to the south end of Manhattan. Michael Terry was waiting by the South Ferry MTA entrance.

Terry got in the car and waited for John to speak.

"What I'm about to ask you to do could be very dangerous, Michael. These people have already killed two people that I know of. You're putting your life at risk. Are you sure you want to help me?"

"This have to do with the building on 43rd & 8th ?" Terry said.

"It has everything to do with that."

"Jimmy Park was our brother. Now tell me what to do."

"Slide your seat back," John said. They both slid their seats back and John started taking his clothes off. "Switch with me."

When they had swapped pants and shirt, John pulled the string on the envelope and showed Terry the bonds. "This is five million dollars in U.S. bearer bonds. It's been in my possession since I checked it out of Midtown South Evidence about an hour ago."

Terry regarded the envelope, checked the signature and the record of contents. "What do I do?"

"Take the Red Line back to 42nd. Stand outside of the Port Authority. Somebody is going to meet you there. I don't know who, or how many. You flash the bonds to show them you're me. Do not get in any cars. Tell them you want to see Jackie, and then you take off on foot. Tell them to eat your shorts. Whatever. Do not let them take you."

"I understand."

John looked at him as seriously as he could. "You're dead if you do, Michael."

"I can do it. Who's Jackie?"

"Jackie Fairbanks. The reporter. They have her."

"What's our timeframe?"

"You have to go now."

Terry looked in John's back seat and grabbed a BFI cap. He pulled it low over his face. "How's that?"

"I think you'll pass. I'm not certain that whoever is going to meet you has ever seen me. Like I said, the bonds are your calling card. Do not let them out of your possession for any reason."

"I can do it. Am I authorized to handle the evidence? What happens to continuity?"

Terry was a peace officer, not a police officer. There was a big difference. At a fire scene, he could guard evidence for the marshals and maintain continuity of evidence, but that was at a fire scene. He'd been studying for the marshal's exam, but hadn't taken the test. "We're a little gray," John said. "I don't have time to ask anyone about the legal particulars. So I'm going to deputize you under my powers as a federal agent."

Terry sat taller in his seat. John trusted him almost as he trusted himself. In their business, you had to trust the guy next to you, and if there were anyone he wanted next to him fighting, it was Terry.

"Under the original *Posse Comitatus Act of 1878*, I am deputizing you as a deputy federal marshal." *Posse Comitatus* said a sheriff or a marshal had the power to deputize all the male members of a county over fifteen to assist in preventing a riot, the rescue of prisoners, or other unlawful disorders. "You're deputized."

"Don't I need to take an oath?"

"There's nothing that says so. You're official. You're due there at 9AM. Answer your phone if you get a call from me or a number you don't recognize. Otherwise don't answer. Give me your Blackberry."

Terry handed it over and John programmed a number into the Contacts database. "I want you to give me text updates if you can. One-worders. Don't let them see you do it."

Terry handed John his keys. On the ring were special keys that would open any New York building that was outfitted with Emergency Fire Access. He opened his door and stood on the street. "I can do this," he said.

"Michael," John said. "This is life or death for you, and Jackie Fairbanks."

"You can count on me, John. Nobody's going to take me. I'll show them the goods, demand to see Jackie, and set off on foot. I know just the route to take to be safe. I'll be waiting for a call and only pick up if it's you or a number I don't recognize."

"Close the door," John said.

Terry shut the door, walked briskly to the subway entrance, and disappeared down the stairs.

John rounded the tip of the island and drove up South Street towards the piers. At the Ferry Pier, he saw what he was looking for, all two hundred feet of her, tied up at the South Street Seaport Museum maintenance dock.

There was an inlet under the up ramp to the FDR. He parked behind the orange and white-striped traffic barrels and went around to the back of the Explorer. He had a backup gun in the rear in the side compartment. A .38 Snub-Nose with belt holster. He shoved it in his pants and wove his belt through the clip. Next he grabbed the Russian's phone and went into the menu. It was a standard Blackberry like Terry's, like the one he'd used in the field for years. In the Forward Calls menu he input the number to an HTC Droid he had sitting at home on his bench, the same phone he'd programmed into Terry's Blackberry. Where he was going, he knew a phone wouldn't survive, and he had to keep the line of communication open with Walken.

It was 8:35 and the heat was coming on. Tourists and locals walked lazily up and down the East River. Behind him, helicopter tours took off from Pier 11 every so often. The river was choppy. Fat luxury cruisers with their sterns sunk low in the water pushed along in both directions. A yellow and black Manhattan Water Taxi was tacking in swiftly for a landing. The 1885 schooner *Pioneer* pushed through the water under full sail.

There didn't appear to be anyone above decks on the two-hundred-foot boat. He'd have a hard time walking up to her on the dock. The South Street Seaport Museum rented out space to vessels like her on a temporary basis, but the entrance to the dock was caged and most likely locked. There didn't appear to be any maintenance guys working out there, but he'd call attention to himself if he tried to scale the fence. There was only going to be one good way to get over to her.

He approached the metal grating at the edge of what was planned to be Pier 13. Unfinished for many years now, the entrance to the cement tab was blocked with a makeshift fence. The thin steel striping connecting the chain link to a post had been pulled away so there was a triangular opening at the bottom big enough to crawl through. There was graffiti on the Keep Out sign.

The crowd was thin. The guy at the pretzel cart under the FDR ramp looked over at him a couple of times, but he was more concerned with setting up his cart than checking out someone standing by a restricted area on an unused dock.

He slipped under the fence, and without hesitation, he ran for the edge of the cement and dove into the East River. He closed his eyes and swam under the surface like a dolphin towards his quarry.

He rose four times for air to cover the two hundred yards to the ship and then silently broke the surface under the pier. Treading water, he caught his breath for a minute and then swam around to the stern. The platform extending from her transom sat low enough in the water that he was able to kick hard and get a hand up on its course decking. He pulled himself up, threw a knee onto the deck, and climbed aboard. He was in plain view of anyone who wanted to see, so he sat up and looked around, acting as if there was nothing abnormal about a man emerging from the East River and boarding a two-hundred-foot boat tied up on a protected dock.

Certain no one was watching, he made his way to the covered cargo area. He knelt by a coil of rope, pulled the .38 out of the holster, released the wheel, spun it around, and then pushed it home. He cocked the gun, picked up the coil of rope with his left hand, and continued on into the belly of the ship.

He smelled smoke. Heard voices. They sounded angry. It was English, mixed with a few Russian words he took for expletives. Was he going to get lucky and find the guys who had jumped him in the van? They were probably nursing their egos after the beating he'd given them.

As he approached the voices, the stench of their cigarette smoke grew stronger. "He is going to fucking kill us. We cannot follow him out of the country. We have to go back to Russia."

"We have no money, Terenty!"

"We could catch that fucking fire marshal and get those bonds."

"The fire marshal will be back. He wants that little piece of ass."

"And Condor wants him and the bonds. He will lure him into the city."

One of them said something in Russian. The other said, "Da." And repeated what the first man had said.

John repeated the words to himself a few times. They sounded a little different each time. He didn't do Russian.

Stepping into the galley, he said, "You'll never get those bonds. But you're right, I am back."

The Russians' eyes fell dead upon him. Disbelief grew to hatred. Hatred grew to seething anger because each knew they'd been had. Two Glocks sat on the table along with a radio, a bottle of Crown Royal and half-smoked packs of Winstons. These guys liked fine guns, good whiskey, and well, John never could understand why people smoked.

John pointed the .38 back and forth at them and said, "Terenty, your eye looks... not good." It was swollen shut and black all over.

Terenty spit at him and some of it landed on his arm. John scooped it off of his skin with the tip of the .38. "I'll make sure to return it to you, Terenty."

Terenty said something to the other guy in Russian and they both smiled.

"You two aren't going to go easy, are you?"

"We're not going anywhere," the other Russian said.

His hatred grew to defiance, and his Russian bravado was almost convincing. "What's your name?" John said, resting his sights on the Russian's forehead.

"Fucking pig," Terenty said. He grabbed for his gun and nearly had it raised when John dropped his sights and shot Terenty's Glock out of his hand.

The Glock dropped on the table and spun around. Terenty grabbed his right hand with his left and yelled Russian obscenities. John had hit the butt of Terenty's gun intentionally. The Winchester .38 Special 158-grain round traveled at almost 900 feet per second and had plenty of mass. The impact sent a shock wave through Terenty's entire body. He'd be sore for days, and he'd be too stunned to do much of anything for many seconds.

The other Russian dove for the table. By the time the Russian had hold of one of the Glocks on the table, John had closed the distance and jumped up in the air. He came down with a crushing kick to the top of the Russian's head, while simultaneously landing on his right wrist. While his head bobbled, the Russian managed to squeeze the trigger. The round bounced around the galley several times. John delivered another kick to the Russian's head, and he fell limp to the ground.

John bent down, put Terenty's Glock in his pants, and picked up the other.

Terenty took a few steps forward, still holding his hand, but stopped. John looked him solidly in the eyes and said, "I have two guns. One for each of ya." He was quoting Doc Holiday from the movie Tombstone, the movie Terenty had incorrectly referenced earlier.

Terenty scowled at John. The other Russian was beginning to recover. He tried to crawl to Terenty.

"I don't have a lot of time," John said. "This is how we're going to do it."

Terenty was a Russian thug to his core. Standing there out-gunned and out-manned meant nothing to him. He charged John with a crazed look, ready to fight to the death. Terenty was strong and fast and his endorphins pumped. But he was no match for John who was faster and stronger, and also ready to fight to the death. John ducked under Terenty and delivered the butt of the .38 to his nose, crushing it over and pasting it to the front of his square face.

The other Russian, dazed as he was, tried to lunge in with a haymaker. John caught the punch, twisted the wrist, and threw him into Terenty. John followed the Russian and, straddling the two of them, he choked the top Russian into unconsciousness. He was alive, but he'd be out for several minutes.

Grabbing hold of Terenty by his broken nose, John stood him up. Terenty wailed like a raging beast and swung at John's ribs. John parried the swings, lifted his knee, and sidekicked him in the gut. Terenty fell gasping for air on the deck and John finished him off with a crushing blow to his temple.

SEVENTY-THREE

Terenty kicked and pulled at the binds that held his feet and hands behind his back. John and his older brother used to practice hog tying each other when they were kids. If you couldn't free yourself after an hour, the other guy got a point. When he was ten, their mother put an abrupt end to the game because his brother forgot him and went out to play for five hours. He hadn't hog tied a person since that summer, but some things you never forgot.

He pulled on the rope that ran through the galley's ceiling supports, hoisted Terenty up off the deck, and tied the rope off so Terenty hung upside down like a bound fly in a spider web. Then he did the same to the other Russian.

Standing in front of them, he took a phone he'd found in Terenty's pocket, dialed his phone server, heard his voicemail greeting, and pushed # to leave a message. Then he put the phone on speaker and set it on the ground so that it was recording.

He slapped the other Russian awake. When he was lucid, John said, "I'm going to read you your Miranda rights now. You're both under arrest for a whole host of crimes. You do not have the right to remain silent. Understand?"

They both looked quizzically at him. "Good, I just wanted to make sure you were paying attention. Terenty, what's your buddy's name?" Terenty struggled defiantly against the binds. "I really don't want to do any more damage to either of you, but understand, I will."

"This is fucking illegal," Terenty said, gurgling his own blood and spit. He hocked and spat a huge mouthful at John, but John saw it coming and stepped aside.

"I've snapped, Terenty. Clean forgot what's right and wrong. All I care about is getting the girl back. Now, I'll ask you one more time. Then, well, this picture here, it's a Saturday morning cartoon. What comes next is more Wes Craven. I'm guessing a movie buff like you knows Wes Craven, Nightmare on Elm Street? Clear? Now, who's your buddy?"

"He's my brother," Terenty said. "Silanty." Even a crazy Russian knew that when you were hog tied and hanging upside down from the ceiling it was over.

"Thank you. I really want this to go well for both of you."

"Fuck you, pig." Silanty spit at his shoes.

"I'm not a pig. I'm a federal fire marshal." John stepped forward, raised his leg up, and cleaned his shoe off on Silanty's shirt. He felt around with his toe and then delivered a quick shot to Silanty's liver. Not enough to incapacitate him, but enough that he really felt it.

"Oh, you, fuck you," Silanty groaned.

"Okay. Fuck me. Fine. That means nothing to me. I'm going to ask you this just once. And I think I know what your answer is going to be. So I'm just going to get the preliminaries out of the way." John stepped behind the two. Picked up a gallon can of white fuel he'd procured from the storage closet. Poured it over the Russians so that it ran all down their chests and over their heads and onto their faces.

"If you don't tell me what I want to know, I'm going to light a fire under each of you. You ever smelled burnt human? I'm guessing yes. I'll put you out. Let you live. Then I'll really start to torture you. Now, like I told you, I don't have a lot of time. Where is Condor Walken? And where is Jackie Fairbanks?"

Silanty was the first to speak up. "How the fuck are we gonna know? You can burn us, pig. We don't know nothing."

Fighting against a current of reason, John took a rag from the table, put a lighter to it, and tossed it on the ground under them. They both yelled and stretched to get away from the flame. He was pretty sure they wouldn't ignite unless he moved the rag closer, but having actually gone that far, he knew he could burn them to get the answer he needed. Of course, he'd given it a lot of thought. Most guys he knew would have loved to have had the chance to torture some terrorists if it would have stopped the 9/11 murders. He knew now how far he could go. These two were killers. At the Hilton, Terenty had threatened to send Jackie to the bottom of the river. They killed Rodney. Either of them would kill an innocent for pocket money. The value of their human life was nothing to him. Jackie's safety meant everything.

John knelt down and moved the rag directly under Silanty. "Maybe I'll burn him first, Terenty," John said calmly. "While you watch. Give you a chance to think."

"I think I know where he might be," Silanty said quickly. "I think I know. Promise to let us go. We just want to go back to Mother Russia. We've done nothing."

"I'm a federal officer. You tried to kidnap me today. That's one thing. You participated in the kidnapping of Jackie Fairbanks. I think one of you killed her brother. I'm sure I could go all day long. Now I told you, I don't have a lot of time."

"We tell you, and you forget about all that," Terenty said.

John pulled the rag away and said, "Be quick."

"Okay. The Norwegian. Torval. He told us after we lost you to be ready to leave the country."

"How? And when?"

"We don't know. The big guy usually tells us right before we are supposed to do something. We never know what is happening ahead of time."

"Makes sense." John dragged the burning rag closer with his foot. "But that does not tell me where he is."

"He'll hold up some place in the city until the heat clears. He was there and he won't risk exposure right now."

"Keep talking."

"He has space in a Midtown highrise that he never uses. If he wants to be safe, he might go there."

"Terenty, be clear. Where is this place?"

"An old business. It was an Internet betting center. Online poker. Feds closed it down. Madison and 53rd. Suite 4811. That's all I can think of. He won't go to his penthouse or the offices on 61st. He's freaky about being trapped."

"What's this place like?"

"Quarter of the floor. It's mostly gutted now. Just a couple of offices left. He was getting ready to turn it into executive offices for lease. Something like that."

"The 48th floor of a Midtown highrise is about the least secure place I can think of." John inched the rag closer. "You're making things up."

Terenty snorted and spit out another mouthful of blood and spit.

"He'll have security."

"Security?"

Silanty cut in, "Let us down. I'll tell you the whole thing."

John moved the rag closer. "I set the terms, Silanty. Now what kind of security will he have?"

"The big guys that pulled you out of the van earlier for sure. Maybe a couple like the two you took last night," Terenty said. "He has a few more people loyal to him. Young guy. Couple of chicks. That's all we know about."

"And the big guy with white hair?"

"Torval, the Norwegian," Terenty said. "Yes. He never goes anywhere without him."

John walked across the galley and picked up the radio from the deck. "They all have one of these?"

"Yes. Yes," Terenty said. "Let us down. This is bullshit, man. I can't breathe."

"If you can talk, you can breathe, Terenty." The volume dial showed the radio was on and at half volume. "When do you check in next?"

"We're on radio silence until they contact us. We're supposed to be ready to move."

"Do they know where you are?"

"No, it wouldn't have been too smart to broadcast that over the airwaves, now would it?"

"You're a smart guy, Terenty, I like you. Now hang tight." John picked up the phone, hit the # key again and listened to the message. It had recorded successfully so he hit # again and the computerized voice said,

"Your message has been sent." He hung the phone up and started to walk away.

Silanty called out. "Hey! You said you'd let us go."

"When I get Walken."

"You can't just leave us hanging here!"

He walked back to them. "You're right."

He pulled the free end of each hitch and let them drop the three feet to the deck. Terenty hit the hard and course surface with his swollen eye and cried out with a string of expletives in Russian. With the rest of the rope, John quickly tied them together and then to a nearby vertical support.

Silanty struggled against the binds and yelled, "What if this shit spontaneously combusts?"

John stopped, thought for a second, and said, "Unlikely, but it could happen. So be cool, honey bunny. Name that one, Terenty, and I'll let you go."

"Pulp Fiction. Pulp Fiction," Terenty cried.

"Eh, that one was too easy for a gangster like you. I'll come back later with something harder." With that, John left the galley, Terenty and Silanty screaming obscenities after him.

SEVENTY-FOUR

She'd made the mistake of calling Tolliver. He entered the Midtown South evidence room, and before greeting anyone in the room, he said, "Play that again."

Fitzgerald was there along with the Precinct Chief Andy Adams.

Stiles pressed the rewind and play button on the DVR and they watched again as John took the envelope of evidence through the slot and then left.

"And he told the evidence clerk he was taking them to One PP?" Tolliver said with a mocking tone. "And then wrapped his car around a light pole a block away? And was then hauled off by two assailants? And then he stole a motorcycle, which you have recovered at the Hilton. And you found a dead man in his hotel room? And you've apprehended no bad guys? And you don't know where Kane is and he's not responding to any calls?"

"That's where we are," Santiváñez said. "You've forgotten that Jackie Fairbanks is missing."

"Oh, yes. Jackie Fairbanks. The cause of all this mess. You have got to be kidding me. Chief," Tolliver said to Andy Adams. "Put out an APB on Kane. He can't be that hard to find."

"All due respect, sir," Santiváñez said, "we think Kane is running a protocol to get Jackie Fairbanks back. We need to find him, but we need to not get in his way. If we alert every cop in this city, we could ruin whatever hope he has of getting her back from Walken."

"What do you mean get her back from Walken? We don't know that he has her."

"It only makes sense. Everyone in this room agrees."

"So he's going to make a trade? The bonds for the girl? You have to be kidding me. We'll throw him in prison."

"Easy, Tolliver." Fitzgerald had been leaning against an old metal desk. He stood ramrod straight. "My man has done nothing wrong. Nothing illegal. We don't know what he is doing. And I agree with Agent Santivánez, we need to find out without running over him."

"Well that's very nice that the New York City Bureau of Fire Investigation has commentary on a federal case," Tolliver said in his most mocking tone. "*My* federal case. Now, Chief Adams, call out an APB on Kane before I do it myself."

Fitzgerald took another step forward as if he were going to deck Tolliver. Andy Adams put his arm out to stop him.

"Ease up, Tolliver," Santivánez said. "That's not the way this is going down."

"You do not speak to me like that. I am the Assistant Special Agent in Charge of the New York City FBI Political Crimes Division. You, young lady, are but a Supervisory Special Agent. You work for me. Now Chief Adams, issue an APB for Kane and bring him in."

Stiles stepped in front of Tolliver. He was trying to control his territorial anger at the way Tolliver had just spoken to the woman he loved, who was also his boss. He said, "Sir, why don't we step away and talk about this. There are four professionals in this room that want to go another way."

"You, Agent Stiles, will be reprimanded with Agent Santivánez. I'll bust you both back down to a GS-13, and I'll be damned if you'll ever go past it again."

"If anyone is getting a demotion around here it is you, Agent Tolliver," Santivánez said.

Stiles knew to step away.

"You've run this investigation into the ground at every step of the way," she continued with a calm tone. "First by refusing to inform another federal agent that we had information on his case. Then by refusing to let me intervene on Marshal Kane when you should have. When we find Marshal Kane, he will testify to that fact himself. You're also ignoring the judgment of four experienced law enforcement professionals. Your ego continues to do you disservice. Now, we have a respected law enforcement professional out there running a protocol, and his chief and I think we know what it is. If you'd like to listen up, we'll tell you. But I promise you, I will burn every bit of political capital I have if you cross me on this, and it is you who will be busted back down to a junior agent, if you're that lucky. Two people have already been murdered. Two more have been accosted. Now it is time for you to let me take over this investigation."

Tolliver jerked his head with indignation, but he knew who had the strongest political backing between the two of them. Her mentor's office was next door to the director himself. And she was right, his actions could be called into question if this thing were examined, when this thing were examined. So maybe it was better to let her run with it and screw it up. "Okay, Agent Santiváñez," Tolliver said with a curt smile. "You have my full support. Your call."

She turned to Stiles. Inside she was boiling, but she kept her cool. "Stiles, what are we missing here?"

"Well," he said. "We want to find Kane. And we want to find Walken. Haven't a clue where Kane might be, but last place we saw Walken was on the *Minnow*. She's probably still docked at the South Street Seaport dock. I suggest we go down there and have a look."

"We'll lead the way," Santiváñez said. She walked out of the evidence room, stopped and turned to Tolliver, and said, "Would you like to ride with us?"

"No," he said. "You're in charge, I'll follow."

"Fine," she said. "Chief Fitzgerald, let's roll." She didn't look back to see who was following her. She was in charge now, damnit, and she was going to turn this thing around.

SEVENTY-FIVE

He threw the heavy lines off the bollards and jumped back aboard the *Minnow*. At the helm, he fired off the engines and dragged the heavy throttle bars backwards. Clear of the dock, he swung the *Minow's* lines around. Bow facing the docks at the northwest tip of Brooklyn, he buried the throttles and pushed all 900 tons of her across the East River at twelve knots. The crossing took three minutes.

His approach to the Brooklyn docks wasn't graceful, but he landed the *Minnow* without crushing the dock. After tying off the stern and then the bow, he jogged across the empty lot towards the Brooklyn Ice Cream Factory. Several families were sitting under the covered porch enjoying the day.

Passing the ice creamery quickly, he stopped at the street and held the door open for a man getting out of his Porsche. "Federal marshal. I'm commandeering this car."

The man wore silk Tommy Bahamas and leather sandals. "Like hell you are," he said.

John grabbed the back of his neck and firmly assisted him away from the car. He snatched the keys from his hand, and sliding into the driver's seat, he said, "You'll get her back as good as new." With that he turned the sporty Carrera over, slipped it into first, and redlined it to second.

It was a quick rip up the 278 to his home in Jackson Heights. At his back door, he punched in the 8-digit code to open the lock. Since Peggy had left, he'd had the whole house wired for security. There were cameras all over, sirens you could hear from four blocks away, and wired and wireless police notification modules.

He dropped down the stairs into his basement, a small, dirt-floor area lined with shelves for canned goods and small boxes. Pulling firmly on a rack of jarred peaches and pickles, he revealed what was really below the house. He stepped through the opening and onto the cement slab. The rows and arrays of LED lighting came to life, and in seconds the entire area was brightly lit.

One summer when he was a boy, he and his brother had helped his father burrow the basement out. They'd carried more 5-gallon buckets of dirt up the stairs and into the driveway than he could remember.

They'd built everything from Pinewood Derby cars to science fair projects in this room. It was fully finished now. In one area, burrowed under the driveway, was a gym. On one wall, there was a martial arts wooden dummy, pads, gloves, wraps. On the other wall, a rack of free weights. Mirrors lined the joining wall. A heavy bag hung from the ceiling in the middle of a small fighting ring. He'd made this room on his own after Peggy used to complain that the whole house shook when his heavy bag hung from the floor joists. Now the room was framed in steel and not connected to the house at all.

Opposite the gym was the lab. Open to the rest of the basement, devices and gadgets in various forms of completion sat neatly grouped on one workbench. Scopes, testers and myriad tools sat on another. On the third wall, servers and power supplies filled racks that hung above three separate work stations, each with its own desktop and organizational system.

A picture of Katie and him sat on the desktop of the far workstation. Her workstation. It was a recent photo. Her white hair hung straight down to her shoulders, bangs trimmed neatly and pushed to the side. Her blue eyes stared back at him. She was a mirror image of her mother.

Peggy had snapped from the stress of her job. The doctors said her schizophrenia was genetic and lay latent until stress triggered it. If Katie were predisposed, stress could ruin her life. It was one of the main reasons he'd retired. "One more time, darling," he said aloud. "One more time and I'm done for good."

He hit his keyboard and three screens rose from sleep. Each was split into six zones, representing the 18 cameras inside and outside the house.

An algorithm he'd written identified when there was movement across the frame and stored the images in a separate file. A click of the mouse and he watched a series of images. A couple of cats jumped the fence. He came home yesterday to shower before going to Malley's. Left for Malley's. At 5AM, the back security lights had come on. He slowed the video. Terenty and Silanty were right there in full color, sneaking up to his home. They looked around, checked the door, saw it was security-enabled, and then they left. Walken had sent them there to pick him up. They'd have kidnapped Katie if they'd had a chance. John sat back and breathed deep. Katie was safe, and they couldn't get to her, but a rage welled up in him at the thought of the Russians touching her.

He minimized the windows showing the security footage and brought up his phone system. He clicked on the one voicemail showing in the Inbox and listened for a second to make sure it was the right one. Then he pulled up a voice analytics program. He imported the voicemail and ran it through the analyzer. The graph on the screen showed the three distinct voices – his, Terenty's, and Silanty's. He labeled them on the graph and saved them into their own files. Then he used the text-to-voice feature and told the program to compile a library. It took about a minute and then the program returned a message that said the library was 93% complete. That only meant some words would sound unnatural. He would keep things very basic so it shouldn't matter. There simply wasn't any other choice. He couldn't go back to Terenty for more samples.

He typed in, "We are coming up. There is nowhere else to go." Then he listened to the output. It sounded good. Almost too good. So he put in some background noise. A little light traffic, barely perceptible. And a little static. He played it again, and satisfied with the result, he loaded the profile into the HTC EVO Droid's text-to-voice application. Now all he had to do was cable the EVO to the radio and type in what he wanted Terenty to say. He grabbed a cable with dual male 2.5" jacks and then walked to the other end of the basement.

At a steel door, he punched in 8 digits on a keypad. There was a dull thud and the door cracked open. He threw the door to the side revealing his armory. The walls were lined with various fighting weapons – guns, knives, bows, staffs, swords, daggers, ropes, chains. He'd inherited most of them from his father, who'd hauled them back from overseas military missions and return visits to the countries where he'd fought as a Marine.

He looked around the room and quickly set his eyes on Max, a Saiga 12-gauge with pistol grip. It was basically an AK-47 that shot 12-gauge shells. He slung the shoulder strap over his head and grabbed the 20-round circular magazine off a shelf. It was loaded with ordinary Winchester slug shells that would take a rhinoceros down at close range. He was extremely accurate with it at close range, and could blow a man's arm or leg clean off from a hundred yards. Or his head if the situation required.

He put on a leather trench coat that was pre-loaded with an assortment of knives and a few guns. He'd save the low caliber stuff for Walken because if there were one person he wanted alive, it was Condor Walken. Prison would be a living hell for him. He'd see that every day was worse than the last until he either killed himself, or someone him.

With what he packed, he could take out an army of thirty men in short order. A hundred if given enough time. He didn't figure Walken had that many men left to guard him. Certainly Torval and the two goons who had dragged him from the Crown Vic earlier. But based on what Terenty had said, it might be just them. If not, it was going to get ugly quick, and he minded not one bit, because he was in a very ugly mood.

SEVENTY-SIX

Stiles came to a swift stop in front of the South Street Seaport dock's metal security gate and they jumped out of the Suburban. The gate was unlocked. Santiváñez swung it open and looked down the dock. "It's gone, Stiles," she said.

"Let's go have a look," Stiles said.

Fitzgerald, Tolliver and four FBI agents who carried long barrel shot guns followed. Before they had reached the end of the dock, Stiles saw the *Minnow* across the river. He pointed and announced, "There she is."

Santiváñez turned to a mechanic who stood on the deck of a small tug. He was wiping grease off his hands with a rag and looking skeptically at the agents who carried the shotguns.

"That thing run?" she said.

The mechanic said, "She sure do."

Santiváñez motioned to the agents and they threw the lines off the bollards. They all hopped aboard and the mechanic fired off the noisy diesels without being told. "Where we goin'?" he yelled.

Stiles pointed across the river to the *Minnow*.

The mechanic eased the throttle back and slowly pulled the tug away from the dock.

Stiles stepped between him and the controls and said, "Excuse me. We're in a hurry." He jammed the lever down and cranked the wheel when they were far enough away from the dock. When her bow had swung almost fully around, he lifted the throttle out of reverse and jammed it down hard the other way. The tug's diesels responded without a hiccup and

Stiles pushed them across the river. When they were close, Stiles put the mechanic back in control and said, "Land us right up on her stern."

The mechanic brought the tug up expertly on the *Minnow*. First off the tug were the agents carrying the shot guns. Everyone else followed with their weapon drawn and at the ready.

They moved into the belly of the boat and soon came upon the galley. Terenty and Silanty let loose a string of expletives when they entered.

"Kane's been here," Santiváñez said to Stiles.

"Let's see what these guys know," Stiles said. He knelt down in front of the Russians and said, "Be quiet."

"Untie us, goddamit," Terenty screamed.

SEVENTY-SEVEN

John's Droid rang. It was Walken calling the Russian's phone, which was forwarding to him. He quickly pulled the Porsche to the curb on Madison at 50th.

He'd find out quickly if his ruse with Michael Terry were playing out. He knew by his texts that Terry had ducked into a Thai restaurant on 42nd by Grand Central. He was sitting in a window having a staredown with the guy in the truck who was leading him. John called Terry over the Porsche owner's phone. When he answered, John said, "Turn your head so he can't see you and act like you're talking to Walken." Then he slid the screen lock down on his Droid and said, "Kane."

"John, what the hell are you doing?" Walken said. His tone was familiar, as if he were talking to a friend who had just done something stupid, but was still a friend nonetheless.

John held the two phones close together so Terry could hear him. "I told you. I'm not getting in any cars."

"Jackie is not in the city," Walken said. "How stupid do you think I am?"

"How stupid do you think I am?" John said. "Bring her here. To this restaurant. I'm not moving." He hung up the Droid and said to Terry, "We're almost home. Hang up the phone and keep up the act." Then he hung up on Terry, dropped the Porsche in gear, and sped up to 53rd.

At the Madison gate, he inserted the round key that fit in the Emergency Fire Access box and turned it clockwise to a stop. The metal gate began to roll up. When the gate was high enough, John gunned the Carrera through the opening and down into the parking garage. He drove all the way down to the loading dock and scanned around for anyone who might be a lookout for Walken. The loading zone was empty and quiet. He got out of the car and walked to the elevator. His assumption had been right so far. Walken didn't have any people at this stage guarding him. Maybe on the 48th floor.

Seventy-eight

"Cut them loose, Stiles," Santivánez said. "Let's see what they have to tell us."

Stiles took out his Buck knife. It was a simple old-fashioned Chairman Series with leather handle. He'd had it since he was a kid and he loved it because it stayed sharp forever, and it had served him more times than he could remember.

He cut the Russians' hands free but left their feet bound. Then he sat them up and said quietly so only they could hear, "Now be polite to the lady. It looks like the marshal already had his way with you for the disrespect done to Ms. Fairbanks. You don't want a second whipping from me."

"Look at my fucking nose," Terenty said.

"The crazy ass tried to burn us," Silanty said. "Smell this shit on us."

"We don't know anything about that," Stiles said. "But I'm sure he had his reasons."

"Look," Terenty said. "He said he gets Condor Walken, he's gonna let us go."

"Is that so?" Stiles said.

"That's right. You make some kind of deal with us to send us back to Russia, free, and I'll tell you where we sent him. Good chance Condor gonna be there."

Stiles looked back and motioned for Santivánez to come closer. She'd heard everything the Russian had said, but if there were a deal to be made, she was going to be the broker.

"What kind of deal do you have in mind?" Stiles said.

"Immunity," Terenty said. "No prosecution."

"You kill anyone today?" Santiváñez asked him.

"Us? We don't kill no one. We just get the marshal and try to bring him in." Terenty looked down at the ground and shook his head. "Just want to go home to Russia."

"Cut the theatrics, man," Santiváñez said. "If you're telling the truth, and we find Marshal Kane and Condor Walken, we'll send you home. But if you're lying to me, all bets are off."

Terenty looked up and said, "Okay. We sent the marshal to the building at 53rd and 8th. Suite 4811. Condor has old office space there. We think maybe he goes there to get away from all the heat on him."

"That's it?" Santiváñez said.

"That's all there is to it," Terenty said.

"We'll check it out," Santiváñez said. "Sit tight." She and Stiles walked away.

"Hey!" Terenty said. "How about some medical attention? Look at what he did to my nose."

"You," Santiváñez said to one of the agents with a shotgun, "stay here and guard them. Make sure they don't die."

"Yes, ma'am," the agent said.

They could hear the helicopter Santiváñez had called in landing on top.

On the stern, as they were about to climb the stairs to the waiting helicopter, Fitzgerald yelled over the whine of the rotors, "Drop me on the other side. I'll cover the ground."

Santiváñez gave him a thumbs up and they all loaded into the bird and flew north over the water.

SEVENTY-NINE

The jet touched down at Ronald Reagan National Airport. Malley recalled when the airport was a badly worn, pockmarked, two-strip regional port for light aircraft. His father had worked with Congress to appropriate funds for its repair and upgrading over the years. Then it was just called National Airport. The eponymous President Reagan, though the enemy at the time, had turned out to be a beloved leader of the country. He himself would be like a Ronald Reagan. He had a vision to bring back prosperity. To reignite production in the country. His mind cycled through his platform. But he only got through a few points and then drifted off. His heart wasn't in it. Could he still lead this country? After what he'd done? After what he was about to do?

The jet taxied to the hangar. It was a standard metal structure amid rows of identical housings. His father bought the unit from a contractor that had won the project decades past. Malley was pretty sure the contractor had given it to his father as a kickback.

The hangar was empty, save a single limousine and driver, who stood dutifully by the vehicle.

Malley thanked the pilot with a big smile and a heartfelt handshake, and then he and Henry walked down the flight stairs. Malley strode confidently to the waiting car. Henry followed close behind. They got into the back and watched the jet taxi away. The car didn't move. Henry looked around. "What are we doing?" he said nervously.

Malley put his finger to his mouth, motioning that the limo could be bugged. When the plane had taxied away, Malley quickly got out of his door and firmly shut it behind him.

Inside the back of the limo, Henry tried to open his door, but it was locked. He thrust himself over to the door Malley had used. Locked. He knocked on the glass separating him from the driver. Nothing. He pounded more violently. Nothing. Malley stared absently at him. So this was how it would end. He'd chosen the wrong side after all.

The limousine started to move. Henry sat back in the seat. Soon he'd face very serious men who would ask him what he had done, and he wouldn't be able to talk his way out of it. He'd tell them what they wanted to know if they promised to finish him quickly and painlessly.

He took the vodka decanter from the bar rack and guzzled it. Took out the small pill box and gulped the last six pills. Would the FBI come swooping in and save him? Probably not. Was it Walken's men, or Black's that would kill him? He took another drink of the vodka and then put the bottle between his legs. He couldn't feel a thing now. It was amusing that he was being driven to a sure death, and he hadn't a care in the world.

Malley looked at the limousine driving away. Henry had been his confidant. His protégé. His friend. But he had been something else that outweighed all his goodness. "You betrayed me, boy," he said aloud. Later he would call the FBI and report that Henry was missing. Black had fixed it so that some "interesting characters" would visit Malley after Henry's disappearance. Malley would report this to the FBI, that these men claimed Henry owed them money, and now they wanted him to pay. They'd be seen by some people, and then disappear forever. That way they would have a reason to refute anything Henry might have told the FBI. Henry Douglas would take the fall for all his indiscretions, and for the good of the country.

Black was to take care of Walken by nightfall. Soon all trace of this mess would be gone. He would rewind the clock back to the night he met Antoinette Lassaut, and he would never repeat the mistake again.

A few minutes later, a Town Car drove into the hangar and stopped before him. Twenty minutes later, they were crossing the Arlington Memorial Bridge. He instructed his driver to stop on Lincoln Memorial Circle.

The driver protested, as the road was fast with traffic. Malley snapped back to stop the car and turn on the hazard lights.

When the car was stopped, he placed his glass in the bar. He'd drunk two screwdrivers to steady his nerves and he was getting mean. He apologized to the driver for snapping at him, but asked him to hold their position.

He tuned out the honks and shouts and looked through the back side of the memorial. As a young senator, he ate his sack lunch with Honest Abe at least twice a week when Congress was in session. The 16th president was his role model, and he'd done everything to be like him. And it had worked. According to the polls, the American people saw Michael Malley as a symbol of honesty, integrity, and humility. He and Abe were the same. In fact, he was going to call his party the Nationalist Party after Lincoln's 1864 National Union Party.

We were facing down the greatest economic trouble our nation had ever faced because a great part of the economic machine that fueled the middle class, production, was gone. There was another war coming to America. The country needed a man to stare it down. Take it head on. It would be an economic war this time, but there was a war looming. To look at a county by county chart of unemployment rates was heart-rending. The country was black and blue from coast to coast. The working man had been beaten senseless. Only select bands of farming country seemed immune. Anywhere there was dense population, unemployment was a staggering ten percent or greater. America had engineered the greatest industrial revolution, created the highest standard of living in the history of the world, and unwitting politicians on both sides of the aisle had unraveled our greatness into a gigantic mess. The working man and woman of this country needed, they wanted, a leader to show them the way out. They needed an independent mind like Michael Malley to do the job.

The current administration had run up an unfathomable debt. It turned the Republican spending binge under the previous administration into a minor blip on the radar. The 21st century Keynesian approach to economic revival had produced the same results as it had for Roosevelt. And there was no world war on the horizon to save us this time. The past two wars were great contributors to the impending national insolvency.

The previous three administrations had driven us into the ditch, one hand on the wheel, the other waving the free trade banner like a checkered victory flag. Instead of a flag, it turned out to be a plague. A diseased, banner of corruption and greed that had decimated the middle class.

Now the elites in the know said those jobs were never coming back. Never was a long time. His plan saw into never, and scaled it back a few millennia to the here and now. He had a plan to turn things around. Michael Malley would do it. He would do it.

He opened his eyes. The driver's window was dropping and there was a police officer on the other side. He'd dozed off. The police officer stared back at him with a polite but quizzical look. "Is there a problem, Senator?"

Malley took off his sunglasses and rubbed his eyes. "Matter of State, officer. We'll be moving on now."

The officer patted the driver's window and waved them on.

"Continue on, driver," Malley said.

The driver wasted no time clearing the lane, made his way to Constitution, and headed east towards The Monocle.

EIGHTY

To Condor, this was like old times. In the 70s when he was running cocaine into the USSR, he and Soviet General Servaya Varvarushka spent a lot of time holed up with captive women. During the 70s, Varvarushka was the high authority and they acted with impunity. It had been years since those times. He'd spent his whole adult life building his empire. Becoming a new-age gangster, staying out of the small stuff. He'd always laughed at the Italians. They attracted the FBI like flies. But now he'd done it. Immunex was dead. When he was gone, the government would seize it. The land at 43rd & 8th was gone. But Malley was ruined, and that's all he really cared about. He could always remake himself. He'd simply have to lay low in the south of France for awhile. Get surgery to change his appearance. He didn't need money. He had plenty of it stashed around the world in bank accounts and safe deposit boxes.

He doubted now that he'd ever get the five million back from The Marshal. He just wasn't playing ball. It was too bad really. The sport was over. He'd have to forget about the money and keep the consolation prize, Jackie Fairbanks.

He took the hood off Jackie and ripped the duct tape off her mouth. "Ah," she said, moving her lips and mouth around. "Thank you."

***

There were four men. One she assumed to be Condor Walken. There was a giant with white hair, and two guys that ran around 300. They were ugly. Steroids had done funny things to their faces. Their necks were shaped like beer kegs. She looked around at the surroundings. Nothing but a gutted-out suite with a couple leftover offices, in what she expected was a Manhattan high-rise.

The one she assumed to be Condor said, "I hope you weren't mistreated."

"You must be Condor," she said.

"Yes, Ms. Fairbanks. I am Condor Walken."

She sat in an old wooden ladder-back chair, her feet and arms bound. "Well, this is very uncomfortable. I'd appreciate it if you at least untied my hands." She'd stay calm with these guys. Because she knew one thing, her Marshal would soon be there to save her.

Walken motioned to the two guys that stood behind her. She felt the cold of a steel blade against her wrist and then her hands were free. She brought them around in front of her and rubbed her wrists. "Thank you," she said. "The legs are a bit much, too. It's not like I'm going to run away with the likes of you four guarding me."

"Not yet, Ms. Fairbanks," Condor said. "But in time."

"Well, then, I'd say it's time we all got on a first name basis. What's your name?" she said to the big guy with white hair.

Condor said, "He is Torval."

"And where'd you pick these guys up? The meat plant?"

Condor laughed. "You're very relaxed for a woman who has no hope of ever returning to her previous life."

"Well," Jackie said, "that all depends."

"I suppose you think John Kane is organizing some rescue mission to save you?" Walken smiled and rattled his hand in the air. It was an odd thing, but she figured it was one of his idiosyncrasies.

"He is," she said confidently.

"I just spoke to The Marshal. He is not far away. Very close indeed. But he is not coming to save you. He is waiting for me to bring you to him in trade for the five million in bearer bonds he stole from me last night."

"I'm sorry?" Jackie said shaking her head. "He stole five million in bearer bonds from you last night?"

"Yes, and sadly, he knows he cannot give me the bonds. So I am forced to take you instead."

"Well, I'll give you five million. Cut my legs free and I'll give you a little extra."

"You are a very interesting lady, Ms. Fairbanks, and I am going to enjoy getting to know you."

EIGHTY-ONE

The service elevator door opened on the 48th floor. John stood in the corner and checked the service bay. It was all clear, so he lowered his silenced 9mm and concealed it behind his coat. He looked at his watch on his left wrist. It was 9:30AM.

The service bay led to the main part of the floor. It was a typical setting in any high-rise USA. The walls were white. On every door there was the name of a lawyer, doctor, counselor, or some other business. He stepped into the hallway and followed the numbers as they descended in order. After two corners, he was looking down the hall at 4811. The entire floor was quiet.

He stepped back around the corner, secured the pistol in its holder inside the coat, and took out his Droid and the radio. He connected the two with the cable and then brought up the text-to-speech app and chose Terenty's profile. Then he typed in, "We are coming up. It's not safe out here."

He pressed the transmit button on the radio and then pressed play on the Droid.

***

"Oh, what?" Jackie said. "You think you are going to kidnap me? Please. Do you know who I am?"

"Yes," Condor said. "I do. That is the beauty of it."

"Condor, you've made a lot of mistakes. I mean, you're hiding out in an empty floor of a Manhattan high-rise. I have a feeling it's only going to get worse for you from here."

"Ms. Fairbanks, do you think I got to where I am without backup plan after backup plan? And well-trained people?"

"We are coming up. It's not safe out here," came Terenty's voice over Torval's radio.

Walken looked at Torval. Torval said into the radio, "Hold your position. We will come to you." He nodded to one of the meat packers.

The meat packer walked swiftly across the open floor to the door, which was about a hundred feet away.

"Over," Terenty's voice came back.

"Something tells me you didn't want him showing up here," Jackie said. "Sounded like the Russian who abducted me this morning. And why is it not safe for him out there? Things not going as you planned?"

"Ms. Fairbanks, everything is going to be okay. You are going to be very well taken care of. You will have to perform, if you want to live a nice life. If you know what I mean."

"Condor," Jackie said, "if you try to lay a hand on me, I'll rip you to shreds. If you know what I mean."

Condor stepped close to her. He raised his hand in the air as though he were going to backhand her. She lunged up at him with everything she had, but the meathead behind her caught her and sat her back down. He had his massive hands gripped tightly around her biceps, and she couldn't move. Condor completed his swing and slapped her across her face with the back of his hand.

"Shut up," he said

She screamed out and tried to shake her body free. "Do that again and I'll bite your finger off!" she screamed.

Condor laughed and said to Torval, "A lively one. Very good. Very good indeed. Call our man on the street. Tell him to take the next clear shot he gets on Kane. I want his head splattered all over the side of a building." If there were one person he now hated more in the world than Michael Malley, it was John Kane.

***

John could hear the footsteps approaching around the corner. Whoever it was, whatever it was, it was big. It grunted while it walked. Probably one of the guys who broadsided his car earlier, dragged him to Terenty and Silanty's van. He knew he came out of 4811 because he'd seen the door move before ducking back behind the corner. And no matter how much he just wanted to blast him through with Max, that wasn't the move. He'd have to quietly incapacitate the guy, and then go to work with Max. Judging by what he remembered about the men who'd grabbed him, taking care of this guy quietly wasn't going to be easy. He was big and strong. Big and strong guys didn't bother him, but they usually took a long time to bring down. Especially big and strong guys that hired themselves out for protection. It usually meant they knew how to fight, and had seen plenty of action.

From the inside of his coat, he removed an eighteen-inch-long piece of mahogany attached to three feet of a new leather jump rope. The club was an inch and a half in diameter. If he hit a man with a full swing, he could easily snap a femur, or cave in a skull.

He listened to the man's gait as he approached. He was in a hurry and he walked with some kind of impediment. Instead of a natural step, step, step, step, it was step step... step step... step step. This guy was big. Probably an old NFL offensive guard with a bum knee. Well, it wasn't going to feel very good after this.

John got down on one knee, extended the club out behind him, and just when he thought the man was close enough, he swung it around the corner with all he had.

He heard a crack, but not like a bone breaking. It was more like one piece of wood hitting another piece of wood, or worse a piece of hard plastic. He continued his momentum around the corner, and brought himself around in front of the man. He'd simply snapped the man's artificial leg in half.

The guy looked at him with the ugliest snarl he'd ever seen and lunged forward with his good leg. John didn't mind the snarl. He was pretty fed up himself. And lunging at him when you only had one good leg was not a good idea. John grabbed the man's right arm and pulled down hard and to his own right. He stumbled, but hopped with his right leg and came out of the arm drag. It was a good arm drag, but the guy was extremely heavy. And strong. Like a rhinoceros. And he had good balance. This guy definitely knew how to handle himself.

Now he was standing up straight. He lost the snarl and smiled at John. He had three gold teeth on the left of his mouth. They all had an impression. The rear most had the Chicago Bears logo. The other two had raised Roman numerals – an X on one and another X on the other. Superbowl Twenty. This guy played with Singletary and Payton. Very impressive. He hopped forward and extended his arms as if he were going to strangle John.

John was impressed, but this time, John wasn't going to underestimate the guy. One leg or not, this guy knew what it meant to win. He outweighed him by at least seventy pounds, and it was all muscle. The best way to take a horse like this down was to hit him where it really hurt. He didn't imagine those were fake. Still holding onto the end of the rope, he wound it quickly around his hand several times and jerked the club forward. The Mahagony club connected with the guy's testicles. His eyes exploded with pain and he made a wheezing noise. Still, he advanced and grabbed John around his neck quicker than he'd ever seen a man of his size move. It was like the grip of Frankenstein. John tried to peel the guy's thumbs away, but they were as big as bananas. If he didn't do something quick, it was going to be over.

John jerked the rope hard and caught the Mahogany club in his hand. Firmly in his grip, he rotated his arm and drove the butt of the club into the giant's mouth. John felt his teeth break away and his grip loosen ever so slightly. That was progress. He swung again. This time he hit him on the temple and drove and twisted the club when he made contact. The rage fell from the beast's eyes quickly and they rolled back. His knee buckled and he dropped to the floor like a felled moose.

John caught his breath and shook the guy to make sure he was completely out. His jaw was slack and his gold teeth lay in a pool of blood on his tongue. "Sorry, pal," he said panting. "I'm a Giants fan."

He left the guy where he lay and ran to 4811. The 20-round magazine snapped home into Max's receiver with a quiet click. The well-oiled slide whispered destruction as he jacked the first shell into the chamber. Then, without a second's hesitation, John kicked the door open and stormed forward. He saw them thirty yards off and began to fire. His shots were purposely off the mark. His tactic was to get them to scramble, and scramble they did. Being assaulted by a 12-gauge semiautomatic was like being charged by a Grizzly. No matter how big you were, the bear was eight times your size and speed, and it scared the living hell out of you. In the case of the 12-gauge, it was simply eight times louder and more powerful than what you were carrying, unless of course you were carrying one yourself. No matter what you were packing, pulling a weapon and aiming it when someone was blasting away at you with a shot gun was a difficult task.

Walken's arms flailed and he looked wildly around. After he figured out what was happening, Torval grabbed Walken and dragged him into an office.

John fired a few rounds after them but let them go for the time being. He was twenty yards out and advancing on the guy holding Jackie. The guy took out a 10-inch bowie knife and held it to her throat. She struggled against him with both hands on his wrist. At ten yards the guy looked at him with sinister eyes and smiled. He, too, had gold teeth, only on the other side. John had Max trained right in the center of his mouth. He wasn't going to wait to find out which team this guy had played for. He simply pulled the trigger and kept advancing. A one-and-a-quarter ounce lead slug left Max's snub barrel traveling at nearly a thousand feet per second. The slug blew his mouth away and warbled his face. The kinetic energy released its heat, boiling his brains along the slug's path. The back of his head exploded like a compressed can of pasta sauce. His body was tipping backwards. John saw that Jackie was struggling to get the knife free from his heavy, dead hand. He ran forward, grabbed the dead guy's wrist and turned it away from her. Jackie was a strong woman. In a flash, she had the knife in her own hand. Then she bent over and cut the binds off of her legs. John freed the dead guy and he fell backwards to the floor.

Automatic fire erupted from the room where Torval had taken Walken. John grabbed Jackie and threw her to the ground behind the dead guy, and then returned fire with Max.

He flanked left but kept his fire in the right of the room. By his count, he had fired twelve shots. Eight more was not a lot. He ran for the door to the room and rapid fired the gun seven times. With only one shot left, he kicked the door open and dropped to his knee.

The window in the room was completely blown away. Walken was gone. Torval had his right foot up on the window sill. He had a pack on his back that had to be a base jumping parachute. He raised the automatic toward John with his left hand. Before he could point it at him, John squeezed the last round from Max and blew Torval's arm away from his shoulder. Torval fell on the sill in a straddle and leaned out the window. John dropped Max, slipped out of his leather trench coat and ran to Torval. He grabbed onto the pack with his left hand and locked his right arm around Torval's left leg. Torval slapped the side of the skyscraper with his right hand, trying to gain purchase on the glass, struggling and throwing his weight downward. He got his right foot up on the ledge and pressed away.

John scanned south, the Met Life building stood out like a billboard. Central Park spread out to the north. Walken was gliding through the air. He was dropping fast, close to the pavement, rounding the corner at 6th Avenue and 52nd Street. Given enough time he thought he could pull Torval up, but Torval wasn't his quarry.

They were five hundred feet up. If he fell with Torval, he'd hit the ground in less than ten seconds. He had a floor of two hundred feet to deploy the parachute and still have a fifty percent chance of living. If he latched onto Torval and managed to deploy the chute in two to four seconds his odds increased, but not by much.

Everything Walken had said to him flashed through his mind, and without further thought, he lifted Torval's leg and dove over the sill with him. He locked his left arm around Torval's neck and clamped his legs around his torso. There was still a lot of life left in him. He kicked and tried to fight with his right arm.

John heard Jackie yell, "John! No!" No time to look back. They were falling fast. He reached for the pull chord. Missed it. Four one thousand. Missed again. Five one thousand. Hand on chord, he pulled. Six one thousand. The chute erupted from the pack and caught air. Seven one thousand. Eight one thousand. There was a bus making its way north on 6th. It was coming fast. Nine one thousand. He had no control of the chute. They had to be going sixty miles per hour. Ten one thousand. John focused on the big plate-glass windshield. Eleven one thousand. Twelve one thousand. Just before the moment of impact, he loosened his legs and curled his heels to his butt. They crashed through the windshield. John held tight to Torval's neck with his left arm. Tucked his head behind his back. Gripped his belt with his right hand.

He'd been hit hard in football when he was a kid. He'd been laid out so flat it took every bit of pride and courage and strength he had to get back up. This was different. He wasn't sure if he could move his limbs. He didn't feel a thing. Then it felt as if his brain were rebooting. "Move your legs, damnit!" He screamed inside his head. His left knee jerked. His right knee jerked. He moved his head and pushed up from Torval. He looked around. There were only a few people on the bus but their faces were a blur. The driver was out of her seat trying to help him. He grabbed on to her and let her help him up. Then he staggered to her chair.

"Hey. What are you doing?" she said.

He could hear that she was a Chinese woman. He was just beginning to regain his focus, and he could see that she was absolutely irate that he was taking control of her bus. She advanced on him and tried to reach for the controls. He was regaining strength. He blocked her advances with his right arm and pushed her back as gently as he could.

"I'm a federal marshal, ma'am," he said and then coughed up blood. He had to spit it out on the floor. The bus driver backed away, saying things in Chinese under her breath.

He dropped the shifter into reverse and floored the pedal. Looked back and forth in the two side mirrors. Traffic was very light. The Level-Two at the intersection of 52nd & 6th saw him coming and stopped traffic in both directions.

The right-hand turn onto 52nd was clear. The Level-Two was blowing her whistle, waving madly at him. He was doing at least thirty in reverse now. Looking in both mirrors. The way was clear. He cranked the wheel over to the right. Kept the pedal to the floor. The rear wheels chirped. The front end slid out from under him to the left. He cranked the wheel to the left and straightened the nose. A few seconds later he slammed on the brakes in front of '21' Club. He threw the shifter into park, hit the lever to open the door, and staggered down the steps to the street. Walken's parachute tumbled with the breeze down 52nd. He had to be inside '21' Club.

John hobbled over the sidewalk. He had broken ribs. His breathing was guarded. He knew he was bleeding internally. His organs hurt, and he felt swelling in his stomach. He bent over and vomited bright red blood. Definitely internal bleeding. But the only blood he tasted was another's.

Sirens rang in the distance. There was no time to wait. Throwing open the door, he stepped boldly into the entryway of '21 Club.' Using the wall as a brace, he made his way around the corner and into the restaurant. A few waiters were placing silverware on the white tablecloths. They looked at John. Then to the back of the dining room. John followed their looks.

A man in a suit who appeared to be the manager stood at the top of a stairwell.

"Federal marshal," John said, panting, spitting blood. "Where did he go?"

The man pointed down the stairs. Without waiting, John took them sideways one at a time. He came to the kitchen. Followed the looks of the prep cooks. They led him through the long galley to a short set of stairs.

He'd seen the History Channel show on '21' Club's Wine Cellar at least three times, and he knew exactly what was at the base floor. Turning back to the prep cook behind him, he choked up some blood, spit it on the ground, and pointing to the cook's Santoku knife, he said, "I need that."

The cook looked wide-eyed around the kitchen for approval. He found the manager who stood by the top stairs. The manager nodded aggressively to him and he passed it over his station to John.

John took the knife and descended the ten stairs. These were the stairs where Hemingway had famously "made love" to Legs Diamond's girlfriend. At the bottom, John cautiously looked around the corner.

A waiter sauntered up the hall from the other end. He carried his freshly cleaned uniform on a hanger.

John walked toward him, stopping in front of the alcove leading to The Wine Cellar. He said, "Did you see anyone go down that way?" John's chin and neck were bloody. He was sweating and he gripped the Santoku knife.

"No," the waiter said cautiously backing away. "Just me."

"Give me that," John said. He pointed to the dry cleaning the kid carried.

Bag in hand, he ripped the plastic away, tore the clothes from the hanger, and cut the hook off with his blade. He straightened the hanger out and handed it to the manager, who had bravely followed him down the stairs. "Open it," John said. Part of the foundation of the building, the door weighed over four thousand pounds. He was in no shape to push it open himself.

The manager took the hanger, and keeping an eye on John and the knife, he sank the straight hanger into the proper hole in the wall. John heard the click. "Help him," John ordered the waiter, who stood there wide-eyed.

John moved cautiously, staying low, ready to spring forward or back. He wasn't sure if Walken had a gun, but it was a safe bet he did. It was a fool's hiding place, because it was a dead end. But Walken was in here. He could still smell his cologne in the air.

He stepped through the foundation wall and into the dining room. He could smell Walken still, but there was no man to match the scent. There was just no way. He'd disappeared into thin air.

He stepped into the small closet at the back of the dining room. There was a bottle of cabernet on the ground. John felt around the shelf. It obviously opened. He could smell Walken in here. There was just nowhere else for him to go.

"Sir... marshal," the manager said. "This shelf does not open. There are many secret passages in '21' Club. This is not one of them."

John ignored the manager and kept looking. Walken's trail stopped cold here.

Next to the shelf on the brick wall there was an outlet box. A stretch of half-inch conduit ran vertically to the ceiling. He looked closely where the conduit joined the wall. There was a crack in the paint at the tangent point. He pulled hard on the box. It came out a few inches from the wall. But the shelf did not move. He looked around his immediate area. Within reach there was only a bronze plaque bearing the name and visage of some long forgotten Broadway star. He held the outlet from the wall and tried to reach up and manipulate the plaque. He couldn't stretch that far. The manager stepped in without a word and turned it clockwise. It turned freely, but nothing happened.

"Go the other way," John ordered. His voice was pained and he struggled for breath.

The manager turned it back the other way. When the top of the plate hit nine o'clock, the shelf separated from the wall.

The manager stood there with a bewildered look and said, "We had no idea."

John said to the waiter, "Give me your lighter."

EIGHTY-TWO

Jack Kriendler and Charlie Berns had built '21' Club in 1929. In the 80s, the second set of Kriendlers and Berns took over running the place. By that time '21' was old and weathered and it had taken on the unofficial moniker of '61' due to the elderly patronage, poor lighting, and dated design. Walken had bought the restaurant from the partners in the early 90s and renovated it through one of his shell companies. Part of the renovation was the tunnel he'd built from The Wine Cellar to the Donnely Library on 53rd. When he'd had the tunnel built it was a busy public library, but it had been shuttered the past several years after the budget crisis had cut off funds for such luxuries as reading and research. He'd used it to impress his old friend General Servaya Varvarushka when he came to town, and he hadn't used it for many years until the other night with Carlos Esperanza.

With no light to guide his way, he felt along the sedimentary walls of the crudely burrowed tunnel. It was never meant to be pretty, simply an escape route if the police ever tried to descend on him while he dined in The Wine Cellar.

He came to the end of the tunnel. He was almost home free. Feeling for the handle, he grabbed hold of the steel bar and pulled as hard as he could. The pony door cracked open and then swung away from the old library's foundation.

The door opened just above the recording studio's ceiling tiles in the building's sub-basement. Now abandoned, there was nobody to disturb if he came crashing through the ceiling. He didn't have to be careful to return the tiles as he had the other night with Esperanza. '21' Club was gone with Immunex when he fled the country.

Heart pumping, he dropped the rope ladder, and kicked through the ceiling tiles. He heard footsteps behind him and saw a flicker of light. They'd found their way through and were on his tail. Who could be chasing him? The Marshal? There was no way.

He dropped down the ladder too fast and turned his ankle upon landing. Limping along, he felt his way to the door and then through the empty room to the stairs leading up to the main basement level. Still pitch black, he started up the flight, and then heard a noise come from the recording studio. He had a gun, but stopping to fight right now was not a good idea. He wanted John Kane dead, and he wanted to pull the trigger himself, but now was not the time. He turned and hobbled up the stairs as fast as he could.

EIGHTY-THREE

Jackie ran barefoot down 52nd. She'd watched helplessly as John crashed through the front of the bus. Her heart leapt when the big steel horse began reversing the wrong way down 6th Avenue. She'd taken the regular elevators to the ground floor, sprinted out of the building past the advancing PD and FBI agents. Down 6th Avenue to 52nd. And down 52nd to '21' Club.

PD cruisers were speeding up to '21' Club now, screeching to a stop. Cops jumped out with service pistols and shot guns drawn.

The manager was rambling. "The guy broke through the door. Ran through here like a feral beast. The other guy came in looking like he just got hit by that bus. Said he was a federal marshal. We went to the Wine Cellar. He opens up some secret passage, goes I don't know where. That's all I know."

"Which way did the passage go?" the cop demanded.

The manager motioned around like he was trying to get his bearings, then pointed north.

A Ford Expedition screeched to a halt. Fitzgerald started to get out. Jackie ran over to him. "I know where he is! Get in!"

Jackie ran around the front and got in the passenger's seat. "Donnell Library," she yelled.

Fitzgerald dropped the shifter into drive and laid the pedal to the carpet. "What the hell happened?"

"John killed them with a big gun." She was panting, trying to catch her breath. "He jumped out the window. Drove the bus around the corner."

"He jumped out of a skyscraper window!"

"Parachute, Chief," she said, trying to calm her breathing. "Walken went first. John jumped on the back of another man." She held on tight as Fitzgerald took 5th north, and swerved to miss an oncoming motorcycle.

EIGHTY-FOUR

The flame wavered and went out periodically as he hurried through the underground passage. He could feel his abdomen filling up with blood. He'd be in decompensated shock in thirty minutes. If he didn't get to a surgeon soon, he was a dead man. His watch showed 9:35 AM.

He could smell Walken's cologne in the still air. The scent quickened his resolve. He grunted. Spat. Ran as fast as he could. Flicked the lighter back on when it went out. He was aware of his singular focus. He embraced it. It was a duel to the death with Walken, and before he died, he would see his opponent either dead or in cuffs.

He came to the pony door and found the ladder. Without looking below he climbed down the rungs. At the bottom, he flicked the lighter on. He knew exactly where he was. When he was a kid, he and his brother used to come here and mix cassette tapes.

He moved quickly to the stairs. Made too much noise taking the first few steps. His heavy breathing echoed up the old, hard walls.

At the top of the stairs he stopped. Listened. Nothing. He flicked on the lighter and could see the stairwell to the ground floor was forty feet ahead. He bounded over the floor with no light, counting out the yards with his strides. At 20 paces he stopped. He sensed someone ahead. He could smell Walken stronger now. Closing his eyes, he drew his arm back and held the Santuko knife above his shoulder. He stepped forward with his left foot and launched it across the dark expanse. He heard it turning through the air and then "ugh." He'd hit Walken. There was no doubt about it. Then the knife clanked on the floor. Had he dropped him?

He held the lighter up and away from his body. The second it sparked, Walken fired at him. John immediately took his thumb off the gas and dropped to his knees.

Five more shots blasted through the air. From the sound of it, Walken was firing a 9mm or a .40. John bear-crawled forward as quietly as he could. Getting to Walken before he shot him seemed a better idea than hiding in the darkness waiting to get shot, especially since he now had no weapon but his own hands.

The shots stopped and he heard footsteps retreat up the stairs. Walken was at least 20 yards ahead of him.

John crawled a few more feet and felt around for the knife. It was precisely where he thought it should be. He picked it up and moved to the stairs. Cautiously ascending the flight, all he could hear through the still air was his own labored breathing. Walken could be laying in wait anywhere. But he had to keep moving up. If he stayed down here, two things were sure to happen. Walken would get away, and he'd die from internal bleeding.

He rounded the corner at the landing and made his way up to the first basement. It was still pitch black, but he knew where the stairs leading to the first level were. Trudging across the floor, he listened as best he could through his heavy breaths. There was nothing ahead. Walken had probably fled the building. He was lost. He would get away again.

He labored on in agony, feeling the sting of defeat more than the visceral pain from his wounds. Then he heard in his mind, "I am not beat. I will persevere. I will win. I am not beat." He continued toward the stairs. At the well, he grabbed the rail and pulled himself up the flight one by one, gaining speed and strength with each step. "I am still strong," he told himself. "I will find him. I will find him." He held the knife by his side, ready to swing it or fling it.

He rounded the corner on the landing and though it was still pitch black around him, he could see muted light above. The street was close. He was almost out. Then a shot rang out. He felt the bullet go through his left side. The force pivoted him, which caused the next three shots to miss him completely. With all the remaining strength he had left, he whipped the knife through the darkness, up the stairs to where the shots had originated. He heard the knife enter Walken for the second time in as many minutes. This time the gun hit the ground and he heard a gurgling sound, as though he'd hit Walken in the neck. He heard him strain at what he thought was his effort to pull the knife out. Then the knife dropped on the cement stairs and he heard Walken staggering away.

John took the lighter out of his pocket and flicked it on. The gun lay a few stairs up from him. He crawled to the top of the stairs, and now with the gun in his hand, he set out to finish it.

The floor was empty. Scattered beams of light peeked through tears in the paper that hung on the 53rd Street windows. By the light, he could see Walken holding his neck and leaning against one of the support pillars. John felt the blood pooling at his waist. He saw the blood pouring from Walken's neck.

"Condor Walken!" he yelled with everything he had left. "Stop where you are. You're under arrest."

Walken looked back at him and staggered towards the double doors. John fired at him, not to hit him, but to scare him and slow him down. If he were going to kill Walken, it would be with his bare hands.

He took off in a run. It felt as though hundred pound weights were tied to each leg, but he put them one in front of the other with everything he had. He continued to fire until the slide locked in its back position and then he dropped the gun. He was only two feet away from Walken and the double doors when he dove out and tackled him from behind.

EIGHTY-FIVE

They both saw the doors fly open and John tackling Condor Walken onto the sidewalk. Fitzgerald yelled, "Stay here!" to Jackie, but it was a useless effort. She was out of Fitzgerald's Expedition before he had it in park.

She ran barefoot to them. John had his left arm around Walken's neck. His weight ground the old man's face into the sidewalk. If there were ever a time she wanted to kill a man, it was now. The slimy threats he had made flew through her mind. When she was close enough, she planted her right foot in front of Walken's head and came through with the inside of her left with a great cry. She connected her heel with his cheek bone and moved his head along the course ground a few inches. She was winding up to do it again when Fitzgerald grabbed her from behind. She screamed and fought and tried to break free. But his long arms were locked tight around her torso and he was just too strong. "Ease up, girl. We got him."

John rolled over, stared up at her with a relieved look and said with a guttural exhale, "Goal."

She dropped to her knees and examined his wounds. She tore open his shirt and felt the bullet wound and his swollen abdomen.

He swallowed a couple of times and said, "Did he hurt you?"

She shook her head no. "No. He didn't." Tears rolled down her cheeks. John was starting to shake. She knew he'd pass out soon. He'd lost too much blood and he was in shock. She looked over at Fitzgerald and said, "They're on the way, right?"

"They're on their way, Jackie," he said. "Just stay with him."

EIGHTY-SIX

Several black Suburbans sped up to the scene. Agents jumped out and covered the area with automatic weaponry, adding to the PD presence that was steadily accumulating.

Santiváñez and Stiles leaped from the lead vehicle. From the other direction, a Battalion 8 ambulance pulled up on the curb. Two paramedics jumped out and ran over. Two more emerged from the back of the ambulance with a gurney.

John looked into Walken's eyes. They held the look of a beaten and dying man. The Santoku knife had gone clean through at about the C4 region on the right side of his neck. He'd pierced the carotid because blood spurted out with every heartbeat. He'd also cut into the larynx. With every breath, Walken made quick and irregular gulping noises. Fitzgerald had Walken's right hand behind his back and he applied pressure on his shoulder with his knee. "Keep him alive," John said.

"You know it, old pal," Fitzgerald said. "You keep yourself alive." Fitzgerald called out to the advancing paramedics and pointed to John. "Scoop and run, boys! He's one of us!"

The paramedics put him on a board in the Trendelenburg Position – flat on his back, legs higher than the heart. It was going to be okay now. They had Walken. Jackie safe. Katie. Where was Katie? She was with Aunt Mary. She'd be okay.

He was still well within the golden hour, that crucial period after a traumatic incident. These guys would have him to Roosevelt in under ten. He was aware of his shaking, sweating, chills. Legs felt weak. Body was compensating for the blood loss – constricting vessels, shoving all the blood to head and core. This was shock.

He was in the back of the ambulance now. Moving. Jackie held his hand. One paramedic put an occlusive dressing on the bullet wound. The other stuck him with two large VOR IVs. Squeezed the saline bags. By the book, he thought. He looked at one of the paramedics' watch. 9:42AM.

One paramedic listened to his heart. "No cavitation. Pulse is strong."

The other guy pressed on his stomach. "He's one strong son of a gun. We've got a rigid abdomen." John flinched when the guy pressed on his spleen. "Hot belly, Marshal?"

Blood was impinging on his peritoneum. His belly burned. He couldn't talk. All he could do was squeeze the guy's wrist.

Keep it going guys, he told himself. He was drifting away. Ten minutes to get to the hospital plus a few for prep. They'd cut him open. Irrigate. Fix anything that was broken. Maybe remove his spleen. Stitch him up. In a day or two he'd be good as new. So tired. And thirsty. He wanted to tell them how much blood he thought he'd lost. The heart pushed six liters of blood per minute. He probably suffered a small tear in his spleen when he hit the front of the bus. That would be, what? Gunshot. Mathematics… to figure it out. Simple formula.

Then he went black.

EIGHTY-SEVEN

Just a thousand paces from the front steps of the Capitol Building sat a restaurant called The Monocle. Established in 1959, it was an institution unto itself. As you entered the front door of the old building, you had the choice to turn right and enter a small dining room, go straight up a flight of stairs, or turn left and enter the bar area that abutted another small dining room. Wherever you went in the Monocle, you were reminded of the names and faces that lead and led the country, all hanging on the wall and framed in the fashion popular at the time they served.

Carl Peterson met him in the parking lot. He'd been waiting, pacing. He calmed himself before opening the door for the man who could soon be president. "Michael," his Chief of Staff said. "I've been calling. Where have you been?"

"I had my phone off, Carl," Malley said when he had both feet firmly planted on the rough pavement.

"Where is Henry?"

"He took a different car from the airport. Said he had to see to something personal."

"Something personal? At a time like this?"

"That's what he said," Malley said absently. "I don't know. He's been acting very strange. I just let him go."

"Alright. That doesn't matter right now. These people have been waiting. You were supposed to eat with them, Michael."

Malley straightened his tie in the reflection of the tinted window. It was time to put on the air of a man who would be president. He stood straight and as tall as he could. "They'll understand, Carl." And then he walked for the door.

Malley waited for Carl to lead him up the steps. The president was never the first to enter a room like this. They were in the middle of the flight of twenty stairs. Malley looked back. When he was president, there would be Secret Service in front and behind him.

Carl entered the Federal Room, one of three small banquet rooms on the Monocle's top floor. "Ladies and Gentlemen, at long last, Senator Michael Malley."

Malley worked the room from front to back, shaking everyone's hand, apologizing for being late. William Cohen, the Senate Majority Leader, sat in the back of the room, watching the crowd. He was pleased at the genuine support for his old friend. If there were any man who could win the presidency as a 3rd party candidate, it was Michael Malley. He just hoped there was no scandal brewing. He remembered the story about Immunex. Remembered that the reporter had died shortly thereafter. Now his building explodes? And he was nearly an hour late to a multi-million dollar fundraiser that was to be a launching event for his candidacy? They had hugged when Malley came to him and he detected alcohol about him, too. There were whisperings among some of the elites that Michael Malley may have skeletons in his closet. He hoped for the country's sake that he was right with his past.

And then he began to speak. Cohen smiled through his entire speech. If there were a more likeable fellow than Michael Malley, he had never met him. Like the rest of the crowd, he was emboldened by the old man's simple way of presenting himself. He talked of getting back to the American way. Returning to American-made products and American industry. He talked of the middle class, and private investment into industry. Never once did he speak of government. Government programs. Government subsidy. It was beautiful. Michael Malley was exactly what the country needed right now. A true independent.

Eighty-eight

A few hours later, Malley sat alone in the back of his Town Car outside of the Russell Senate Building, asking himself if he really wanted to go inside.

Where was Henry, he asked himself? An unexpected wave of emotion passed through him. He wished he had never called Black. He could have taken care of it himself. Could have tried to level with Henry. Find out what he had told the authorities. If he had told them anything at all. Maybe Henry was telling the truth. Maybe Condor's men had tried to kill him and taken the bonds. He would never know now, and it was as if he had killed the boy himself.

After chewing up a few antacids and washing them down with water, he thanked the driver and got out of the car. With great deliberation, he descended the four steps leading down to the double-door entrance.

He made his way past the security guards. No need to pass through the metal detectors required of every other person that entered the building. He was one of the most well-known and trusted people in the country. What used to be his greatest comfort all of a sudden was a cruel irony.

He took the elevator up to the second floor. The hallway was long and quiet. Normally a well-lighted corridor even on weekends, the lights were dimmed for the holiday. The tall oak doors lining the hallway were passages into rooms where the deals that had molded this nation had been made and administrated. History rang out to him and he heard whispers and echoes in the back of his mind.

In the basement, he walked the short corridor to the underground tram that ran from the Senate Building to the Capitol. He got into the open four-seat car and the operator got him moving right away. The Capitol was largely deserted, but there was always someone there to ferry senators and congressmen back and forth for the nation's last minute business.

In his father's day, they rode in modified, battery-powered Studebakers. The Congress was different then. The country was different. There was not so much wealth. Not so many millionaires and billionaires. The country was more humble. The American Dream was on everyone's mind. They all knew they could achieve it if they worked hard enough. Today, most people doubted it still existed. Instead, they were occupied worrying if they'd be able to keep their house and pay their fat credit card bills.

It would take generations to turn the train around and get the nation's priorities straightened out. He was the man to apply the brakes and get everybody to work pulling, dragging, pushing the country back in the right direction. It was going to take a Herculean effort, but he was the man that could do it. He'd need a Congress to support him. That would be part of his campaign slogan. Give me your vote and a Congress. Something like that. There were men and women on both sides of the aisle who would join him. He'd campaign for anyone who shared his vision, Republican, Democrat, Independent, Tea Partier, Libertarian. He'd do it, and when he was done they'd put him on the currency. Maybe take Grant off the fifty.

He was at the door of his hideaway office — deep in the maze of the tunnel-like passageways that ran under the Capitol Building. He put his key into the slot of the old wooden door and entered the small room. Actually two rooms in one, his father had commandeered an old storage room next door and turned it into a full bathroom with a separate shower area. No other member of Congress had one of these, and they all envied him. It was a shame he didn't have a son to whom he could bestow it.

He locked the door behind him and tossed his keys on an old end table that had been in his family for generations. He used the lavatory and then sat behind the small desk that fronted a window looking directly out to the U.S. Supreme Court.

He pulled the drapes and touched the mouse on his desk. The screen on the notebook PC came to life. He double clicked on the browser icon, and while he waited for the CNN home page to load, he reached into the credenza behind him and poured a another Macallan. This time from a bottle of Distillery Exclusive he'd received as a gift from the Sultan of Brunei.

The page finished loading. The 4th of July imagery was gone and they were transitioning back to regular news. Front and center was a story about a wildfire in Malibu. Twenty-five people had been gunned down in Syria. "Terrible. Terrible," he said aloud. Below that, in the Don't Miss section, there was his picture. The caption under his smiling face read, "Looks Like He's In." The image they chose was flattering. It was a good thing Carl had kept the reporters away from the event. He felt his mid section. He had to get back to an exercise program.

His eyes fell dead on a story listed under Latest News. It read "Bizarre Police Chase in New York City."

He clicked on the link. At the top of the page was THIS JUST IN. He read the story – NEW YORK, Manhattan, Three unidentified men base-jumped from the 48th floor of a Midtown building Sunday afternoon. Witnesses reported a lone man landed on 52nd Street and then fled into the historic restaurant and bar, '21' Club. Concurrently, two other men using a single parachute crashed through the front windshield of a Metro Bus heading north on 6th Avenue. One of these men, described only as very large and with white hair, died in the crash. The survivor of the crash, an unidentified white male, then chased the first man into '21' Club. NYPD then rushed to the entrance of the old Donnely Library on 53rd. Witnesses there reported that two men broke through the entrance to the old library and fell to the cement. FBI agents immediately took control of the scene and the two men were both hauled away in separate ambulances. There is no official comment from either the FBI or NYPD. Check back often for updates to this late breaking story.

He unfroze his hand from the mouse and sat back in his chair. A large man with white hair. That was definitely Torval Tangval.

There was a noise in the hallway. Or was there? Were they coming for him? He sat still and listened for a long while. When he was sure it was just his mind playing tricks on him, he read the story again. Base jumping out of a Manhattan high rise? And how did a person get from '21 Club' on 52nd Street to the old Donnely Library on 53rd? He surfed through the other majors' websites. There were no other stories. No more answers.

What would Condor say if he were in custody? Nothing, he was sure. Absolutely nothing. He would lawyer up and sit like a clam. Besides, he'd really done nothing that they could prove. He'd never spent a dime of the money Condor gave him. He had complete deniability. Henry was gone.

Walken's lawyers would turn to him immediately for help, and Walken would try to turn the screws even tighter in lockup. Black could have him killed in jail. Yes, Black had the power to silence him anywhere.

Snatching his phone from the desk, he held down the C on the pad and speed dialed Carl. "Carl, it's Michael. What's going on?"

"Ah, I'm working, Michael. What's –"

"Where are you?" Malley cut him off.

"Home, Michael. Where are you?"

"I'm at the office. Working."

"Is Henry with you?"

"No. He, ah. Have you heard from him?"

"No."

"Well, he's probably out having a good time."

"Very well. Can I call a car for you to take you back to your town-house?"

"No, no. I'll take care of it. I'll talk to you later." Malley hung up the phone and read the story again. He hit the desk with his fist, stood up, and walked toward the adjoining room. He stopped abruptly. Returned for his Scotch and drained the last of his double. His hand shook when he returned the glass to the desk. He leaned against the edge and tensed both arms. Bitterness welled up inside of him. He took the Macallan and poured again. The bottle's neck clanked and rolled on his tumbler as he filled it.

He gulped the Scotch down greedily and walked to the adjoining room and small bed. Lying down, he thought one of two things would happen next. He'd get a call from someone representing Condor Walken. Or the FBI would come calling. But Condor wouldn't talk. No, he'd sit tight and wait for help. Black would send in the Cavalry, and then the problem would go away. But not too fast. He'd make sure Black's people killed Condor slowly. Maybe he'd have them burn him alive. Or perhaps throw him from a plane miles above the Earth.

As he drifted away, he forgot about Condor Walken, and he saw himself on a cold winter's day. Instead of standing under the oak with his dying father, he stood on the Capitol steps being sworn in as president. But there were only nameless faces. No family. No friends. The faces drifted away, and he was all alone. And he was bare. And confused.

Eighty-nine

Katie was there. He sensed her. Could smell her. He turned his head. Willed his eyelids to open. They fluttered. She was blurry, but he saw her face outlined by her fine white hair. Her bangs needed a trim. So innocent. So pretty. Her warm glow was his comfort.

He was in the hospital. Then his mind rewound and he saw it all. Jumping from the building. Chasing Condor through the tunnel. Collapsing on the sidewalk.

Katie was rubbing his arm. Her little hand went up and down his shoulder. It was how she woke him up in the middle of the night when she was scared. She was probably scared now. He must be an ugly sight. He wanted to open up his arms and snuggle her tight, as he did at home. He willed himself to sit up. He just wanted to tell her he was fine.

There was a hand on his chest. It was Jackie. He smelled her perfume. Prada L'Eau Ambrée. With hints of citron, rose de mai and amber. He'd asked her what it was at Jersey Boys two nights ago. Googled on his phone when he was waiting for the sun to come up at the fire. It promised a graceful presence, empowering but never demanding. Fitting. Very fitting. He turned his head to her.

"Stay there," she whispered. She kept her hand on his chest to prevent him from moving. Her hair was pulled back. She wore no makeup. Such a beautiful, strong woman. Since the last time he saw her, she'd cleaned up. Changed clothes. Sprayed on that perfume for him. He felt love on both sides of him.

He turned back to Katie. Tried to speak. Cleared his throat. He was becoming more lucid now. He looked at his wrists. Followed the lines on his left side up to the bag hanging at the head of the bed. It was blurry, but he saw the word Morphine. He reached over with his right hand and pulled hard on the line. "Oh, John," he heard Jackie say.

The next thing he knew a nurse was standing there. He was pushing her away. "Marshal Kane, you need this," he heard the nurse say.

"My daddy doesn't like drugs," he heard Katie say. "At all."

The nurse stopped. Pressed a button on the head of the bed. "Doctor, I need you in here right away."

Then the doctor was there. He was talking to Jackie and Aunt Mary in the corner. Randy Fitzgerald was there. He stepped over to the bed and said, "Hey, old pal."

John smiled big. "Hey." Much of the haziness was fading. He could feel a dull pain in his ribs and stomach.

Katie was still there rubbing his arm. He looked over at her and smiled. She smiled back.

The doctor stepped up. "Marshal Kane, we had to sedate you to cut you open. Sorry. But we couldn't have you moving around while we operated."

"What did you do?"

"We opened up your belly. Cleaned the blood. You ruptured the outer wall of your spleen. About a half centimeter lesion. It was clotted off by the time we got to it. Didn't touch it. Bullet went in and out. Took off a piece of your large intestine. We sewed that up. Ribs will heal on their own. You're a lucky man."

He tried to sit up but couldn't. He winced at the pain, which was steadily becoming more acute. "Raise the back of this thing up," he said through clinched teeth.

"That's not a good idea, Marshal," the doctor said.

"What's the worst that could happen?"

"I don't want to have to open you up again. Please just stay there."

John found the control with his right hand and raised the bed himself. "Where is Michael Malley?" he said.

"Washington," Fitzgerald said. "He's in the Capitol. Feds are convening a grand jury as we speak to draw up a warrant for him. They'll take him later today."

"You got the bonds back from Michael Terry, right?"

"Santiváñez took them. They're safe."

"What about Henry Douglas?"

Fitzgerald took a few to answer, cleared his throat. "Washington PD found Henry's body."

"He was playing both sides of the fence. I don't believe for one minute that Mack Washington helped do that deal."

"We might not ever know now," Fitzgerald said.

"Maybe Walken will tell us," John said. "If Jackie didn't kill him with that place kick." He looked at Jackie and Fitzgerald, and he didn't like the absent stares they were returning to him.

"What?" John said.

"Walken got away," Fitzgerald said.

John swallowed a few times and coughed. "Doctor, please bring me some water." The nurse stepped up and put a straw in his mouth. He took the cup from her, gave her the straw, and drank it down. "How?"

"A group of about thirty Colombians. They came from the roof and the ground. Huge firefight. FBI and PD killed all but five of them. We lost eight PD. They got away off the roof in a helicopter. Santiváñez said it had to be a Colombian drug lord named Carlos Esperanza."

"What time is it?" John asked.

"Seven AM," Fitzgerald said.

John sat up further, and with a pained growl, he said, "We're not finished."

"Ease up, old pal," Fitzgerald said. "You're done. The FBI has it from here."

John threw the sheet off himself and said, "We're going." He swung his right leg out as if he were trying to stand up. The doctor put out his hand and blocked him.

"Please, Marshal Kane," the doctor said.

John growled out in pain through clinched teeth. "Get. Me. A wheelchair. Or I'll walk out of here."

"Marshal Kane," the doctor said. "I won't release you."

"All due respect, doctor," John said. "You said my spleen capsule is healing. That means it's filtering red blood cells like it's supposed to and producing lymphocytes. Am I right?"

"Your spleen is functioning."

"So my immune system should be strong as ever. I'm assuming you know how to suture, so my colon will be fine. Nothing but time will heal my ribs, right?"

"There's more to it than that."

"It'll take a couple of days for the collagen to start healing the tear in the organ. So I'll be careful. I don't want you to have to open me up again, either." He looked at the doctor now with every bit of seriousness he possessed and said, "Now get me a chair before I split this thing back open."

The doctor looked over to Katie, appealing to the only blood relative in the room.

With a shrug she said, "If my dad says he can do it, he can do it. I think it would be best to get him a chair."

In that moment John forgot about the pain. He didn't have to look over at Katie to see her face. He knew it was calm and free of emotion. Her words played back in his mind. She was such a practical girl. So much like her mother. Or maybe it was that she was like him. He just wanted to finish this and let her be a little girl, free of police work and all the insanity that came with it.

With great consternation, the doctor turned back to John. "Let me have a look at you." He pulled his gown up and examined the sutures on his abdomen. There was still a lot of subcutaneous bruising. "Lower your left leg."

John did so and groaned.

The doctor felt around his abdomen. "Why is this so important to you, Marshal Kane?"

"Because I was would have voted for him," he said through gritted teeth. "I'll look into his eyes when they take him away."

"Nurse," the doctor said with resignation. "Please bring a chair in here."

The nurse left the room and quickly returned with a wheel chair.

"I'll accompany you to Washington," the doctor said.

"Doctor's orders?"

"It's the only way you're getting out of this room."

"That's good," John said, "I make it a point to always listen to my doctor."

NINETY

7:30AM. Washington, DC. Dick Culling, head of the Republican National Committee, sat in his Georgetown home and waited on the line for Bill Bryan, a Special Agent in Charge at FBI headquarters in DC.

Bryan came on. They exchanged pleasantries and then Culling got down to business. "What can you tell me about this thing in New York, Bill? I have a source telling me it's got something to do with Michael Malley."

Bryan sat in his office downtown. He looked out a window high up in the Hoover Building. "What thing in New York?" he said.

"Oh, come on, Bill. I'm not looking to start the rumor mill, but I'd also like to stop it before it starts. People are talking."

Bryan had been in on some of the briefings and he knew full well what was going on. "I don't think it's anything to worry about, Dick. These things have a way of working themselves out."

Culling considered what his old friend had said. "These things have a way of working themselves out." He was being coy, and Bill Bryan was never coy. Something big was coming. If Malley blew up, it would be an ugly mess. His knee twitched with excitement and he smiled into the phone. "I'll see you next week," Culling said.

Bryan didn't need to check his schedule. It was their standing round the second Friday of each month at the Congressional Country Club. "We'll play the Blue Course," Bryan said.

"Fine," Culling said. "See you then."

"Dick?" Bryan said before hanging up. "The Senate Gallery might be a nice place to hang out this morning. I hear the FDA debate won't be as an innocuous affair as usual." Bryan hung up his phone and shrugged it off. A guy had to throw an old friend a bone once in awhile.

NINETY-ONE

Through half-open eyes, Malley poured a glass of water from the decanter on the small bedside table. He gulped it down and then pulled a little aspirin tin from his pants pocket. Feebly pressing the edges, he opened the small tin, swallowed its contents, and then, with a shaky hand, he drank more water. This was his morning routine for the past many weeks, and it was getting very old. He'd seen his father wake like this half his life. How he'd tried not to become his father, and yet here he was in much worse a predicament than his father had ever worked himself into.

Placing his feet on the ground, he took his phone and woke the screen. 8AM. No texts. No emails. No calls. If the feds had Condor, they could hold him for a long period before they allowed him to contact a lawyer. But Condor's people would come calling, and they would want help. Help he would be only too glad to supply. Black would be in Washington today, and it would be his people taking care of Condor Walken. For good. Soon, he thought. Soon he'd be back to a normal life. He simply had to get up and face this down. He rose and walked to the shower.

Two hours later, he left his hideaway office and made his way back through the basement halls. The emails had begun to pour in shortly after he woke. He had everything he needed for the debate, so he sent out a blanket email to everyone on his staff that he wasn't to be disturbed until he was finished on the Floor. He was annoyed when his phone buzzed and Carl's name popped up on the screen. His head pounded and his mouth felt raw. He could feel the goodness of the protein drink he had for breakfast, but he wished he'd had a Bloody Mary. After the debate, he'd cut over to The Monocle for lunch and a few drinks.

He passed by the Senate Book Store, which was but a small outlet that sold select books, tourist novelties, and candy and soda. It was intern season. Many smartly dressed late-teen and early-twenty-year-old college kids hurried about. Malley passed by one particularly beautiful young black girl who reminded him of Antoinette. Her beauty stirred his senses, and he was reminded, ever so bitterly, of how Condor had used her to entrap him.

Could he still be president after all he'd done? By his actions, or his inaction, he had effectively helped Condor commit arson and innocent people were now dead. He'd just allowed Henry to be murdered to save his own skin. He'd been lying for years and years.

He kept walking and shook it off. Now was no time for fear and panic. It was his enemies who had done all this, not him. God had called him to lead his country out of despair. Just as Joshua had led Israel to the Promised Land, so would he lead his country back to prosperity. He would face his enemies down, toe to toe, and they would fall. He would defeat the giants and victory would be delivered unto him. Yes, he was about to have Condor Walken killed, but mankind had been killing one another for the greater good since time immemorial. When Israel fought its enemies, it was a battle to the death. Whatever he did, whatever he had done, was for the good of the country. For a stronger America.

Minutes later, he entered the Senate Cloakroom. The carpet was a deep, dark red with an elaborately embroidered inlay abutting richly stained oak wainscot running the perimeter of the rectangular room. There was ample lighting from antique fixtures and lamps. Hanging between beveled and raised panels above the wainscoting were paintings and portraits – storied canvasses of our nation's history framed in heavy wood and gilded encasements. Senators from both parties, sitting on leather couches and chairs of different configuration and style, greeted him with smiles and handshakes. It was comforting that he was truly one of the most liked politicians in the body.

After some brief small talk, he excused himself from the other members. It was time for the debate to begin. Only a few senators would be on the floor at any given time – one or two from each party. There would be a few aides scattered about, and members would enter and exit as they were called to take their part in the debate. The Presiding Member would quietly read his newspaper at times, staying just present enough to do his Parliamentary duty if called upon. It wasn't a high profile topic. The mood on the floor would be calm. Each side would present their argument, emotions would run cool, and then there would be a vote which would be attended by only a bare minimum of the senators.

Malley walked onto the Senate Floor. Matthew Cohen looked up from his table and greeted him with a heartfelt smile and firm grip of the hand. He said in a hushed tone, "You knocked them dead yesterday, Michael."

His spirits soared at seeing his old friend and hearing his words. He was home, and all his paranoia last night was just that, nervous doubt that he must cast from his mind. He was Michael Malley. He would be the next president of this country.

The Presiding Member called the session to order and deferred to the chaplain for the customary prayer. The chaplain began, "Let us pray."

Malley hung his head and listened to the holy man.

"Lord of creation, lead us through this day. Control our thoughts, words, and deeds as we serve as Your ambassadors. Show us the tasks that deserve our attention. Keep us from the wrong focus. Continue to sustain the Members of this body. Answer their prayers; protect them from dangers; keep them faithful. Help us all to remember that those who take refuge in You will never be put to shame. Bless our military men and women. Be their light in darkness. In Your great mercy defend them from perils and dangers. We pray in Your holy Name. Amen."

The Presiding Member stood up and led the Pledge of Allegiance. Malley put his right hand to his heart and tuned him out. He looked around to the empty seats that climbed the floor. In this hallowed chamber, he had sworn to uphold the Constitution. The image of him holding up his hand and saying "I solemnly swear" so many times echoed in the back of his mind. He had listened to prayers many times like the one he just heard. Now he squinted his eyes and prayed again to God to help him keep his focus, to keep him faithful, as the chaplain had prayed. There were so many tasks that deserved his attention. He called for God directly to control him. His mind was like a flickering switch on this thought. Back and forth, from God's control to his need to have Condor killed. Control me, God. But let me kill Condor Walken. Show me the right way, God, but look the other way while I have Walken killed. It was right to have him killed. He had been in a war not of his choosing for what seemed a lifetime. And the only way to end a war was to vanquish one's enemy. Condor Walken would only be completely defeated in death. He knew that God would show him what was right. Condor Walken was an unholy man and he must be removed from the Earth. I am a righteous man, he cried inside, and I will do so much good. He prayed with all his might for forgiveness and direction. "So be it," he said out loud as everyone else finished the Pledge. Everything would be fine now.

The Presiding Member commenced to announce the Reservation of Leader Time. Just as he began to speak, the side doors opened and men wearing FBI coats filed into the Chamber. His chest seized and his knees weakened. He fell back into his chair. Were they there to protect him, or arrest him? Then it all became clear. They pushed a wheelchair into the Chamber. John Kane sat in it. It was he who had jumped from the building in Manhattan yesterday and chased down Walken. They weren't there to protect him at all.

A female FBI agent walked to the Presiding Member and apologized for the interruption. She showed him her badge and gave him a document. The Presiding Member scanned its contents and then handed it back. They had a few quiet words. Then the Presiding Member looked up. "Senator Malley, Agent Santiváñez would like to have a word with you outside."

Malley tried to clear his throat, but felt as if it were glued shut. He poured water from a pitcher sitting on a table nearby, and drank with an unsteady hand. Then he stepped down to the floor.

"Let's step outside, Senator," Santiváñez said.

Malley tried to clear his throat again and managed to utter, "What is the meaning of this?"

"I have a warrant for your arrest, sir," Santiváñez said. "We'd prefer not to do this on the Senate Floor. Please step outside." She'd been given instructions not to arrest Malley on the Senate Floor. C-Span was in the wings taping.

Malley hung his head and the cacophony in his mind cleared. It was finally over. The charade. He was not a righteous man. Instead of a

Joshua, he was a modern day Judas. God had smote him. His name would not be celebrated in history, rather, the Malley name would live in infamy.

When he was in front of John he stopped and looked up. "I'm sorry, John. I truly am."

***

Up above in the Gallery, Dick Culling looked down with a solemn frown. Several people with Capitol Visitor badges pasted on their chests looked around confusedly. Culling was up the stairs and out the door before the Floor door latched shut behind the last FBI man. He nearly sprinted to the C-Span control room. This video was gold. Pure political gold. "I'll give you five thousand dollars for a copy of that tape," he said to the camera operator.

The young kid looked at him and said, "Deal."

NINETY-TWO

A week later. World's Fair Marina – Flushing, NY. Water lapped quietly against the sides of *Investigator*. The 2010 Hinkley-built Sou'wester ran seventy feet and three inches from bow to stern, and eighteen feet across her belly. She was a seven-million-dollar yacht and had few equals in her class. Jackie's father had named the ship after his only daughter and presented it to her on her thirty-fifth birthday.

John untied the hitch from the dock cleat and spun the nylon rope up on the bow. He gave *Investigator* a shove, stepped onto the starboard gunwale, and down to the wheel. The Cummins diesel purred as he eased the throttle forward, and they were off.

Once he was clear of the dock and safely out in the bay, he poked his head down through the companionway. Jackie and Katie were sitting at the small table in the salon drawing dresses. They didn't even see him, so engaged with their drawing were they. It seemed they were immediate best friends, and he wasn't sure who needed the other more. Jackie blamed herself for the loss of her brother, but seemed to be healing with Katie. He hadn't seen Katie so animated since well before her mother got sick. He watched them for a full minute, trying to not so much as breathe, lest he interrupt them.

Back at the wheel, he queued up *Sinatra, The Capital Years* and set it on random play. "South of the Border" played. The plan was to make their way down the coast to Charleston, South Carolina. Take in a little history. Buy some dresses. Maybe have one or two made. Maybe they'd keep going after that. They hadn't talked about it. To get away was enough.

Malley's defense was urging an insanity plea, but he refused. He confessed to all his dealings with Walken and to giving the order to have Henry killed. After a reserve was set up to compensate Mack Washington's and Jimmy Park's families, he was voluntarily giving the federal government all his assets.

Terenty and Silanty weren't getting any deals and they weren't going back to Russia. Hotel cameras had them coming and going when they took Jackie away in a laundry cart. And they had them coming and going when they killed Rodney. Santiváñez was charging them with both crimes. John had confessed to pouring the white fuel on them. Owned that he would have burnt them to death to find out where Jackie was. Nobody at the FBI seemed too interested in pursuing anything about it.

He ran the boat under power for thirty minutes, just around the southern tip of La Guardia Airport and out of Flushing Bay. Riker's Island lay just ahead.

Just into the East River, it was time to cut the power and get down to business. There was a fresh northwest wind blowing, perfect to take them where they wanted to go. John let the girls stay below. It seemed a hurricane couldn't wrest them from their time together.

John opened the cover to the sail controls just to the side of the wheel. He hit a button and the stowaway main began to unfurl. In just under a minute, the mainsail was fully up and locked into place. It billowed and then filled, grabbing firmly its part of the sky and extracting just a small portion of the fresh Canadian wind. John hit another button and the genoa unfurled on its rolling. In another minute they were doing six knots down the East River.

The boat leaned slightly with the wind. *Investigator* could handle seventy-knot and better winds and any water he cared to venture into. What would it be like to pilot this thing in the raging sea? He was going to find out one day. But for now he concentrated on rounding Riker's Island and navigating them through the tight passage that ran under the Triboro Bridge called Hell Gate. He'd call the girls up on deck for that.

As he was trimming in the genoa, "I've Got the World on a String" started to play. It brought a smile to his face. He felt that he did have the world on a string. He wasn't wearing shoes. He was fully retired and free.

He was heading out on an adventure, and he wasn't conflicted as he joined Old Blue Eyes in singing the line, "I'm in love." It might have been premature to say he was in love with Jackie Fairbanks, but at least it felt okay to go there. His Twitter and Facebook accounts were gone, and so was his desire to keep tabs on Peggy.

His phone buzzed against his leg. Fishing it out of the cargo pocket of his shorts, he saw a blocked caller ID. It had to be someone from the FBI or BFI. Maybe it was Santivañez. He really didn't want to talk to her right now but he hit the talk button out of habit. "Kane."

There was no sound on the other end. He realized he wasn't a marshal anymore, and he should answer the phone like a civilian. "This is John."

"John?" the voice said. It was Peggy. She sounded strung out and her voice wavered. "Why have you abandoned me?"

The End

My Dear Reader,

I hope you've enjoyed The Marshal – 43rd and 8th. Thank you for your support.

Please visit my Website www.corysanders.com to read the beginning of the next book in The Marshal series, The Marshal – Sakhalin.

You'll also find information on The Marshal series and The FDNY Foundation.

Yours in discourse,
Cory Sanders

1158919R00186

Made in the USA
San Bernardino, CA
26 November 2012